HATTIE BREAKS A LEG

PATRICK GLEESON

NO EXIT PRESS

First published in the UK in 2026 by No Exit Press,
an imprint of Bedford Square Publishers Ltd,
London, UK

noexit.co.uk
@noexitpress

ISBN
978-1-83501-007-5 (Paperback)
978-1-83501-008-2 (eBook)

2 4 6 8 10 9 7 5 3 1

Typeset 10.75 on 13.8pt Minion Pro
by Avocet Typeset, Bideford, Devon, EX39 2BP
Printed and bound in Great Britain by
CPI Group (UK) Ltd, Croydon CR0 4YY

The manufacturer's authorised representative in the EU for product safety is Easy Access System Europe, Mustamäe tee 50, 10621 Tallinn, Estonia
gpsr.requests@easproject.com

HATTIE BREAKS A LEG

Also by Patrick Gleeson

Hattie Brings the House Down
Hattie Steals the Show

For Stella, Denys and Solomiia

The Larry Lloyd company presents

WHAT YOU DESERVE

By Larry Lloyd
Directed by Larry Lloyd

Producer: Larry Lloyd
Costumes: Roxie Duff
Lighting: Nick Cocker
Stage manager: Hattie Cocker

Starring
Larry Lloyd

Other parts by
The Ensemble of the Larry Lloyd company

(Programme © Larry Lloyd)

Prologue

It was freezing cold and chucking it down with rain, Hattie's hip was sheer agony, and to cap it all off the van wouldn't start.

Ordinarily this last item wouldn't be a problem, or at the very least it wouldn't be Hattie's problem. Nigel the technician had insisted on driving the (hugely temperamental) van from the very start of the tour and Hattie was more than happy to cede responsibility to him. But Nigel was an inveterate alcoholic, and on nights when they didn't have to pack up straight after the show then *as soon* as he had the lights rigged and focused at each new venue Nigel would disappear in the direction of the nearest pub and not be seen again until the morning. Hattie didn't mind his absence in the slightest, except in cases such as this, where the venue manager insisted that the show van be moved out of the car park half an hour before the doors opened in order to make space for paying punters, and of course it went without saying that in Nigel's absence that responsibility fell to the stage manager.

This wouldn't happen on a proper tour, thought Hattie, as she hauled herself out of her seat, yanked up the bonnet and stared hopelessly at the gubbins beneath. *A proper tour would stop at proper venues with proper car parks. A proper tour would hire a technician who didn't smell of old farts and rubbing alcohol at all times. A proper tour would have a van that was worth more than its scrap value.*

Worst of all there was a car in the car park that, from the occasional flick of movement in the darkened interior, seemed to be occupied. Presumably a punter had turned up early for the evening's show and, the south coast village of West Rimesdale seeming to be utterly devoid of intelligent life, had nothing better to do before the venue opened than wait in their car. Hattie wasn't able to make out the face or expression of the occupant, but couldn't shake the thought that they were watching her, from the warmth and comfort of their driver's seat, and having a jolly good laugh.

But that was neither here nor there. She had to get the van moving. Now, what was it she'd seen Nigel do? Hattie shivered, wiped a rain-sodden curl of hair out of her face, and poked disconsolately at a couple of wires sprouting from behind a pipe. He'd said there was a loose connection in one of these, hadn't he?

She spent the next few minutes alternately twiddling the wires then limping back to the driver's side door and trying the ignition. She was eventually rewarded for her efforts with an ugly coughing sound that announced that the senescent engine was now running as healthily as it ever could. She closed the bonnet, got back into her seat with a wince, and drove the van a few hundred yards up the road to a lay-by.

Her thoughts returned to a comparison between her current situation and the norms of a 'proper tour' as she stomped, on foot, in the rain, back to the venue. Hattie had been on many proper tours in her life. She had staged productions in Madison Square Garden, Wembley Stadium, and the Théâtre des Champs-Élysées in Paris, and she could safely say that compared to such illustrious venues, the West Rimesdale Village Hall was even more rubbish than you'd expect.

It wasn't just a matter of scale, or upkeep, or even cleanliness. Hattie had put on shows at tiny, grotty London pub venues, in bombed-out buildings in the Baltic states, in 'theatres' that were barely more than cupboards at the Edinburgh Fringe. But what those places had, uniformly, and what West Rimesdale Village Hall lacked, was charm. No, not exactly charm. Magic. Ugh, again no, that didn't cover it. It was that *other* thing that sat just beyond the limits of Hattie's vocabulary. That essence of theatre-y-ness. That sense that, when the lights went down at the start of the first act, the rules of reality shifted slightly, and the venue, for an hour or so, became Somewhere Else.

Hattie would have given her left leg to be Somewhere Else, but instead she was stuck in West Rimesdale for the rest of the evening, in a sterile, boxy red-brick hall that had all the magic and transportive power of a piece of Tupperware.

It was her own fault, she reflected, as the gloomy outline of the village hall hove into view through the icy February rain. First for being a silly bint and falling off that loading ramp in Birmingham four years back, fracturing her hip and putting an end, it seemed at the time, to her touring career. Then for managing to make an enemy of the most influential person in non-West End theatre during her first non-touring gig. Then for managing to make an enemy of the most influential person in West End theatre during her *second* non-touring gig. Then, having made herself effectively unemployable within a hundred-mile radius of London, for panicking about her prospects, ignoring all medical advice and taking the first and only job she could find, that happened to be worst of all possible worlds: all of the hip-wrenching agony of a proper tour, but none of the normal and reasonable amenities. Just a dead-end show touring dead-end rural venues with a dead-end cast, crew, and van.

By the time she dragged herself past the presumed-occupied car (*laugh all you want now, you won't be laughing when you have to sit through this god-awful show later*) and back through the rear entrance of the building (what would in a proper venue have been called a 'stage door', but that in this depressing case deserved no such title) Hattie was cold, wet, in considerable pain, and in a *very* bad mood.

'We've got a problem,' announced Lucy Preston, one of the actors.

'Oh?'

'They're not letting me put the hamper stage left.'

'No?'

'It's a trip hazard,' explained Glynis, the secretary of the local amateur dramatic society and therefore also, apparently, the venue manager of the village hall, appearing in the corridor with an armful of plastic glasses and a box of wine.

'It won't fit on the props table, so I tucked it under the table on the floor,' explained Lucy.

'But it sticks out, so it's a trip hazard!' called Glynis over her shoulder as she disappeared out into the foyer.

'God, I could kill that woman,' muttered Lucy. 'So officious.'

'Rules are rules for a reason,' Hattie forced herself to say, trying to suppress the unreasonable surge of animosity she felt towards Glynis, and all venue managers, for making her life harder. 'I ignored a trip hazard and now I get shooting pains up my side every time it rains.'

'So where can I put it?'

'Is there any space stage right?'

'But… I bring it on from stage left in scene six,' said Lucy, bewildered.

'Yes, but you've got plenty of time after your previous exit in scene five. You can just go fetch it from stage right, bring it round with you to stage left, and come on as normal.'

'Oh.' Lucy frowned. 'Then where do I put it afterwards?'

'Stage right, where you got it from.'

'That could get confusing… can you just bring it to stage left for me so it's there when I need it?'

'I have to be at the lighting desk during the show. Like I always am,' said Hattie, trying to be patient.

'And you couldn't just nip out from the lighting desk during the scene change to bring the hamper round for me?'

'You mean the scene change where the lights go down, there's a few seconds of darkness as the actors reset, and then the lights come up again? I'm afraid I'm rather busy then. At the lighting desk. Making the lights go down and up. Look, all you have to do is pick up the hamper stage right after you come off from scene five, walk round to stage left, and then when the lights come up for scene six, you walk on holding the hamper. I'm *sure* you can handle it,' said Hattie firmly.

'Well… maybe if I practise it…' said Lucy uncertainly.

'Great idea. Why don't you go and do that now?' suggested Hattie, and marched away before Lucy could argue. She made it ten paces forwards before a voice called out from the men's dressing room, 'Ah, Hattie! Is now a good moment?'

'What do you need?' asked Hattie. She stopped and turned and looked into the room, then found herself immediately averting her eyes. Julian Hodge was mid-change, with many wobbly, hairy parts of him unashamedly exposed to the world. If she had been in a better mood, Hattie would have reminded herself that it was unfair to complain about an actor getting changed in a changing room, and that a certain level of intimacy with one another's bodies was part and parcel of being in a touring company, and that realistically, if Julian were a few stone lighter and a decade younger she'd have had no problem with him exposing a bit of skin and therefore her discomfort at his semi-nakedness was her problem, not his. As it was, it was all Hattie could do not to visibly grimace.

'It's about Kitty.'

Kitty was Julian's niece, about whom he seldom stopped talking. She had recently turned eighteen and apparently had shown some interest in following her uncle into the acting profession, about which he could not be more thrilled, as he told all and sundry at regular intervals.

'Oh yes?'

'So I've been thinking about it, and I think ACDA really would suit her more than RADA or Bristol. I don't think she should go anywhere too stuffy, she might lose her alternative *edge*. And you taught at ACDA, didn't you?'

It was true: Hattie had survived a little over a year at London's second most prestigious drama school as a stage management tutor, until, just as she started to get comfortable, the entire technical department had been abruptly shut down. It had been, she thought, one of the more creative ways in which fate had intervened to screw her over in recent years.

'Ye-es,' she said cautiously.

'Well then, I hate to ask, but I wondered if you could be persuaded to write a letter of recommendation to support her application?'

'I see two problems with that, Julian. The first is that I don't think the recommendation of a former stage management tutor would carry much weight among the admissions team for the acting course, would it?'

'Oh come now, Hattie, you're too modest. I'm sure everyone there knows you and respects your judgement. If you say a girl has talent then—'

'And that's the second thing: I've never even met your niece. So I can't exactly recommend her acting abilities, can I?'

'That one's easily solved! I was thinking perhaps a lunch?'

'Can we talk about this after the show? I've got some jobs to get through before the doors open.'

Hattie whisked herself away before Julian had a chance to reply, and took herself off to the lighting desk. Not that any of the more urgent jobs that needed doing waited for her there. It was simply that the little lighting booth at the back of the hall was the furthest place from where the actors were prowling. Short of hiding in the store cupboard, going there offered her the best chance of being left alone for a bit.

She was just running through the lighting cues when her phone rang noisily. It was her husband, Nick. That was unusual. It was unusual for Nick to ring at all, frankly, and more unusual still for him to call in the early evening when he knew she'd be working on a show, but most unusual for her to have forgotten to have put her phone on silent less than an hour before curtain up.

I'm slipping, thought Hattie as she picked up the phone.

'Hello?'

'When do you next get paid?' asked Nick without preamble.

'Wednesday.'

'Bugger.'

'Why?'

'Have you seen the joint account lately?'

'Is it bad?'

'I'm beginning to regret the fancy pillow.'

'Didn't you say it helped your neck?'

'I didn't realise helping my neck meant my card being declined at the offie.'

'Well, you've been meaning to cut back on drinking anyway. So the pillow's good for your health in two ways. Look, it's fine, I paid for petrol a couple of times this week so I'll be reimbursed for that. Move a few quid from the savings account to cover us until Wednesday, then move it back after.'

'We still didn't move back the "few quid" from last time.'

'Well then. Less beer, more neck exercises, so you can get back to earning again. Now if you'll excuse me, I've got a show.'

Hattie hung up before Nick could start grumbling. He'd only tweaked his neck, she told herself. He'd be back up and running in no time. Everything was fine. And even if it wasn't, now wasn't the time to worry about it.

However, now *was* the time to go backstage again and check on the actors. She made her way back to the corridor outside the dressing rooms (keeping her eyes firmly *away* from the men's doorway, just in case) and called out, 'Ladies and gentlemen, this is your half hour call. You have thirty minutes until curtain up.'

'How long til the house opens?' asked Lucy.

'Ten minutes,' said Hattie.

'Can we warm up on stage?'

'If you're quick.'

The actors all trooped out of the dressing rooms, mostly wearing most of their costumes, and formed a circle on the stage. Julian led them through a game of Zip Zap Boing, a round of Energy Ball, and a rousing chorus of One, One Two One, all staples of the vocal warm-up process. Hattie used the time to set and check the props and costumes backstage. She found the hamper balanced precariously on a fire extinguisher stage left, presumably Lucy's cunning plan to avoid having to carry the thing around backstage, and quietly brought it round to stage right, where there was ample space for it.

'What are you doing?' a voice suddenly hissed at her.

Hattie turned round. It was Glynis who had spoken.

'Just setting up,' said Hattie.

'You can't have actors on stage. The house is about to open!' Glynis wailed, her eyes bulging.

'I thought the house opened at quarter past?'

'It's nearly quarter past now!'

'Then everything is on schedule, isn't it? I'll get the actors off stage so that you can open the house at quarter past,' said Hattie slowly.

'Thank you!' huffed Glynis, and she stalked off.

Shaking her head to herself, and again trying not to wish plagues upon all venue managers, Hattie called out to the actors, 'Ladies and gentlemen, the house is about to open. Can you clear the stage please?'

'Righto,' said Julian. 'Break a leg, everyone. Big show tonight. "I love touring" on three. One, two, three…'

'I LOVE TOURING!' the actors all yelled.

Three hours later Hattie was alone in the building, finishing writing up the show report on her phone to send to the producer. One of the lanterns had slipped out of position at some point, meaning that in scene eight Mr Hensby had been in near darkness delivering his monologue, while the head of one of the patrons in the front row had been unexpectedly illuminated. In response Hattie had unplugged the offending light from the dimmers so that it didn't keep lighting up the audience in subsequent scenes, but in doing so she'd ended up being late for sound cue sixteen (Hattie knew that no one would ever know if she didn't own up to this, and that she was effectively telling on herself to the producers for no benefit, but professional pride prevented her from omitting her mistake from the report). Inevitably, Miss Preston had failed to locate the hamper backstage during scene five, so had come on without it in scene six. Other than that, it had been a comparatively clean show.

The final part of the report was a brief statement about how the show had been received by the punters. If they laughed and clapped a lot, she'd typically write 'Warm response.' If they didn't, she'd write 'Quiet audience.' Tonight there hadn't been many of them, and they'd been pretty abstemious with their applause, but one thing they hadn't been was quiet. It seemed that the majority of attendees were members of the West Rimesdale Amateur Dramatic Society, and as such it was to be expected that they would have strong opinions about the show, and not so surprising that many of those opinions would be critical. What was perhaps unexpected was how happy they all were to share those critical opinions with one another during and indeed throughout the performance. From her little booth behind the seats Hattie had heard a fairly continuous hum of scornful mutterings, rising at times to a crescendo that must have been clearly audible from the stage. It didn't help that there wasn't much of a division between stage and auditorium in this village hall – the actors were basically on the punters' laps – so the constant negative chatter must have been hard to ignore for the actors.

How to sum this up for the producers, though? Hattie thought for a second, then wrote down, 'Tough crowd.'

Report sent, Hattie started her final checks of the building. They had been engaged for a single performance in West Rimesdale, but venues like these didn't have such packed schedules as to require a tight turnaround of shows, so they didn't need to pack everything up on the night of the performance. They just needed to make sure all costumes were hung up and all props accounted for, ready to be packed and loaded onto the van the next day.

She got everything tidied away and was just having a quick sweep of the stage (Ricky and Lola always managed to get crumbs all over the floor in scene twelve) when she heard the click of a door closing.

'Hello?' she called out.

Silence replied.

The building was empty, and the exterior doors were all locked. Had she just imagined it? Hattie was suddenly aware of just how out of the way the village hall was. There was unlikely to be another soul within screaming distance. A ghastly premonition made its way unbidden into Hattie's brain. In her time, she had witnessed some terrible things in theatres that were supposed to be deserted.

'Oh bloody hell, Hattie, don't you start,' she muttered to herself.

Gripping the broom handle tightly, but trying to force herself to walk casually, so as to convince herself that she wasn't actually scared, she made her way backstage. There was no one in the wings… nor the men's dressing room… nor the ladies'. The rear exit wasn't *locked* locked, but it was one of those push-bar fire doors that didn't have a handle on the outside, so as long as the door had been properly closed then no one outside would have been able to get in unless—

There was a sudden roar of noise behind her, and as Hattie spun around there was a flood of light and a silhouetted figure loomed out at her, hands raised. Hattie shrank back and a cry escaped her lips…

… and then the sensible part of her brain intervened and pointed out that the noise was the sound of a toilet flush, and that the light and figure were both emanating from the bathroom doorway, and the raised hands were clasping a paper towel. And besides, she knew this person, even if he was the last person she'd have expected to see in a place like this.

'*Steve?*'

'Ey-up, Hattie,' replied Big Steve Felton, Hattie's former colleague, a now-retired production manager she had last seen at the end of a disaster-ridden production of *Love's Labour's Lost* in London. 'Sorry, did I startle you?'

'A bit,' Hattie admitted. 'I spooked myself. You might remember, I've got form for coming across dead bodies backstage.'

Steve nodded.

'I remember. And I'm sorry to do this to you, but I'm afraid you've just found another one: me.'

Act One

Actors are a jealous and competitive lot, and have been fervently hoping that their contemporaries and rivals will fall on stage and break their legs since time immemorial. When they utter such a hope out loud, however, the meaning is rather different. It is considered extremely bad luck to wish another actor good luck before the start of a performance. Instead of saying 'good luck', therefore, one says an alternative phrase, and the standard alternative is, perhaps surprisingly, 'break a leg'. The exact origin of the use of these words in this context is unknown. The simplest theory is that breaking a leg is the epitome of bad luck, and that actors superstitiously believe that the opposite of whatever one wishes for will come to pass. More complex theories posit that the phrase is a contraction of something like 'I hope one of the stars of the show breaks their leg so that you can step into their role' or 'I hope you cross (or "break") the part of the stage known as the "leg line" and in doing so get closer to the audience, thus gaining more attention for yourself.' My personal favourite interpretation is 'I hope your performance evokes such yells and shouts of appreciation from the drooling groundlings in the audience that their spittle liberally covers the front of the stage in enough quantity that you slip and break your leg.' Wildly implausible but delightfully gross, so I choose to believe it is true.

– from *A History of Theatrical Superstition*
by Freya Barnsworthy

1

They made a brew. Hattie had to grudgingly admit that the facilities offered by the kitchenette built into the multi-purpose village hall were better than many of the proper venues' 'green rooms' that she had encountered in her day. Once she and Steve both had mugs in their hands and had found two relatively comfortable chairs to sit in, by which point Hattie's heartbeat had returned to something resembling its normal rate, Hattie started to address the obvious questions.

'So what on earth are you doing out here in the middle of nowhere, anyway?'

'I came to see you.'

'You could have called.'

He shrugged.

'I'm not based in London any more. I was visiting my old mate Ivan who lives nearby anyway. When I saw you were in the area, I thought it was easier to drop in.'

'Late at night. Unannounced. In a locked building. How'd you get in anyway?'

'Doors like that aren't really built to keep people out,' was all Steve said by way of explanation.

Hattie remembered that Big Steve had always had something of a reputation. Theatre had been his second career. Before that it was rumoured he'd done something slightly more insalubrious and hands-on in north London. His bald head, broken nose, and broad physique did nothing to dispel the impression of a bruiser.

Hattie frowned.

'Hold on. What do you mean you're not in London? I thought you were up Archway way?'

'I was. But before I moved there, I was based a bit west of here, near Portsmouth. Came back to my old digs when I tried to retire. Thought I'd live out my days as a country gent.'

'I remember you saying you wanted out. Aren't you a little bit young to retire, though?' asked Hattie. She didn't know Steve's exact age, but she'd have been surprised if he was much older than fifty.

'I had a bit of money put away. Thought it would be enough to last me.'

Hattie nodded, beginning to feel she grasped the situation.

'But life turned more expensive than you thought, did it? Downside of a long life expectancy is a lot of financial planning needed. So, what, you looking to get back to earning now?'

Steve let out a rare bark of laughter.

'No, my problem's more or less the opposite of that. First week of being officially off work I get a cough. A week later it's full-blown pneumonia. As soon as I get over that I pass out in Tesco, the doctors tell me my heart's forgotten how to beat properly. They patch me up, give me enough pills to last a lifetime, and just when I think I'm squared away I get another call from the hospital. Different department. Turns out after the heart doctors had finished with all the scans they'd done on me, they passed them round the rest of the hospital, and one of them caught the eye of one of their lung people… anyway, it's a long story, but the final word of it is "cancer", and the one before that is "inoperable".'

Hattie was shocked.

'Oh, Steve, I'm so sorry.'

Big Steve scratched his big bald head awkwardly.

'Cautionary tale, I reckon. About the dangers of retiring. I spent my entire career stressed out of my mind, never took a sick day. Then as soon as I take my foot off the gas, everything starts falling to pieces.'

'So what's the… what's that word? The outlook?'

'Prognosis, you mean? Like I said, you're looking at a dead body.'

'I'm so sorry,' said Hattie again, before adding, 'you're… you're looking well, at least.'

'That's because I've not let them at me with any of their treatments. No chemo, no radiation. They said they'd buy me a little time at best, and near incapacitate me all the while. In the meantime, I've barely got any symptoms yet, but they warned me that when it all starts to go downhill it will go pretty fast.'

'Is there anything I can do?' asked Hattie. 'I mean, I know there's nothing I can do about *that* but—'

'Well, as a matter of fact, Hattie, there is,' said Steve, sitting forward in his chair with a new energy. 'That's why I came to see you. Truth be told I need your help with something.'

'Anything you need, Steve,' said Hattie forcefully. 'What can I do?'

'Well, the first thing is, you can keep this conversation to yourself, right?'

'Of course.'

Discretion was part and parcel of being a stage manager. Theatres were places that abounded with secrets, after all.

'Right. So, ever since I found out I had limited time left, I've been keeping myself pretty busy with something. Partially because it turns out that *not* being busy is literally killing me, but partially… you know that I didn't always work in theatre, right?'

Hattie nodded.

'Before that, I mostly did… let's call it planning and logistics. Mostly of the legitimate kind from the 2000s onwards. But before that I worked on some things that were… less legitimate. There was a group of people, see, that were very interested in the discreet movement of certain things that arrived in the country on the south coast to what you might call distribution centres in north London. As part of a broader transportation network, shall we say. And I had quite a lot to do with the planning and execution of all this. And at the time I didn't worry too much about the right and wrong of what I was doing. I was good at it, and it paid well. But now that I'm older and recent events have me feeling a bit more reflective, it doesn't sit well with me.

'Because Conor's lot… I mean, the group of people I worked with… well, they're still working today. They've built up something of an empire, and a lot of it is built on top of the foundations I laid for them twenty, thirty years ago. They're not good people, Hattie. And because of them, a lot of good people get hurt. And knowing that they're sitting pretty in large part because of me, well, it's stopped me sleeping so well this past year. So I started doing something about it.'

Hattie took a big slurp of her mug of tea.

'Why do I have the feeling you're about to tell me you did something a bit foolish?'

Steve winced.

'You know me, Hattie. I believe in solving my own problems. I started digging, working out who's still in the game, who's new on the scene, how everything works these days. And alongside that I started writing down everything I could remember about how it worked in the old days, and who did what, and who they did it to. I realised just how lucky I was to get out unscathed, given what I know. And I began thinking about how I could use what I know about before to maybe put a stop to some of what's going on now. See, back in the day what we were doing wasn't exactly good, but it wasn't so bad either. No one got hurt. Well, not seriously hurt. Not many people, anyway. But these days… well, they've got into some bad stuff. Some really bad stuff. Same transportation network, different cargo. And I reckon if I can put a stop to at least some of that, then my conscience will be a bit clearer at the finish.'

Hattie's tea was now unpleasantly cold but she kept drinking it anyway. This was wildly unfamiliar territory, making her deeply uncomfortable, and she didn't know what to do or say. Sipping her tea seemed like the least worst thing to be doing right now.

'Anyway, after a while I realised I'd put together enough dirt to give me a bit of leverage. I've got a neat little dossier of information that would be of great interest to the police, and even more interest to certain other parties too. So I got in touch, and let it be known what I have, and made it clear that I want certain parts of the operation shut down. Obviously they don't like it, but I've got them over a barrel and they know it.'

'Isn't that *incredibly* dangerous?' asked Hattie, horrified. 'If they're the sorts of people you say they are, and you're standing in their way… aren't you in quite a lot of danger?'

'I'm taking precautions. You may have noticed that I didn't waltz up to you in broad daylight today, for example. I've spent most of the day skulking in the car park outside. I know how to take care of myself.'

'So that was you watching me faff about in the rain, was it?'

'Yep.'

'I hate that van.'

'I figured.'

Hattie began to get an uneasy feeling.

'Steve,' she said. 'Why did you come and see me tonight?'

Steve smiled awkwardly.

'Well, now we're getting to it. I need your help. There's a

very simple job that needs doing in a couple of days' time, and it needs doing by someone who's discreet, reliable, and totally unconnected to any of what I've just been telling you about.'

Steve reached into his pocket and fished out a crumpled envelope.

'Do you remember the old workshop in Bow? The one they built the set for the *Skunktown* tour in?'

'Oh crikey,' said Hattie, thinking back. 'Yes, I remember. They couldn't book a rehearsal space big enough to stick the carousel in so we ended up rehearsing half the scenes in the workshop yard. That was Desi Treader's place, wasn't it?'

'That's right,' nodded Steve. 'Although Desi shut up shop years ago. But there's some sort of dispute between the landlord who owns the workshop and the rail company who owns the railway arch it's built into, so the place has been empty ever since. They stashed all the scenery from *Skunktown* there in case anyone ever wanted to revive it, then the whole place was forgotten about.

'Point is, that's where I'm having a final sit-down with Conor to thrash out the… actually, do me a favour and forget I said that name just now, would you?'

'Righto,' said Hattie. 'I'll forget you said it earlier, too, shall I?'

'Maybe I'm not quite as sharp as I like to think, eh?' said Steve. 'Anyway, on Sunday I'm sitting down to talk things over. Like I say, I've got some precautions in place to make sure I keep some leverage, and one of them is this envelope. It's got some things written down inside it that would greatly inconvenience these men even if… even if I'm not around to corroborate them. Once they know the envelope exists, they'll know they can't get rid of their problems by simply getting rid of me. So all I need you to do is hold onto this envelope for now – keeping it *completely* secret, mind – and then give it back to me on Sunday night once everything is concluded, and I can hand it over to them. That make sense?'

'No,' replied Hattie immediately. 'Not a bit of sense. I'll admit I don't know the first thing about organised crime, but it sounds to me like you're trying to blackmail a criminal gang, and you've got it into your head that there's *any way* this thing could end well for you. You've told them that you know secrets that could harm them, and you seem to be expecting that you can use that to convince a bunch of hardened career criminals to stop doing crime in exchange for you not spilling the beans, then you also expect to walk away, still knowing the secrets that could harm them, and that they'll just leave you alone and carry on not doing crime in perpetuity. Oh sorry, no, you're happy for them to keep doing some crime, just not the *bad* crime, is that it?'

Steve gave Hattie a look. She shifted uncomfortably, and not just because she'd been sitting too long and her hip was giving her grief.

'There's a lot I'm not telling you, Hattie. On purpose. I get that from the outside it might sound a little...'

'Stupid?' offered Hattie.

'... *risky*,' countered Steve, 'but I need you to give me the benefit of the doubt here.'

Hattie sighed.

'All right. So you want me to hold onto this envelope full of deadly secrets that bad people would potentially kill to keep quiet. For a couple of days. And then you want me to bring it to you in London.'

'Yes.'

'To the place where you're meeting the bad people, at the time when you're meeting them.'

'Yes.'

'The bad people who are prepared to kill to keep the contents of this envelope secret.'

'You'll be perfectly safe, Hattie. I promise you. Just... don't open the envelope, yeah?'

'Steve, I am a stage manager. I am well on my way to being a little old lady. You are talking to me about a world I've never been close to, and that I want no part of. I am not the person you should be dragging into this mess you've made.'

'Hattie *please*,' said Steve, his voice filled suddenly with as much emotion as Hattie could ever remember him exhibiting. 'Look, I know this is a big ask. I didn't come and track you down in the arse end of nowhere just to borrow a cup of sugar. I promise, this isn't going to be dangerous for you. But… it is for me. I know I've got limited time left, but I really don't want to go quite yet. Which is why I need someone I can trust to do this for me. Someone genuinely reliable. Take the envelope. Keep schtum. Then bring it to Bow at ten o'clock on Sunday night.'

'I don't even know if I can be free on Sunday night,' said Hattie, and she realised she was almost pleading. 'The last performance is Saturday, down near Hastings, and Sunday we'll be striking the set and returning everything to the props stores.'

'Oh come on, Hattie, you'll have that all done by mid-afternoon and you know it,' said Steve. He was an old pro, she was an old pro, and they both knew how these things went.

'Oh… bloody hell. Fine. Give me the sodding envelope.'

He handed over a thick A5 package, and Hattie wedged it straight into her coat pocket. As far as she was concerned, she didn't even want to have to look at the thing.

'Thank you, Hattie. This means more to me than you know.'

'In return, can you at least give me a lift to the B&B? It's only a quarter mile down the road but I'm not sure I can face the walk.'

'I… I think I'd rather we leave this building separately,' said Steve slowly. 'I'm sorry, but like I say, I'm taking lots of precautions. I can't believe anyone would have followed me here to West Rinton—'

'Rimesdale,' Hattie corrected him.

'—but just in case, we're safer if we're not seen together by anyone. Sorry.'

Hattie sighed.

'All right,' she said sourly. 'You bugger off, then, and I'll finish sweeping the stage, shall I? And hopefully your murderer pals who are waiting outside will follow you away and leave me alone. What a lovely end to a perfect evening.'

'I'm sorry,' said Steve, getting up awkwardly. 'How… how are you doing anyway? How's Nick?'

'Oh don't bother. Clear off, and I'll see you Sunday. Ten, was it?'

'That's right.'

Steve dumped his empty mug in the sink and made for the door. Hattie waited until he'd left then washed up his mug and hers. She went back to the stage and tried to finish sweeping, but found that she quickly spooked herself. Every sound from outside conjured up images of violent gang members lurking, ready to storm in and seize the squat white envelope from her.

It was madness, she thought, that in the space of half an hour she had let herself be sucked into such a right royal mess. What on earth was Big Steve thinking? Was he out of his mind, getting mixed up in something like this?

Then she realised that yes, he probably was out of his mind. He'd just been given a death sentence by the doctors, in a period of his life when he had all the time in the world to mull over it. Steve wasn't the sort to shy away in denial about anything. He'd have met this head on, and had some cold, hard conversations with himself about how he was going to spend the time that remained to him. Presumably the prickings of his conscience from the life he had led as a younger man wouldn't let him alone. Hattie had always known him as a rigid, moralistic man, and she could imagine that he found it very difficult to reconcile himself with his past.

If only he could have found a way to salve his conscience that was a little bit less blindly idiotic…

Once fifteen minutes had elapsed since Steve's departure, Hattie took a deep breath, steeling herself, and, buttoning up her coat, stepped out of the fire door and into the night. The car park was now entirely deserted, with no roving mafiosos gunning her down on sight. It was drizzling though, and achingly cold. With a grimace Hattie hunched her shoulders and stomped off in the direction of her B&B.

2

Morning came, and Hattie's memories of the previous evening's events took on the amorphous quality of a dream. Especially since she had immediately tucked the portentous envelope at the bottom of her suitcase and refused to let herself think about it, let alone look at it, lest by doing so she somehow alerted this mysterious and alarming 'Conor' to its presence in her possession.

She returned to the village hall and started to pack up. After half an hour Nigel appeared, hungover and irritable, and immediately took umbrage with the van's absence from the car park. Hattie apologised for not having driven it back first thing from its spot down the lane, but this idea only outraged Nigel further, and it became clear that his real grievance was that she'd driven the thing at all. Hattie's explanation that it was the venue's non-negotiable policy that the car park had to be cleared before performances fell on deaf ears. Eventually, after rollicking her enough to significantly worsen his own headache, Nigel stomped off to retrieve the vehicle, leaving Hattie wishing for the hundredth time that she'd never touched this tour in the first place.

Half an hour more and the actors started to appear in dribs and drabs. Their contracts demanded that they provide 'assistance as required' with the fit-ups and get-outs at each venue, but the assistance they gave varied tremendously. Lucy clearly believed her greatest strengths were orchestration and delegation: she would turn up clutching a large flask of tea and immediately start telling Hattie, Nigel, and the others what to do, according to some plan that existed only in her own head. Jim Hensby was always after any excuse to get up a ladder, which was a blessing when there was something that needed doing up a ladder, but could be a right curse when there wasn't. And then there was Julian, who was genuinely keen and willing to make himself useful, but was so unutterably cack-handed that he could be relied upon to mess up even something as simple as folding a pair of trousers and putting them into the costume bag.

On the whole, though, it was marginally faster to put this makeshift crew to work than to send them all away and do it herself, and having someone else do a lot of the bending and crouching was appealing, so Hattie did her best to divvy up tasks and provide supervision in a way that, even if it didn't maximise efficiency, at least minimised the potential for catastrophe.

She was coiling cables and overseeing Tonya Markham and Pippa West (who she had privately christened Morecambe and Unwise due to their propensity to creatively and elaborately fail every task assigned to them) loading two flight cases of kit onto the van when Julian loomed up behind her.

'Nearly there, then,' he opened, and Hattie replied, 'Hopefully we'll be off in the next hour.'

'I meant the tour as a whole. Just one more venue, and then… puff. The thing we created evaporates and is no more.'

'Oh. Yes.'

'Tragic, isn't it?'

'Yes,' Hattie lied. 'Could you possibly go and fetch the red tool kit fro—'

'I think that's the one downside of theatre compared to film,' Julian reflected, settling his hands into his pockets as he watched Tonya and Pippa struggle to lift the flight case. 'The performance of theatre is so much more satisfying, the way you tell the whole story in one go. It's not just a thousand tiny snippets spread out across months. But at least with film there's a tangible end product, something that survives once the project has finished. A show only exists for as long as the cast keeps performing it. Once the actors disperse at the end, that's that, and all that's left is memories.'

'That's right, Julian,' said Hattie, leaning in to get a hand under the corner of an unsecured case that was threatening to make a break for it out the back of the van. She was used to Julian's occasional need to wax lyrical, or at least to wax verbose. Once he got started there wasn't much you could do to derail him, so it was best to just let him get it out of his system.

Julian hadn't always been an actor. He had been a partner in an extremely successful law firm somewhere up in Yorkshire, and had made enough money to put his children through private school. Once they'd come out the other side, he found he no longer needed to be earning such fantastic sums, so had decided to reinvent himself as the thing he had always secretly wished he could be: an actor. Consequently, despite being in his late forties, he was relatively new to the whole industry, and still had a naivete about it that was endearing if a little tedious.

The thing about people like Julian, though, was that they were necessary to keep theatre ticking along. Lots of bright young things threw themselves into the industry in their early twenties, and from there on it was a game of attrition: some dropped out after a year or so, some stuck it out into their thirties. But it was a hard and demoralising life, as only the most successful actually made a living, and the rest had to subsidise their careers with whatever paid work they could find in the gaps. By the time any given cohort of actors had reached their forties, almost all of the unsuccessful ones had been weeded out. Which was fair enough. The problem was that you didn't want to do shoestring tours round provincial village halls if you were a successful actor, and the sorts of shows that could cover their costs doing provincial village halls almost always had parts for actors over the age of forty (as successful plays tend to reflect their audiences). So whence could producers draw their supply of actors old enough to fill the roles and unsuccessful enough to consider a badly paid, unglamorous, no-frills tour of the country? From second-career-ers like Julian, who were fresh enough to believe that a show like this was a stepping stone to bigger things and besides, still found it all new and exciting.

So it was worth letting the Julians rabbit on (as Julian was doing while Hattie thought these thoughts), since the whole enterprise depended on people like him.

'… which reminds me: Sunday. Kitty's on board, so we just need a place and a time. What do you think?'

'I'm sorry?' said Hattie. She hadn't really been listening, but she was pretty sure Julian had only a moment ago been saying something about Peter Brook's production of *King Lear*. What on earth was he on about now?

'Lunch,' he explained. 'Kitty's free at the weekend, and I know that you'll be jetting off to the next project next week, so I thought Sunday would be the best day.'

'I'm afraid I've got to spend the day returning props and costumes.'

'No problem, she can also do dinner, after you're done.'

'I have to be somewhere on Sunday night.'

'Where?'

'Er, Bow, in east London.'

'Oh that's perfect then!' Julian exclaimed. 'Kitty's based in Romford. I'll tell her to book somewhere in Bow, and I'll text you the address. Would seven o'clock do?'

Hattie probably could have got out of it. Julian would have taken no for an answer eventually. But it would have hurt his feelings, and besides, Hattie *could* do seven o'clock. She was sure she'd be done with returns by then, and she didn't have to be at Desi's old yard until ten. So she smiled and told Julian that she'd be delighted, and finally managed to shoo him away to collect the red tool box.

They completed the get-out, the actors piled into their cars and drove off eastwards towards Hastings, and after a brief pause to get the van running, Hattie and Nigel followed behind. They passed the drive in silence, which suited Hattie fine. Nigel's idea of conversation seemed to amount to listing his grievances against the world, and he took no great pains to avoid repeating himself in this enumeration, returning with enthusiasm to what he obviously considered his primary antagonists again and again. By the end of their first week on the road together Hattie had heard enough of his complaints, particularly those directed against what he still called the Inland Revenue, to last a lifetime.

They made good time, and knew they wouldn't get access to their next venue, the St Margaret's Community Theatre, until mid-afternoon, so they stopped for lunch at a service station. Nigel disappeared for a long commune with the men's toilets, and Hattie rang Nick to let him know that he should no longer expect her back until late on Sunday, as her day had rather filled up.

'Is she paying for your dinner then? This wannabe actress?' inquired Nick.

'I shouldn't think so. It sounds like she's only a teenager.'

'How about the uncle then? Sounds like he could afford it.'

'He won't be there, as far as I can tell.'

'Still.'

'Don't worry, I won't order the Chateaubriand. And if I go for the lobster I'll try to choose a small one.'

'I'm serious, Cockatoo,' he said.

'I know, my love,' Hattie replied soothingly. 'But we're not that hard up, are we? I mean, we've got savings to fall back on.'

'Yes, but they'll stop *being* savings at this rate. They're all turning into spendings.'

'What's the point of a rainy-day fund if—'

'But they're all rainy days these days. And besides, it's not supposed to be a rainy-day fund, it's supposed to be the retirement fund. It's supposed to be getting bigger, not smaller.'

'All right,' said Hattie, holding back the urge to snap. They'd had this conversation so many times, taking it in turns to be the censorious one. 'I'll get a side salad and tap water. And I hope you're not planning to stop by the Maltby Street Market this weekend either. I've seen you spend thirty quid on snacks between breakfast and lunch.'

'And I've seen you spend fifty quid on stationery when all you went out for was sticky tape. What's your point? Ow!'

Hattie sighed.

'Neck?'

Nick grunted.

'I'm sorry,' said Hattie. Then she added, 'I am sorry. I know you're having a miserable time of it.'

Nick lived to work. He was a tour bug, like Hattie had been, always on the road, never happier than when he was unloading a lorryful of kit at midnight on the outskirts of a city he'd never heard of. These neck problems had forced him to cut short a European tour, and he'd been stuck at home since about the same time as Hattie had set off on her recent travels. She didn't know whether her absence was more detrimental to his wellbeing than her presence would have been. As a couple they'd always worked best at a slight distance.

'It's worse than you think,' he said. 'I just got an email from Davey about *Hamlet*. Said they can't wait and see any longer. They're giving Min-Su the job.'

'What? Your job? To *Min-Su* Min-Su?'

'Yup.'

'The backstabbing little—'

'Oh it's not his fault. He's not been having much luck himself lately. He couldn't afford to turn it down.'

'Well… that's not the only gig in town. Once you're back up and running there'll be plenty more jobs.'

'I hope so. I just feel like every day I'm not working I'm… slipping away.'

Hattie grimaced. What he meant was that he was worried that what happened to her would happen to him: that by the time she came back from injury the industry had forgotten about her, and all the doors had closed.

'Don't be silly,' she chided him. 'You're only out of it for a month tops. And besides…'

She tailed off. What she wanted to say, but didn't, was, 'And besides, unlike me you're actually *liked* in the industry.' Hattie had always commanded respect for her competence, and she prided herself in her ability to get on, at least on a superficial level, with most people. But she didn't befriend people in the same way Nick did. No one came away from a show with Hattie thinking, 'I really want to make an effort to stay in contact with her, and work together again in the future.'

No, Nick would be fine. The phone would keep ringing, and the first time it rang after his neck was better he'd be straight back in the game, off gallivanting round Central America or South Korea or wherever a touring lighting technician was most needed. In the meantime, he was claustrophobic and worried about money and his neck hurt, but all of those things would pass.

Hattie changed the subject and she and Nick wittered on about nothing in particular while she waited in line to pay for her sandwich (she didn't tell Nick how much it cost), and then it was time to get back in the van and head for St Margaret's. Their awkward conversation about money stayed in her head, however, and made her mindful that she only had a couple of days of paid employment left. It was time to turn her attention to the next gig, so she spent the final hour of the journey looking at job listings on her phone.

The pickings were slim. The few shows that were being put on in town were all linked, directly or otherwise, to Sir Geoffrey Dougray, who hated Hattie (long story), or they were such tiny fringe shows that they were listed as 'profit share' (a gentle euphemism for 'unpaid'). There were rather more touring opportunities, but if the current gig had taught her anything it was that her hip really wasn't up to the hardships even of this one tour, let alone a second straight after.

After she'd scoured the official theatrical listings sites, and then the unofficial ones, she moved on to a couple of general classified ads websites that very occasionally had paid theatre gigs. And here she came across her first lead. It was a bit of luck – she'd meant to search for 'stage manager' but accidentally typed 'mangaer', and by the purest chance was presented with an ad that had the exact same typo in the job title field.

It was an odd one. The listing description simply read:

What You Deserve. A new play by Larry Lloyd. Performing on 14 March at the Ashwood Artspace. Rehearsing full time over the previous three weeks. Costumes, props, lighting and so on. Theatrical experience necessary. DO NOT CONTACT IF YOU ARE NOT A SERIOUS CANDIDATE.

Ordinarily, Hattie would have dismissed it immediately: the lack of detail, the fact it was a single performance at a miniscule venue. Everything pointed to this being an amateur gig with no money behind it. But the ad had been tagged as 'paid', and, well, Hattie wasn't exactly swamped with other options. So, she fired off her standard application email to the provided address, attaching her CV, then put away her phone. She would have almost certainly forgotten all about it had she not received, within five minutes of hitting 'Send', a phone call from an unknown number.

'Hello, Hattie Cocker speaking.'

'Ah. Yes. This is… Larry.'

'Oh yes?' said Hattie. That had been the name of the playwright in the job ad, hadn't it? Was this him? Was this about that ad? Or was that a coincidence and this about something else entirely?

'Yes.'

There was an unexpected silence on the line for a few seconds.

'Sorry, I'm in a car at the moment,' said Hattie, losing her nerve. 'My signal isn't great. Did you say something?'

'No. Ah. So I saw your CV. Ah. Very impressive. You've done a lot.'

So this was about the job ad. Hattie's heart sank. If the playwright was the one putting on the show that was another indicator that this was a profoundly amateur production.

'I've been very fortunate in my career,' she said. This elicited no response from Larry, so after a second she added, 'I was very interested to see your job listing. I wonder if you could give me little bit more information about the production?'

'Well. Ah. It's a new play. It'll be performed on the fourteenth of March at the Ashwood Artspace in south London. We'll be rehearsing over the three weeks leading up to it.'

Hattie realised that he was regurgitating the same information she'd already seen in the job add, so she gently cut him off, saying, 'May I ask, is this an amateur production or a professional one?'

Nigel looked over on hearing this, and silently rolled his eyes. *He's right*, thought Hattie. *If you have to ask, that's already a bad sign…*

'Ah. Well. I'm not… My background is in… When it comes

to technical distinctions… Ah. I can pay you, if that's what you mean.'

'All right,' said Hattie. 'And how big is the production team?'

'Ah. I think it would be easier to talk this through in person. Are you free today?'

'I'm afraid I'm working on a tour at the moment,' replied Hattie. Her instincts were screaming that this was a waste of time and she should make her excuses to get off the phone, but with Nick's niggles about money still fresh in her mind she couldn't quite resist the sniff of a paid gig, so she added, 'The earliest I could meet is Monday. Would this be in London?'

'Yes. But I can't do Monday. Tuesday? At three o'clock? Outside the Artspace?'

'Er… sure.'

'That's great. Well. Ah. I'll see you then. And I can tell you more then.'

'Wonderful. I'm looking forward to it.'

Another silence.

'Well, thank you for your time, Larry. I'll see you on Tuesday'

'Yes.'

'All right, bye for now.'

'Goodbye.'

Hattie hung up.

'Job?' asked Nigel.

'Possibly. A little gig at the Ashwood Artspace. But I don't know any details yet.'

'Ashwood? Horrible place. Uptight staff, no facilities. I did a show there once, absolute disaster…'

3

St Margaret's Community Theatre was a marked improvement over West Rimesdale Village Hall. It was tiny and run-down, and the roof leaked in various places, but it was a theatre space, if not purpose-built then at least exclusively used for performances. It had that cosy, worn, slightly mildewy smell, old cupboards filled with bolts of black stage curtains that were disintegrating with age, buckets full of broken cables, and everything was splattered with errant blobs of black stage paint. A play put on here at least felt like a play, even if the actors had to pick their way over the audience's feet to make an entrance from stage right, and the punters on the back row could barely see the stage thanks to the trio of lights rigged from the particularly low auditorium ceiling.

It was as good a place to give the tour its send-off as any, and, having seen the space, the cast's spirits were high as they started to unload the van for the final time. Unfortunately this high-spiritedness translated into a dearth of caution, and Morecambe and Unwise managed to ram the corner of a flight case straight into Hattie's bad leg, causing her unspeakable agony for a few minutes, and a throbbing pain for the rest of the day that served to sour her mood.

The Friday night performance, the first of two, was no more calamitous than most. The only real upset was that Lucy came to Hattie in a panic just before the show started because she couldn't find the hamper she needed for scene six, as it wasn't set where she expected it to be.

'It's next to the props table stage left,' said Hattie.

'Stage *left?* I thought it was supposed to be stage right, now!' yelped Lucy.

'That was only in Rimesdale, when there wasn't room for it stage left.'

'But I'd only just got used to it being stage right!' Lucy complained

No you hadn't, thought Hattie. *When it was stage right you missed it entirely.* But what she said was, 'I think there's room on either side of the stage this time. Why don't you put it where you feel most comfortable?'

Lucy frowned in confusion and walked away. Hattie went and found Jim.

'At the start of scene six, do not let Lucy onto the stage unless she is holding a hamper in her hands, get me?' she told him, perhaps slightly more forcefully than was strictly necessary. He blinked, swallowed, and nodded. Hattie retreated to the prompt desk.

Sure enough, Lucy did manage to come on holding the hamper in scene six, but the mental effort required for this feat clearly took a toll on her, because she utterly blanked on her first line and had to be rescued by a quick bit of improv by Pippa. Hattie resisted the urge to say something unkind about this in the show report.

The Saturday night performance the following day was an altogether messier affair. There is an informal tradition that on the final performance of a show, actors play small pranks on one another backstage. Unfortunately, not all actors have a clear sense of what constitutes an acceptable prank. Hattie, who hadn't slept well the night before, and was consequently in no mood for this sort of thing, intercepted Julian trying to sneak a bag of flour into the dressing room. Upon interrogation he confessed to having intended to empty it into Jim's hat, which the intended victim was supposed to don on stage halfway through the first scene.

'I'm sure it'd get a laugh,' Julian protested when Hattie began to lecture him.

'A laugh? This is a Regency drama, not a bloody panto,' said Hattie. 'If I see so much as a speck of flour, on stage or off, then you will have both me and the producers to answer to, and of those two, it's not the producers you should be afraid of.'

'Yes ma'am,' said Julian, and Hattie glared at him until she was sure he understood the seriousness of her threat.

'Oh, and Kitty's made a booking in Stratford,' he added. 'A Korean barbecue restaurant. Don't worry, I don't think it's too spicy. I'll forward you the details.'

The only other prank came to light in scene four, when Tonya opened the prayer book onstage and tailed off in the middle of delivering a line. She froze, her eyes bulged, then she abruptly closed the prayer book again, cleared her throat, and resumed. The next bit was supposed to be her looking up and reciting a verse from Leviticus, and the scene didn't make full sense when played with the book held firmly shut the entire time. But it was only a minor moment that didn't derail the show. Hattie made no mention of it in her report (there seemed little point given it was the final performance), but once the show was over and the cast had been dismissed, curiosity got the better of her and she picked up the prayer book from the props table and opened it to where it was bookmarked. She was greeted by a crudely drawn but *extremely* graphic pencil sketch, on a Post-it note, of Julian, Tonya, and Nigel (the artist had helpfully labelled them by name) engaged in… well. The three of them were very busy, and beyond that Hattie didn't want to dwell on the details.

And then the show was over. Or at least the performances were. The next morning the company assembled for the final time, and for once Nigel wasn't the most hungover of them. They packed everything up, sorting everything according to where it needed to be returned to, while Hattie and Nigel planned an itinerary connecting the various prop stores, wardrobes, and kit-hire warehouses that needed drop-offs.

'I'll drop you off with the suitcases in Hammersmith, you can take the tube across east,' suggested Nigel.

'There's four of them, that's more than I can manage by myself.'

'I'm not driving to east London. That's well out of my way,' he said sulkily.

'Hold on, after Hammersmith you've just got the lights to return in Wembley and then you're done, right? And then home's not too far from there for you? How about I drop you back home then, and *I'll* drive the van east with the costumes then I can return it tomorrow.'

Hattie made the suggestion reluctantly. She was no fan of driving, especially not driving in and around London, and *especially* especially not driving the van. But it was the logical, efficient solution. Nigel's disapproval of Hattie driving the van evaporated once he realised it would mean him getting home sooner. And besides, her evening was set to involve hopping between the costume store in Barking, a restaurant in Stratford, and an old scenery workshop in Bow before heading home to Chiswick. Her hip was agony as it was. Clumping around between bus stops and tube stations all night might do for her entirely.

So after the inevitable tearful farewells with the actors, and after they had woven their way around the periphery of London, depositing mixing desks, lanterns, props, and cables like a backstage Saint Nicholas, and after Hattie had deposited Nigel as well (*I'd prefer a lump of coal, all things considered*), and after she had worked her way eastwards across London and made her final drop-off in Barking, she realised that, barring tomorrow's drop-off of the van itself, the tour, which had taken up two full and aching months of her life, was finally over. She was, for now at least, a free woman. She wanted nothing so much as to go straight home, hurl herself into a hot bath, and there remain for a fortnight, suffering Nick to approach only as often as was required to periodically replace the box of Merlot she would keep nestled between the taps. But she had made a commitment. Two commitments (although she was on one level aware that she was doing her damnedest not to even think about the second one). And Hattie Cocker was a woman who kept to her commitments.

She looked up the location of the restaurant on her phone. Hattie wasn't particularly technically savvy, but she was up to this task. Identifying a place to park a van within walking distance of the restaurant was nearly beyond her though. She worked it out in the end, got the directions up on her screen, and, with her phone in place in the little holder next to the steering wheel, was pleasantly surprised that the van started first time of asking. She made her way to the appointed place, comfortingly aware that she had over an hour of contingency time to play with.

The first attempt at parking was a minor disaster – the car park she had identified had spaces so tiny that the van wouldn't fit in them (or if it would, it would require the abilities of a more dexterous driver than her). By the time she had found an alternative place, maneuvered the van into it, and paid, the whole of her spare hour had been eaten up, and she had to limp along rather faster than was comfortable to make it to the restaurant on time.

She needn't have bothered. Kitty was twenty minutes late, but, since they hadn't swapped contact details, couldn't let Hattie know. Hattie, knowing she had driving and a long night ahead of her, permitted herself just a single small glass of wine, which she had finished by the time the girl finally appeared, a bustling, beautiful, ginger-haired ball of glamorous energy.

'Wow!' she said as she sat down. 'Look at you! Look at us! What a time to be… er… Goodness. I mean, oh. Er, thank you so much for taking the time. I, honestly, I'm just so touched that you… er… I mean… meeting me… here…'

Her voice immediately dried up, and she looked almost pleadingly at Hattie. Suddenly she wasn't a glamorous young woman any more but instead a scared girl. It shouldn't have been surprising, Hattie reflected. She was eighteen, and that was what eighteen was all about: getting a sense of the person you might want to be, trying a personality on for size, finding sometimes that it didn't fit, or just that you didn't yet know how to wear it. Kitty had led with who she wanted to be, but it seemed that perhaps that wasn't yet who she fully was. She was playing the part, but she hadn't yet learned all of her lines.

'It's my pleasure,' said Hattie. 'I'm always happy to meet anyone who's thinking about joining the world of theatre.'

She shifted position, then regretted it as her hip let off a burst of complaint up her nervous system. Kitty must have seen her wince as she asked, concerned, 'Are you all right?'

'I'm fine. Just a little bit battered by a long tour.'

'Oh yes! With Uncle Julie… I mean Julian.'

'That's right. He tells me that you're thinking of training to be an actor, is that it?'

'Y-yes,' said Kitty, and her nervous smile spoke volumes: she seemed embarrassed to admit to her ambitions, as if they were unreasonably audacious, or perhaps that they were too fanciful and deserving of mockery. Actors were like this sometimes: not all of them were born believing they deserved to be in the spotlight, and in fact the best actors Hattie knew were the more modest ones. So Hattie was careful to smile as warmly and encouragingly as she could in return.

'And your uncle thinks you might do well to apply to ACDA, he tells me.'

'Yes. Well. I don't know. I think I'd go anywhere that would take me. Although sometimes… No I shouldn't say.'

'It's all right. Despite anything Julian may have told you, I have no influence of any sort, anywhere. All I can do for you is offer you information and advice, and the more you tell me, the more I can tell you back.'

'Okay. It's just that sometimes I wonder if I really should go to drama school at all. I've got a couple of friends and they're just… acting. Putting on shows, getting themselves seen. I'm worried that if I go to drama school for three years then by the time I get out, they'll have a three-year head start on me. And I mean, I've been finding auditions. I've not got cast in anything yet, but I think I might, if I keep plugging away at it.'

Hattie nodded.

'I understand the concern. Of course, I'm a stage manager; it's different on my side of the fence. I didn't train, I just got a job and then got another one, and took it from there. My understanding is that as an actor, it's blooming hard to go far without an agent, and blooming hard to get an agent if you haven't trained. But equally it's blooming hard to go far no matter how you do it, so I think you have to follow your gut on that one.'

'I see,' said Kitty seriously. 'I suppose I need to think about it some more. If you're up for giving advice I actually… I had another question. I know acting and stage management are very different but I was thinking, the longest show I've ever done ran for a week. I'm guessing you've worked on shows for a lot longer than that.'

'I did a tour of *Waiting for Godot* that lasted two and a half years.'

'Wow. Well, exactly. And on a show like that, whether you're an actor or a techie or whatever, you're basically doing… the same thing. Every night. Over and over again. And I was wondering whether it ever gets… boring?'

'It can do,' Hattie replied after a moment's thought. 'Some people don't have the patience for it. There's more variation if you're touring, or if you do more fringe gigs. And that's the draw of film and TV for some people: each time you nail a shot you get to move on from it forever, so you're not just repeating yourself. But the way I look at it is that it's only boring if you think of it as doing the same thing over and over again.'

'But how else can you look at it?'

'By seeing each performance as an opportunity to do a better job than you did the night before. Whether you're on stage giving your lines, or in the wings trying to do the scene changes as smoothly as possible, or in the booth at the back twiddling knobs to mix the sound, the satisfaction comes from doing the job well. And once you really start leaning into the detail of it, it's never the same thing over and over again. Each new show starts as a blank slate, and each night forms its own identity, with the things that work, the things you don't get right, and the things that are just different for whatever reason. Maybe you'll get bored of it one day. But if you take the craft seriously, that day should be a long time coming.'

Hattie realised that she was slightly surprised by the words coming out of her own mouth. Not because they weren't true, but because the truth behind them was one that she'd not thought about, and perhaps not necessarily felt, for quite a long time. Theatre was a slog. It was real hard work, and she'd got into the habit of complaining about it. But the reason she had stuck with it all this while, apart from the fact that she was quite sure she was fully unemployable in any other industry, was that it was a craft she had dedicated her life to, *because she loved it*. Or at least, she had loved it. Recently she had stopped thinking so much about the things about theatre that she loved. She only thought about the hard work. It was good to be reminded of the good things.

The meal was very pleasant in the end. Kitty talked about what drew her towards theatre in the first place: the friends she'd made at a drama club, that one teacher who had inspired her. It was the same story a thousand bright young things would tell, but no less joyful to hear for that. Hattie told war stories of disasters and triumphs dotted around the globe over the course of four decades, and was introduced to the joys of bibimbap and hotteok. She came away unsure if she'd managed to offer a single piece of actual advice to her new acquaintance, but optimistic that she had at the very least reinforced Kitty's enthusiasm for the world that surrounded the stage.

'It's a great life,' were her parting words, and to her own ear, at least, those words rang true.

On the walk back to the van, outside the warm bubble of the restaurant table, normality started to reassert itself, choosing the familiar pain in her hip as its first point of contact. Hattie wondered whether she could get away with not mentioning to Nick the cost of the meal (she had insisted on paying for everything), and considered that her only hope of that lay in his already being asleep when she got back, which was likely because… and then suddenly, for the first time in three days, she actually found herself thinking about how she would be spending the rest of the evening. A lurch in her chest caused her to stagger and have to lean up against a nearby lamppost to recover.

Hattie was terrified.

The prospect of doing what Big Steve had asked of her was so distressing that she had successfully managed to put it out of her mind until the last possible minute, but this *was* the last possible minute, and the feelings she had spent seventy-two hours stamping down now ambushed her all at once. She was going to walk into a deserted building, late at night, where a dying man was meeting a gang of hardened career criminals, holding an envelope with information that these men were very keen to suppress. This was madness. Utter lunacy. She should refuse. Go straight to the police, or go straight home, stopping only to throw the wretched envelope into the Thames.

But she didn't do any of those things. Because Hattie Cocker was a woman who kept to her commitments. She took a deep breath, steadied herself, then walked back to the van.

4

Hattie had fallen victim, she realised, to a false sense of security with respect to the reliability of the van. It had behaved so well in the early part of the day that she had allowed its foibles to slip her mind. To be fair, she had still reflexively built in plenty of contingency time for making it from dinner with Kitty to her meeting with Big Steve, but contingency time only helps if your problems come in the form of delays and things that slow you down. A van that won't start doesn't slow you down; it stops you entirely.

She tried everything. She jiggled all the wires that were jiggle-able, she poked and she pinched. She rang Nigel (no response), she rang Nick (no clue), she searched for answers on the internet via her phone (a million helpful-spirited but utterly useless suggestions). She even prayed, in a very general, non-denominational way. All to no avail.

She watched the time slip by, from 'if I leave now I'll be uncomfortably early' to 'if I leave now I'll be early by other people's standards but on time by mine' and when it got to 'even if I left now the best I could hope for would be to be a bit late, and even that's only so long as nothing else goes wrong' she gave up and rang a minicab. One came almost immediately, and she clambered in, only to have to clamber awkwardly out again as she realised she'd nearly left behind the one thing Big Steve had asked her to bring. She opened up the back of the van, pulled out her personal suitcase (the only thing that was now left in it) and hurriedly retrieved the envelope from the bottom of it, grabbing with it a handful of other sheets of paper, schedules, and programmes that it had been sitting with. She shoved them all into her coat pocket before closing up the van and clambering into the taxi once more, moving too fast for her hip's liking and as a result receiving an immediate throb of pain that promised further retribution over the days to come.

As the taxi slid through quieter and quieter streets en route to Bow, Hattie checked her phone. No messages from Steve. Was that a bad sign? Or a sign of any kind? Was he even now in tense negotiations with a criminal mastermind? Would she arrive to find him bound and gagged with a gun to his head and another one levelled at hers? Or was this all a misunderstanding, or a practical joke?

The car pulled up outside the old workshop gates. Hattie had wondered if she ought to get out a street away and walk the final bit of the journey. That did seem like the sort of thing people did in situations like this. But, especially in her flustered state, she couldn't think *why* people did things like that, and besides, the thought of doing any more walking was more than she could face.

In any case, as she stepped out and looked around, standing awkwardly with her weight on her good leg, the place seemed entirely deserted. The whole street was made up of industrial businesses inhabiting boxy warehouse buildings and railway arches. There was a car mechanic, and a print works, and then a lumber yard, all places that would be uninhabited late on a Sunday night. There was only one other car, parked at the far end of the street, a little pink three-door runaround. The whole street smelled slightly of petrol.

Desi's yard had no signage. From the outside it was just a stretch of ten-foot-tall brick wall, broken up by a pair of large steel-plated gates, once painted blue but now predominantly the colour of rust. Hattie knew from memory that behind the gates was a modest enclosure mostly used for storage, and behind that was the enclosed arch that made up the workshop itself. The gates were shut, but on closer inspection the deadbolt was drawn back, and the surprisingly new and shiny padlock that would normally have secured it in place was hanging, neutered, round a different bar off to the side. Hattie reached out to push the gate, then jumped at a sound behind her. But it was only the minicab's tyres going over a plastic bottle as it slithered away into the night. She set her jaw, then reached out to the gate again and this time pushed, and was rewarded by the thing moving easily and quietly open enough for her to get through. She walked in.

The yard was dark, and the petrol smell pervaded. Hattie wondered if there'd been a spill of some kind, either here or in one of the adjoining lots. She pulled out her phone, using its torch to light her way. A series of tarpaulined mounds loomed upwards. In some cases the tarpaulin hadn't survived the ministrations of several years of London weather, and had feathered away, revealing strange and alien shapes underneath.

I recognise that, thought Hattie as she passed a stack of wooden panels. *Those were the prison walls in* Skunktown.

On closer inspection most of them were rotted through. They must have been here, exposed to the damp and cold, for a very long time. This place was no longer a scenery construction workshop; it was a theatrical graveyard.

Hattie made her way across the yard to the workshop proper. Its entrance was protected by a big metal roller shutter, large enough for a lorry to drive through if opened, with a small personnel door cut into the bottom left-hand corner of it. Hattie went up and tried this, but it was locked, secured with a mechanical keypad. There would be no way of opening the main shutter from the outside.

Hattie listened carefully. She couldn't hear obvious sounds of life, but at first it was hard to pick out any nearby noise because a train was rumbling overhead. Once that had faded into the distance, everything was quiet. Screwing up her courage, Hattie knocked on the door.

'Hello?' she called, acutely aware of how her voice quavered.

She heard nothing in reply. The shutter was bent and corroded in places forming small gaps through which Hattie would have expected to see a little light escaping if there was anything switched on inside, but everything was dark.

There's no one here.

Hattie felt the beginnings of a wave of relief. She had no idea what was going on, and that confusion was unsettling, but it was starting to seem like her intended part in this mystery had been cut, and that she would perhaps be allowed to go home and forget all about it, at least for tonight.

She took out her phone, but resisted the urge to call another minicab immediately. Instead, she rang Big Steve. His number was still in her phone from the last show they had worked on together, although she hadn't tried to contact him since then, she acknowledged with a twinge of guilt. As the phone was ringing she thought she heard something quiet nearby, but before she could identify the sound it stopped, and the call went to voicemail.

'Hi Steve, it's Hattie. I hope this is still your number. Just to say, I'm sorry I'm late, and I'm here, but I can't find you. You did say Desi's old yard? In Bow? And it was tonight, wasn't it? Um. Let me know. I hope you're all right. And safe.'

She hung up, and turned to leave, but suddenly she heard a faint sound. A bright little chime noise, the sort that a phone makes when it receives a notification of a new voicemail. The sound hadn't come from inside the workshop, but from somewhere out in the yard.

Hattie turned back round and inspected her surroundings more carefully. There, tucked into the far corner, was a shape, larger and squarer than the others.

Of course. The shed.

It had been there back when they'd rehearsed here. It was where they kept all the really nasty chemicals, the specialist paints and sprays that you weren't supposed to get close to without a mask and goggles. They'd taken their lives in their hands by using it as an impromptu dressing room while working on scenes where the mechanical costume pieces were integral to the action. It was barely larger than a potting shed, and it had been in pretty bad nick even back in the day. Hattie was a little surprised to see it still standing, but there it appeared to be.

She made her way over to the corner. Sure enough, the shed was there, and its door was slightly ajar, although it seemed to be dark inside. Her chest tight and her breath catching, all her senses on high alert, Hattie willed herself to push open the door and look inside.

The smell of petrol was even stronger here. In the near-total darkness all Hattie could make out at first were some shadowy shapes, but as she fumbled with her phone, one of the shapes on the floor suddenly groaned. She got the torch switched on and pointed it down, and there, on the ground, was Big Steve.

He was in a terrible way. He was lying at an unnatural angle, and a terrifyingly large puddle of blood had formed around his leg. There was a filthy rag wrapped, for some reason, around one of his hands, and his face was a mess: there was a huge gash on his cheek, with a small flap of skin sagging downwards, and above it his eye was swollen shut. The rest of him was covered in cuts and bruises and blood.

It didn't look real. Hattie had come across some injuries in her time, but never anything like this. Not in real life. So her brain refused to accept that this was real life, and kept trying to tell her that this must be makeup, or a mask, or even some computer-generated special effect (not that that made *any* sense, of course).

'Steve!' she called, and at the sound of her voice he shifted slightly.

'I messed up,' he moaned, and blood trickled out of his mouth as he spoke.

She started forward to help him, but he called out, 'Stay back! It's not safe.'

'I'm calling you an ambulance.'

'No! Hattie, you've got to get out of here.'

His voice was hoarse and slurring. Hattie wondered if he was delirious.

'Steve, you need to get to a hospital.'

'You don't understand. They're coming back. They'll be here any minute.'

Hattie froze. Seeing the state Steve was in, she didn't need any convincing that it wasn't a good idea to be around when 'they' returned.

'Look,' Steve continued, panting, 'Don't go to the police. Don't draw any attention to yourself. Don't… make yourself a threat to them. I shouldn't have got you involved. I'm sorry.'

'What about you? I can't leave you here.'

'I might… I might have a way. I can still convince them I'm more useful to them alive. I just need the envelope.'

'Give me a second then.'

Hattie reached into her coat pocket and pulled out the bundle of papers, rifling through them to find the envelope. She didn't find it on the first pass. Nor on the second. There was *an* envelope, A5 and white, but this one contained only the receipts for coffees and sandwiches she'd bought with the company kitty. She felt her stomach begin to drop away from her, and her hands started to shake. In her panic earlier she hadn't thought to check *which* envelope she had picked up. She went through the papers one more time.

'Oh Steve,' she said softly. 'Oh I'm so sorry. I was rushing. I… I think I've left it behind in the van.'

'Is it parked nearby? If you run—'

'No it's… it wouldn't start. It's in Stratford…'

Big Steve said nothing for a few seconds and Hattie thought she might just curl up on the floor right there. Then he took a big rasping gulp of breath and said, 'Don't worry. It can still work. You just get out of here. If I don't… don't tell the police anything, half of them are in on it and you don't want to make yourself a target. But if *they* find you, tell them everything, cooperate any way you can to save your skin. And for God's sake, burn that envelope without opening it.'

Hattie tried one last time.

'Steve this is mad,' she said, stepping forward. 'I can't leave you h—'

'Listen! That's them. They're coming back. You have to go. Now!' Steve barked at her, lurching upwards to emphasize his final word.

Fear and confusion finally outweighed Hattie's concern for her friend and she stumbled away as instructed, hobbling as fast as she could away from the shed and back to the gate. She couldn't hear anything, and when she reached the gate and, terrified, peered around it, she saw that the street was still deserted. Wherever the men were coming back from, it wasn't here. She could almost convince herself that this was all Steve's delusion. There were no men. She had no need to leave him. But now that she'd started moving, the fear gave her unstoppable momentum, and she carried on out of the gate, and limped up the street as fast as she could go. Once she rounded the corner, she pulled out her phone and breathlessly called a minicab, asking it to pick her up on the next street along, well away from the workshop. They told her it would be at least fifteen minutes before they got to her, and she was just wondering where on earth she could hole up to wait, when she heard a loud bang. At first Hattie thought it must be a gunshot, but the sound was followed by a sustained roaring whoosh noise, which she didn't recognise at all.

Don't be an idiot, she told herself. *Keep moving away, and don't even turn round to look back.*

But, knowing that Steve was still behind her, some reckless part of Hattie couldn't help itself. She turned around and cautiously made her way back to the corner and very slowly and carefully poked her head round it.

The street was still deserted. There, a hundred yards down the road, was Desi's yard, the gates still fractionally ajar as Hattie had left them. But just above the top of the wall there was movement, a flash of light, growing into a series of tongues of flame as Hattie watched. The darkness above the yard was a different colour to the darkness around it – the dirty grey of a cloud of smoke illuminated from below. Something was on fire, and as the flames grew it became clear that that something was situated right in the corner of Desi's yard. The smell of petrol from earlier popped back into Hattie's memory as she realised, horrified, that 'they' must have doused the shed in fuel and left only for as long as it took them to find some way of setting it alight, with Steve inside. She just had time to visualise the bottles and tins of chemicals lining the walls of the shed before there was a sudden flash, followed immediately by a huge boom, as the whole shed exploded.

Act Two

When there is no show currently in production at a theatre, in other words during a period of temporary or permanent closure, we say that a theatre has 'gone dark'. But a theatre is never truly dark. There will always be a light on in an empty theatre, and I don't mean those wretched health and safety-mandated emergency exit signs. From time immemorial, theatre managers have insisted that 'dark' theatres always have a single light burning in the auditorium, and this is known as a 'ghost light'. This has practical value, of course, in that if you are the first person to enter a darkened auditorium, filled with weights and mechanisms, sudden drops and improbably-shaped scenery, being able to see where you're going in order to locate the main lights is helpful. It has also historically been quite an impractical measure: in the age of gas light, an unattended flame burning in a building largely constructed from wood would inevitably carry the risk of disaster, and indeed, an alarming number of theatres have burned down while dark.

But ask any performer or impresario and they'll tell you the real reason for the ghost light. It is the embodiment of the spirit of the theatre, and represents a silent promise: that, no matter how prolonged and dark the darkness is, the light will one day return, and actors and audiences will once again fill the building with passion and stories and applause.

– from *A History of Theatrical Superstition*
by Freya Barnsworthy

5

Having had no sleep on Sunday night, Hattie spent Monday morning in bed. She didn't manage sleep there either, but after the previous night's exertions she wasn't capable of doing much more than lying supine, and her mind was feeling far too scrambled to do anything productive while there. So she lay still, ghastly images from the previous night playing and replaying in her mind.

She had called the fire brigade, and explained that Big Steve was inside the blaze, although by the time they arrived the probability of any kind of rescue seemed slim. They had questioned her further and, not knowing the practical or legal consequences of withholding relevant information about the cause of the fire, she conveyed to them that it had been started deliberately, with the help of liberal quantities of petrol. The firefighters inevitably, and understandably, treated this information with the severity it warranted, and before they were done extinguishing the last of the flames, a police car had appeared, and Hattie was interrogated more thoroughly.

In her extremely agitated state, Steve's urgent insistence preyed on her mind. *Don't tell the police anything. Half of them are in on it and you don't want to make yourself a target.* Was that really true? Steve had clearly misjudged a lot of things, but he hadn't *over*estimated his adversaries.

So Hattie told a *very* stripped-back version of the truth. Steve had been to see her, and told her that soon after retiring he had been diagnosed with terminal cancer. Something was pricking at his conscience, but he hadn't gone into the details. He had asked her for a favour, to meet him at Desi's yard on Sunday night (Hattie made no mention whatever of the envelope). The van had broken down, so she had been late. The taxi had dropped her off, she had looked around the yard, smelled petrol. She had eventually found Steve in the shed, but he had told her to leave. She was just leaving when the shed exploded.

'So he asked you to come here, but when you arrived he just told you to leave again? Did he tell you why he had changed his mind?' asked the officer.

'No, I… well,' Hattie had replied, uncertain. She couldn't for the life of her think how to describe her last encounter with Steve while still feigning ignorance of anything to do with this awful mess of retributive gang violence. In the end she said: 'He seemed agitated. I think he was in pain. He told me to go. I went back out on to the street while I tried to think about what to do next. I thought I might call the emergency services or something. But that's when the fire started.'

'I see. And when you save Steve earlier in the week, how did he seem? Did he seem himself? Was he agitated then too, maybe about the cancer diagnosis and the prospect of the pain and discomfort the illness would cause?'

You think he killed himself, Hattie thought. Which was a fair assessment, based on what Hattie had said. If the police had any ability, appetite, or resources to investigate the true crime and bring the perpetrators to justice Hattie didn't want to stand in the way of that, but also… *you don't want to make yourself a target.*

'He wasn't one for making big displays of emotion,' said Hattie carefully. 'But Big Steve was always a man of action. I don't think the idea of sitting around waiting to die suited him.'

Everything she said was true, and it fitted together so smoothly. She knew that she was saying what they wanted to hear, and that made it easy. The officer nodded, satisfied, and Hattie was allowed to go. She took a cab back to the van in Stratford, asked it to wait while she collected her suitcase from the van, and then continued on back to Chiswick, hobbling up the stairs to her flat in the early hours of the morning.

Now, lying in bed, her conscience pressed down heavily upon her. Big Steve had been killed, in an awful, brutal way, and she had effectively aided his killers in getting away with it. She should call the police and give them a full account, right away, tell them about the envelope, what Steve had told her, the state she had seen him in. She should at least tell them the name 'Conor'.

But Steve had been so clear. At the best of times he trusted the fuzz even less than she did, sometimes unreasonably so in her opinion, but if he said they were thick as thieves with the very gang that he had once been part of, then surely she should believe him. And if that was really true then perhaps there was no route to justice being done that went via her telling them what she knew. And now that she had seen what these men were capable of, no one could blame her for following Steve's instructions, for respecting his last words indeed.

And yet all of these felt like convenience excuses for cowardice, and so Hattie found herself lying in bed doing nothing, exhausted but not sleeping, and fretting. (That being said, in the midst of this emotional turmoil, she found a moment to email the show producers to explain about the van and make arrangements for its return. She had committed to getting the show squared away, and Hattie Cocker was a woman who kept to her commitments.)

Nick, meanwhile, had been asleep when she got in, and when he awoke in the morning to find her lying next to him, he rolled over and gave her a groggy peck on the cheek before stumbling out of bed toward the shower. When he came back into the bedroom to get dressed he had assumed she was sleeping and she, in no state for conversation, hadn't disabused him of the idea. He had eventually wandered out on the trail of coffee and breakfast and hadn't returned since, although she could hear him padding around the flat.

He looking in again at lunchtime.

'Wakey wakey, Cockatoo,' he said brightly. 'If you don't get up now you won't sleep tonight.'

'I've not been sleeping. My leg.'

'Oh don't you start. Your leg has been bust for years. Time to move over, let someone else have some sympathy for a bit. Now, changing the subject entirely, my neck is killing me.'

At that, Hattie abruptly burst into tears.

Nick was evidently shocked into silence, and not unreasonably so: the last time she had cried in front of him had been soon after she fractured her hip, when the ramifications of the injury on her touring career became clear, and the previous occurrence before that one had probably been at least a decade earlier. Hattie did not cry. She coped. She was a stage manager, after all.

'Er… you all right?' he asked eventually.

'No,' said Hattie. 'Big Steve's dead. He was killed. They beat him up. Then they burned him. And I was there.'

'Oh. Crumbs. Er. I'll stick the kettle on, shall I?'

'Yes please.'

Armed with a fortifying cup of tea, Hattie worked her way through the detail of what had happened, from Steve's visit, to the envelope, to the van not starting, right through to the explosion, with Nick nodding and listening. The good thing about Nick was that while it could be difficult to get his attention at times, when he did listen he listened properly: silently, attentively, and sympathetically. She knew that there were moments when, muddled by tiredness and emotion, she was confused and confusing in her telling, but he gave her the space to sort herself out without interrupting, correcting, or redirecting, and eventually she'd given him as full account as she thought it was possible to give, and she fell silent, a small portion of weight lifted from her. She had kept secrets from Nick in the past, and it hadn't worked out well for her, practically or psychologically. It felt good to impart everything that she knew, and know that they were more or less on the same page at the end of it.

'Bloody hell,' he said in summary.

'Yup.'

'Is there any chance he could have made it out?'

'Not under his own steam. His leg… I suppose the people who started the fire could have carried him… but why would they have?'

'How big did the fire get?'

'How do you mean?'

'Well, if the whole street caught fire I suppose there'd be a news story about it.'

'I don't think much of the scenery will have survived, but they got the hoses going pretty fast, and I don't think it spread out beyond Desi's yard. Not much at least. You never know, though.'

Nick pulled out his phone and did some searching. Eventually he showed her a headline from an east London local news site article: 'Arson suspected in fatal warehouse explosion'.

'Let's see… "Two fire engines and fifteen fire fighters tackled" … blah blah blah… "The blaze, which began at around ten thirty last night" … Ah. Okay. "The London Fire Brigade confirmed that one person died. The victim has not yet been named. It is understood that identification of the body was hindered by the extent of…" Jesus, it sounds like all that was left of him was a couple of charred… never mind. Anyway. "However, certain effects found at the scene, as well as witness statements, have allowed investigators to ascertain the identity of the victim, which will be released once next of kin have been notified. The cause of the fire is not yet known, although arson is suspected."'

'Oh,' said Hattie.

'Yup.'

'Well, that's that then.'

'I'm sorry. He was a good man. I think.'

'How do you mean?'

'Well… by his own admission, he was mixed up in something fairly nasty. Enough that it left him with a pretty guilty conscience. He didn't say what sort of things it was?'

'He wasn't clear. Sounded like it might be bringing drugs to London?'

'Oh. Well. Might be a bit hypocritical to condemn that. Although I suppose there's quite a bit of difference between selling a little bit of herbal recreation to the likes of us compared to, say, enabling and buggering up the lives of a bunch of hopeless crack heads.'

Hattie shrugged.

'In all the time I knew him he had a powerful sense of right and wrong,' she said. 'Didn't always line up with mine, but still. I think he was a good man. But either way. He was a friend, and a colleague, and above all he was a theatre person.'

'That's a point. Who's going to tell everyone?'

'What do you mean by everyone?' asked Hattie. Her head felt fuzzy.

'I mean everyone. Every theatre in London will have someone who worked with Big Steve, and half of the theatres outside it too. Someone's got to put the word out.'

'That's not our problem, is it? He had friends, family.'

'I'm sure he did, but were *they* theatre people? He retired a couple of years ago. You know what it's like. You step out for a bit… you fade from view. 'Specially if you've left town.'

Hattie did know what it was like. It had happened to her and she hadn't even retired.

'So what I'm saying,' Nick continued, 'is that one of us—'

'I know.'

'And I mean one of us theatre people, not necessarily one of us two—'

'I know.'

'But it needs to be a theatre person who knew him and who knows what—'

'I know.'

They sat in silence for a few moments. Hattie knew what needed doing, but she couldn't bring herself even to contemplate it. Not yet.

'I'll make a couple of calls,' said Nick, eventually. 'You've been through enough.'

Hattie had never loved him more strongly.

So Nick took himself off into the sitting room while Hattie stayed in bed. He wouldn't need to call all that many people, she realised. Word spreads. He just needed to plant some seeds. Meanwhile, having at least slightly unburdened herself, Hattie lay back and had another go at a sleep. She could feel her thoughts getting cloudier and dreamier but somehow each time she started drop off, an image of Steve lying on the floor of the shed would pop into her head and her chest would tighten and she'd wake herself up again. So she lay in a half-awake daze for an hour, until her hip informed her that lying down was no longer acceptable, and her bladder suggested that getting up would allow her to resolve at least one other of her many current discomforts.

So she awkwardly lifted herself out of bed and hobbled to the loo. On her way back she overheard Nick, on the phone, in the living room.

'… so Henty's hanging halfway up the side of the building off the railing of a cherry-picker, Donna's marching round below him demanding to know why there's whipped cream on the prompt desk, and Fliss walks in with the mayor of Basel and the British ambassador to Switzerland…'

Hattie smiled. She knew the anecdote. It was nothing to do with Big Steve. But presumably if Nick had been on the phone for an hour, breaking the news and having a natter, with each successive phone call he collected more reminiscences to share with the next person. Good old Cocker One. He had such warmth. Hattie thought that if ever anyone needed to ring round and break the news of her death, she wanted it to be him. Which was lucky, really, given the balance of probability.

Her mood soured, however, as she turned, and her gaze fell upon her suitcase, still sitting in the corner of the hall where she'd left it when she came in. Somewhere in there, she remembered, was an envelope whose contents she both did and very much didn't want to investigate.

6

A job interview was the very last ordeal that Hattie would have chosen to put herself through, but a stern notification from the bank that the heating bill was about to put her into the red served to steer her mind towards the merits of securing gainful employment in the near future.

So on Tuesday at lunchtime, after a quiet morning, Hattie turned her attention to making herself look and feel presentable, and then working out how to get down to the Ashwood Artspace on the outskirts of Lewisham. It was, she discovered, one of those tedious journeys where none of the available transit options were either fast or direct, but that couldn't be helped. She pulled on her big coat, double-checked that her handbag contained all the essentials (the ghastly moment of discovery that she had left behind the envelope flashed into her mind, and she forced it out again) and, ignoring the grumblings of her hip, set off.

An hour and a half later, she was standing awkwardly on the corner outside the venue, and her hip was grumbling rather more loudly. She loitered as obtrusively as possible, aware that she had no idea what Larry Lloyd looked like and that likewise he had no idea what she looked like. So she made awkward eye contact with every man who approached, not smiling of course (because you can't smile at strangers in south London), but trying at least to look potentially friendly in case any of them turned out to be the man she needed.

When he did turn up she was jolly nearly caught out, because of all the men who had walked past he was the only one about whom she privately thought, 'Well at least I know it can't possibly be *him*.' She could hardly imagine anyone who looked less like a theatre person. He was barely five foot tall, sallow-skinned and tubby, with greasy strands of very fine, jaw-length grey-brown hair hanging down at the back and sides, with a little bit teased up and over to half-heartedly cover the bald top of his head. Hattie guessed he was around fifty, but wouldn't have been that surprised to be told she was off by a decade in either direction. He wore a dark grey suit with light grey pinstripes, a white shirt with brown pinstripes, a brown tie with grey pinstripes, and a blue plastic anorak over the top. He wore thick glasses and carried a tattered briefcase, and his too-short trousers revealed grey socks and a very worn pair of trainers. He walked with a bouncing little stride and hunched shoulders. Hattie had met many playwrights and producers in her life, and none of them looked like this. Not in a way that necessarily reflected badly on this man, it had to be said. It was just that theatre, both onstage and off, was all about appearances, and even the people behind the scenes developed a sense of playing a part, and dressed accordingly.

Nevertheless, this was the man who stomped up to Hattie, stuck out his hand and said, 'Hattie Cocker, yes?'

'That's right,' she replied, shaking his hand. 'Larry, is it?'

'Oh. Yes. Ah. We won't go into the theatre. Maybe we can get a coffee somewhere. Ah.'

'Don't they have a café in the theatre?' asked Hattie.

'Ah, no. That is, it's not open.'

They turned to look at the venue. It was quite clearly a converted church, which came with both benefits (such as high ceilings, helpful for rigging lights) and drawbacks (such as poor acoustics, limited wing space and awkward sight lines) in Hattie's experience. It also, despite Larry's assertion, seemed pretty open, with a little illuminated sign by the door that even said 'Café Open', but when Hattie started to point this out she was met with a shake of the head.

'It's closed. I checked,' said Larry. Hattie decided not to question him further. For whatever reason, he didn't want to set foot into the theatre building. He didn't seem to be in any hurry to propose an alternative venue, though. He just stood there, looking expectant and slightly uncomfortable.

'I think I saw a greasy spoon just round the corner,' Hattie suggested eventually.

'Ah. Okay. Okay. Greasy spoon,' said Larry, blinking rapidly.

Hattie smiled encouragingly and led the way. She had been oscillating between feeling optimistic and dispirited, as she tried to work out whether there was a proper job here or not. But now, having met the mysterious Mr Lloyd and found him to be absolutely nothing like what she had either hoped or dreaded, she realised that her primary sentiment was a deep curiosity. Who was this odd little man, and what was he doing putting on a play?

They ordered teas and sat down, and Larry pulled out a laptop from his briefcase, opened it up, and hunched forward so that his face nearly disappeared behind its screen.

'Right,' he said after a second, rearing back so that he could look Hattie in the eye. 'So. I'm not here to do a typical job interview. Ah. I'm not going to ask you where you see yourself in five years' time, or any of the questions you'd normally get.'

No one has ever asked someone where they see themselves in five years in a stage management interview, thought Hattie as she nodded seriously.

'I'll put my cards on the table,' he continued. 'I like your CV. I think you have exactly the experience I need. Ah. I was disappointed by the calibre of some of the applicants I've had.

Ah. I'm a decisive person, and I think… if the right person comes along, you grab them. So I'm probably going to offer you the job. And the pay is… let's just say it pays pretty well. Ah. I've budgeted four grand for a month's work. And it's yours. Ah. Unless this meeting goes very badly.'

Hattie did her best not to splutter. A thousand pounds a week was extremely good going, *far* more than she'd expect for a one-off performance at a fringe venue in south London.

'All right. I'll try not to mess this up then,' said Hattie, in what she hoped was a light-hearted tone. Larry just nodded earnestly.

'I suppose what I really need to do is check that you've got experience doing all the things I need doing. The main thing is, of course, are you able to operate both lights and sound during the performance?'

It was a slightly odd question to ask. You'd never come across a stage manager who'd say they *couldn't* run lights and sound during a performance. It was a bit like asking an electrician if they were comfortable working with wiring. Of course, on most professional shows the cueing would be delegated to the deputy stage manager, or handled by dedicated lighting and sound board operators, so the charitable interpretation of the question was to inform Hattie that this production was the sort where the one stage manager would be doing everything, and to ask if she was happy to work on something that small.

'Yes,' said Hattie confidently. 'I've just come off a tour where I was doing both. I don't know what sort of lighting desk they have at the Artspace…?'

'Ah. I don't think we need to worry about that sort of technical detail at this stage,' said Larry. 'Now, for this production the setting is very specific, so I need the lighting to be just right. If I tell you what I want each scene to look like, light-wise, you can do that for me, right?'

Another odd question, but skewing the opposite way this

time. A bit like asking an electrician if they were comfortable working with plumbing. Hattie began to suspect that Larry didn't entirely know how a theatre production worked.

'That's a bit outside my area of expertise. I'm no lighting designer, and while I know the basics of rigging, I'm not a lighting technician.'

Larry's face creased into a frown.

'This is what the other one said. And what *I* said is that this isn't some la-di-da production. This is real theatre for real working people, and I need a hands-on, can-do attitude. I'm not going to hire a hundred different people each to do one thing. I need people who are going to get stuck in and make things happen. This is why so many shows lose money. Well I'm not going to be like that.'

Hattie could feel the four grand slipping away from her.

'I do understand,' she said soothingly. 'And I completely agree, everyone should be willing to muck in, regardless of job title. I'm more than happy to do what's necessary… It's just that I've got a dodgy hip, and I'm not as fast as you'd need me to be getting up a ladder. And in my experience, the time you get in venues like the Artspace to do all your rigging and focusing is pretty limited. You're better off getting a few hours of time from someone dedicated to lighting to make it all happen. Maybe the Artspace have an in-house technician?'

He shook his head.

'They want to charge me an arm and a leg to use their in-house people. I need to staff this myself.'

'Well,' said Hattie, thinking on her feet, 'as it happens my husband is a lighting technician. And he's probably free. He's at a bit of a loose end at the moment. I bet I can get him to help out.'

Larry's face lit up.

'*That's* what I want. Problem-solving. Not just sitting back and complaining. Coming forward with solutions. Okay. Yes.

Husband-wife team. Right. Ah. Then the next thing is rehearsals. You're happy organising them?'

'Yup,' said Hattie. 'I'm very comfortable being "on book" in a rehearsal room.'

She hesitated, a doubt nagging at her.

'Although, when you say organising them… can I just double-check what you have in mind?'

'I just mean getting the actors together, working through the script, making sure everyone knows where to stand and so on.'

Again, he seemed to be eliding some things that fell within a stage manager's purview with some other things that definitely didn't.

'I see. So I understand it, are you directing the show?'

'Well, I think of myself more as a writer and producer primarily…'

'But, I mean, there's not someone else who's the director?'

'Oh, I see what you mean. No, to the extent that there's a director at all, it's me.'

'Okay. I just wanted to be clear. Traditionally in a rehearsal it would be the director who tells everyone, er, where to stand and so on.'

Lloyd blinked again.

'Right. Yes. Of course. Ah. That's what I mean. Ah.'

He had gone rather red.

He really doesn't know how any of this works, thought Hattie. This was without a doubt one of the strangest gigs she'd ever come across. But if he was really going to pay a grand a week then it was a gig she still wanted. And that meant staying on his good side. She decided to rescue him.

'Just checking we've not got our wires crossed. So you'd be taking the creative decisions in the rehearsal room and telling them to the actors, and I'd be there recording those decisions and making sure that the actors do what was decided.'

'Exactly,' he said gratefully. 'Yes. And you've experience doing all that, don't you?'

'Lots of experience,' said Hattie enthusiastically. 'That's right up my alley.'

'Good. Ah. And then… props and costumes?'

The dynamic was shifting slightly. He had initially seemed like he was trying to bluff his way, pretending that he knew what he was talking about, and quite defensive. It's tricky when you're trying to assess someone's expertise in a field where you yourself are not an expert. Like when you want to hire a builder and you're trying to work out if they're a cowboy who's going to rip you off. But now Hattie seemed to have won just enough trust for him to acknowledge some of his ignorance about the process, at least indirectly. She took this to be a good sign, but tried not to rock the boat.

'Props are straightforward. As and when you know what you need, tell me and I'll try to source it. We can borrow stuff, buy it, and at a pinch make it, depending on the budget. I mean, it also depends on what sorts of things you need.'

'Oh, well it's pretty straightforward. Most of the play is set in a classroom, so it's pretty much the obvious: desks, chairs, blackboards, pencil cases, that sort of thing.'

'All right. Costumes is a bit harder. I don't know what sort of thing you have in mind…?'

'I need school uniforms. White shirts, black trousers, black and blue striped blazers, with a yellow logo on the pocket, and a black and yellow tie.'

'I'm sure the actors will be able to provide their own shirts and trousers. As for the blazers, we might be able to get them from a costume store, but I can't promise we'd find an exact match.'

'It has to be exact,' he said, unexpectedly firmly.

'Oh okay. Then… I suppose if there's an actual school that has that as its uniform then we could order it from their supplier? Would get expensive, though.'

He shook his head.

'They don't make them any more. They changed the uniform years ago.'

Hattie sucked her teeth. In the back of her mind she wondered idly who 'they' were, but now wasn't the time to worry about that.

'That sounds like a custom job then. I can do a bit of sewing where needed, but you'll probably need a specialist. You're sure it has to be exactly as you describe it? No wiggle room?'

'No wiggle room. If you can't do it yourself, I'd need you to find me a costume specialist. Can you do that?'

'Certainly,' said Hattie.

'Well then. Ah. Well then.'

Larry frowned and looked away, then looked back.

'Well then, I suppose I'm going to offer you the job. Unless you have any questions?'

Hattie felt herself relax, fractionally. Money. She was being offered money. It wasn't entirely clear what she was getting herself into in return, but this was a far preferable situation to *not* being offered any money.

'That's great to hear. As it happens, I do have some questions if I may. I understand that you've written this play yourself and are now putting it on. Am I to understand that this is… er… your debut?'

'That's right. Ah. My experience is more… yes, this is my debut.'

'And may I ask what's drawn you to put on a play?'

'Well I don't think theatre should just be the preserve of theatrical types in their ivory towers,' he huffed in reply, and Hattie could sense his defensiveness returning. 'Anyone can make art, and I shouldn't be discriminated against just because

I'm not part of the establishment. New voices, that's what they're always saying they need. And that's what I am.'

'Of course, and I'm very glad to have, as you say, new voices being heard in theatre. Is the script… is it about something close to your heart?'

'Ah. Yes. Yes, it is. I can… Ah. I mean, obviously I'll send you a copy. You can't do the job without a script, can you?'

'I'm looking forward to reading it. And it's just you, is it? No one else involved yet?'

'Well. Ah,' he began, and Hattie realised she was in danger of putting his back up again.

'I just mean, it's remarkable if so, that you've got this far by yourself,' she added hurriedly. 'Writing a script, securing a venue, hiring staff, and you being new to the world of theatre. It shows lots of guts and determination.'

'Ah. Well,' he said, looking mollified. 'And casting, of course. I've auditioned loads of actors. It's not that hard, though, is it? You just have to find people who look right, and if they can act they can act, can't they?'

Hattie was of the opinion that was quite a lot more to it than that, but she kept that opinion to herself.

'How big is the cast, by the way?'

'Not so big. About twenty-five. I've nearly got all of them.'

'Oh,' said Hattie, unable to hide her surprise entirely. For a one-off performance, self-funded at a small venue by a first-time writer, a cast of twenty-five was vast. 'That's quite a lot…'

'I need them, though. I need a full class, plus a teacher. I considered hiring actual children but it turns out that's complicated, so I'm hiring a bunch of adults who look young enough.'

'That sounds sensible. And they're all being paid, are they?'

'That's right, and well paid too. I want my team to give it their all.'

None of it made much sense to Hattie. Getting twenty-five paid actors to rehearse a show, putting it on at a proper venue then only performing it once. Hiring a stage manager and offering double what you'd expect for a gig like this, then quibbling over bringing in any additional crew. And insisting on exactly matching a school uniform for the costumes... his priorities seemed to be all over the place.

'One more question, if I may,' she asked. 'Where's the budget for this show coming from? Are you self-funding it entirely?'

'Yes,' he said proudly. 'I'm a man of... Ah. Let's just say I have the resources to do this properly.'

'Well I think that's great,' said Hattie. 'And hopefully this performance will be your springboard to a career in theatre.'

'Well. Ah. Yes. Yes, indeed. Now. Ah. I think that's everything, isn't it?' he asked, standing. 'I'll send you the script, and a list of the actors, and we'll get started in a week. That's right, isn't it? Three weeks of rehearsals?'

'Yes, that should be fine,' said Hattie, standing as well.

'Good. Well. Nice to meet you. I'll email you. Ah. Yes.'

And with that, he turned abruptly and walked out.

Hattie finished her tea slowly, trying to decide whether to be pleased that she seemed to have scored herself a well-paid gig or horrified about what she had got herself into. Most stage managers she knew would have walked away from this job by now. There were too many red flags, mostly revolving around the fact that this was obviously a one-person passion project where the one person in question knew nothing about theatre. It was almost guaranteed to end in disaster, and when a theatre production fell apart and came tumbling down it was normally the stage manager who got crushed at the bottom of the pile. *However*, whether or not it did come tumbling down, there was still a decent likelihood of a pay cheque at the end (although no guarantee, even with a contract in place), and Hattie was no stranger to being crushed at the bottom of a collapsed theatre production. If it was a choice between surviving that again and not working at all, she'd take the crush.

Deciding, therefore, to acknowledge the risks and look on the bright side anyway, she made her way back home. By the time she got back she was quite worn out. Job interviews always took their toll, and a three-hour round trip didn't help, and there was that other thing that had happened that she didn't want to think about *and* before that there had been the very tiring tour from which she had yet to fully recuperate. So she made a beeline for the kettle upon arrival, and once she had a mug in her hand she lowered herself carefully onto the sofa, planning to stay there for the rest of the afternoon. However, as soon as she had sat down she heard a moan behind her. Twisting herself round, she saw out of the corner of her eye, poking out from behind the sofa, a pair of legs.

It's a body. It's Nick.

Her heart immediately racing, she heaved herself up again, spilling her tea in the process, scalding her hand.

'Nick!' she yelled.

'Oooh,' he moaned.

Hattie pulled herself around the sofa, and saw him lying there. He was sprawled on his back, legs straight out, one arm by his side, the other covering his face. She couldn't see if he was bruised or bleeding, or if his eyes were open.

'What happened? Are you okay?'

There wasn't much room between the back of the sofa and the bookcase, enough to walk behind, but not easily if there was an obstacle in the way on the floor. Hattie edged her way from his feet up to his head and started awkwardly to kneel down beside him.

'I must have… Ugh…' he murmured.

'Did you fall? Shall I call an ambulance?'

'I must have drifted off… Sorry, ambulance? What?'

Nick wiped his face with his hand and gazed up at Hattie muzzily. Hattie, now feeling wrong-footed, gawked back.

'What?' was all she could think to say in return.

'Are you all right?' he asked her.

'I thought you had an accident,' she said in a small voice.

'I had a *nap*, Cockatoo,' he said.

'On the floor?'

'For my neck. I wanted to lie down fully flat, see if that helped. I think the pillow is doing more harm than good if I'm honest.'

'Oh,' said Hattie.

She moved out of the way to allow Nick to sit up. It began to occur to her that her hand hurt rather a lot. The pain reminded her of the spill. She looked and saw that the entire mug's-worth of tea had splashed out across the sofa and was dripping down onto the carpet. Feeling foolish, she went and fetched the kitchen roll and started mopping up, but she found she kept having to stop to massage her scalded hand.

'I'll do this,' said Nick, seeing her struggling. 'You go and run that under a cold tap.'

She did as she was told, and had to concede that the cooling water brought tremendous relief. Also, standing still at the kitchen sink gave her heart a little time to slow its beating and her head a little time to marshal its thoughts, so that when Nick came back in she was able to say, 'I'm sorry, my love. I completely spooked myself, I don't know why.'

'I think I know why,' he said, giving her shoulder a gentle squeeze.

'Maybe I do too. I've spent the past few hours trying not to think about it. And maybe the pay-off was that my brain started thinking about it a bit too much as soon as I got home.'

'I'd believe it.'

They stood in silence for a while.

'Got the gig, though.'

'Yeah?'

'Well paid, too. Grand a week.'

'Really? That's bloody marvellous. What's the catch?'

'It's a weird one. Vanity project, all written, produced, and directed by someone who's never done it before. Mid-life crisis, maybe. Don't know where he got the money from. He wore a suit. Maybe he's got a city job. Oh, and I promised you'd help out.'

'Eh?'

'I need you to do the lights. Shouldn't be too complicated, it's a small venue. Probably a couple of days of rigging, focusing, and plotting, middle of March.'

'Am I getting paid as well as you?'

'I think your work will come out of my pay, to be honest. At a grand a week it's still worth it.'

'I didn't realise we're a two-for-one now. But I don't mind a gentle gig to ease back into things. Who's the lighting designer?'

'That's the other thing: there isn't one. I said you'd do it.'

She winced as she said it. Nick worked on large-scale professional productions, and in his world the delineations between different professions were fairly clear. The line between *crew* like lighting technicians such as himself, and *creatives* such as lighting designers, was thick and straight and rigid, and could only be traversed by many years of paying one's dues.

'I am no lighting designer, my love,' he said, a note of gentle admonishment in his voice.

'Just because it's not your job title doesn't mean you can't do it. You know everything there is to know about stage lighting.'

'That's not the point.'

'I think it sort of is.'

'Cockatoo…'

'Look, as far as I can tell the whole show is set in a classroom.

You just need to set up a basic wash. I doubt the venue has the kit to do anything more than that anyway.'

'I don't like this,' he grumbled.

'It's a paid gig. Would you rather us both sit around the flat for the next month, nursing our injuries and feeling sorry for ourselves?'

He grunted in reply. She felt a little bit bad for railroading him into it. But not too bad.

Her hand was feeling slightly better. She dried it off, took a couple of ibuprofen, made another cup of tea, and had another go at a sit-down.

Then she saw the state of the sitting room.

'Nick, what exactly were you *doing* with the kitchen roll when you were alone in here?'

'I was cleaning up the tea that you spilled.'

'I think you and I need to have a serious conversation about what constitutes… oh never mind. Just bring me the kitchen roll again. And the thing of vinegar under the sink. And maybe a bowl of hot, soapy water.'

'Hold on. Kitchen roll. Water. Soap. What was the other thing?'

'Forget it. I'll take care of it.'

7

Nick had done a good job of putting the word out in theatre circles about Big Steve. The news evidently got around fast, getting so far around in fact that it made a full circle, with Hattie receiving a phone call from her old colleague Moira Macleod, a wardrobe freelancer, to inform her of the news. Hattie was quietly relieved by this, as it meant that her name wasn't already attached to the story of Steve's death. She was already known as the one who found Atlanta's body at the Tavistock and Lel's at the Revue. This wasn't a specialism for which she hoped to earn renown.

'It's a great loss,' Moira announced.

'He was a good man, and a good production manager.'

'Aye, a theatre person through and through. I don't quite understand the circumstances of how it happened. I thought Desi's yard had closed down years ago.'

'It did,' Hattie agreed.

'So what was he doing there?'

'Well,' said Hattie uneasily. Thankfully Moira wasn't expecting an explanation, as she clearly had one of her own that she was fostering, for she continued, 'Did you know that he'd been handed a terminal diagnosis?'

'I heard it mentioned.'

'I wouldn't have waited around for something like that.'

'No,' said Hattie noncommittally. She didn't like that suicide seemed to be becoming the universally accepted explanation for what had happened, especially because she knew she had played a part in the establishment of that explanation. It seemed disrespectful to Steve. But she didn't know how to counter that narrative without revealing some things that she was very keen to keep quiet.

'Anyway,' Moira continued. 'There's a memorial service on Friday. Well, funeral technically, but as there's… well, there's not really anything left to bury. Eleven o'clock. It's a bit rushed but apparently it was the only time they had free. See you there?'

'See you there,' Hattie confirmed.

Moira didn't have to specify *where* the service would be held. The Actors' Church, or to give it its proper name, St Paul's Church, Covent Garden, was where theatre people were traditionally seen off, particularly theatre people who didn't have big families and separate lives outside the theatre. So that's where, at ten to eleven on Friday, Hattie and Nick arrived wearing, as dictated by tradition, clothes that were not *too* sombre. They weren't on the same level as the actors, of course. When one of them was buried their contemporaries would turn up dressed like a tutti-frutti fashion parade. Techies were a bit more restrained, but theatre was theatre, and a bit of colour was seen as appropriate and respectful.

Hattie had had a couple of days to rest now, but she didn't feel rested. Stuck at home together, each nursing their respective ailments, she and Nick had been getting on each other's nerves. While they both were happy in theory to divide their time equally between being the carer and the cared-for, they could never seem to agree on whose turn it was to feel sorry for themselves, and this came to a head at certain points in the day, in particular when it was time for someone to get up and put a brew on.

And beyond that, she still wasn't sleeping. The night time brought with it darkness, and the darkness transported her straight back to Desi's yard, and the half-seen horrors lying crumpled on the floor of the shed. The noises of the nocturnal traffic of Chiswick High Road brought to mind the whoosh and roar of the fire, but again and again she found her mind returning to the moment before the flames, when she had discovered she didn't have the envelope. No matter that it was at the other end of the flat; the presence of the envelope now, in stark contrast to its absence then, felt imposing and claustrophobic.

Steve had told her to destroy it, and she fully intended to do so… just not yet. Not quite yet. She could probably have articulated why she didn't want to destroy the envelope if she thought about it, but the point was that she *didn't* want to think about it, and indeed devoted quite a lot of energy to *not* thinking about it, and it was that expenditure of energy that both tired her out and kept her awake.

The crowd at the church was small. Steve had been known and liked, but theatre people are busy people. Many of his former colleagues would be off touring at the moment, many more contractually obliged to be in fit-ups and get-outs and technical rehearsals and production meetings, or setting up for the Friday matinee show. Even so, it was a decent turn-out, with many faces that Hattie knew, if only a few that she knew well. Nick was off immediately, greeting and chatting and nodding sympathetically, and Hattie had to pull him away to get him to sit down and shut up as the service began.

Words were spoken, and solemnities conducted. Hattie had never cared much for the church. The venues could be pretty and the priests' costumes were nice, but the scripts they read from generally needed a lot of editing and you could always tell from their performances that they hadn't been to drama school. The service was blessedly short (Nick informed her in the few minutes before it started that Caz had told Mike B, who had in turn told him, that the priest was apparently antsy because he had to get the building cleared for a lunchtime wedding). There was no eulogy. When it was over, and they were all filing out to the sound of sad-but-not-too-sad organ music, it occurred to Hattie that she hadn't spotted anyone in the congregation who *wasn't* a theatre person.

'Hey,' she said to Nick. 'Is there anyone here you don't recognise?'

'Don't think so. Why?'

'Just a bit odd. I knew Steve didn't have much family. Didn't think he had none.'

'Oh. Yeah. Er. How about him? He was sitting at the front, I think.'

Nick pointed out an elderly man who was hovering awkwardly at the back of the queue to leave. Hattie thought he looked deeply sad, and rather uncomfortable. She made a sudden decision.

'I'll be back in a sec. You go mingle before everyone scatters. Make sure they don't forget you exist.'

'Righto.'

Hattie peeled out of the queue and looped her way back round towards the man. He looked up as she approached, with the air of a rabbit in headlights. She gave him her most non-threatening smile.

'Excuse me. Did you happen to be related to Steve?'

He nodded.

'That's right. I'm his uncle.'

'My condolences then.'

'Thank you. Did you know him well?'

'We worked together. He was a friend,' said Hattie.

'It seems like he got on with lots of the people he did his theatre shows with,' said the man, nodding towards the exiting congregation.

'He was well liked,' agreed Hattie, and as she said it she thought she detected a slight wince on the man's face.

To fill the awkward pause that followed she added, 'I suppose he didn't have much in the way of family. He didn't talk about his life outside theatre much.'

Again, a wince, and no response.

'Still, it's nice that so many people came out to see him off,' said Hattie.

'Yes.'

Hattie began to realise that, while this conversation was going nowhere, neither were they: the line of mourners looking to exit the church had stalled, as those just outside the doors dawdled and started to chat, blocking the way for those behind them. And Nick had got himself deep into conversation with his old mate Mike B, meaning that Hattie had nowhere to escape to if she excused herself from this man other than to go and stand silently a yard or so away from him, which would be extremely awkward. Yet he seemed to dislike everything she said, and was making no effort to prolong the conversation himself.

'Were you and Steve close?' she tried.

He thought about this.

'As close as we could be, all things considered.'

'Oh?' said Hattie, and quite improbably, that one syllable seemed to be the key to unlock something in the man, because he took a breath and said, 'Well he managed to piss off pretty much everyone in the family over the years, which made him bloody difficult to keep up with without drawing some flak myself.'

'Oh?' Hattie repeated, both as an exclamation of genuine surprise at this new information and because saying it had rendered such successful results the first time.

'Well, it wasn't all his fault. Insofar as you can't help your own temperament. Ramrod straight he was, and a stickler for correctness. Which puts people's backs up at the best of times, but in particular when you think about how he'd been as a young man. Called him a hypocrite, they did. They weren't entirely wrong. But Steve couldn't see it, so he only made it worse. So stupid it all was. An argument on Christmas that started with an off-hand remark about something in the Queen's Speech and ends with Steve accusing his cousin of diddling his taxes, and because they're all stubborn as mules, five years later there's no one come to his funeral 'cause they're all sitting at home gloating.'

The man's voice had started to falter towards the end, and his eyes were wettening slightly.

The line in front of them had started to move again, and Hattie now had a clear route to the exit. She could technically have made her excuses and disengaged. But Steve's uncle was clearly distressed, and this was no way to leave a funeral.

'Listen, I'm not knocking the service, but I don't feel quite ready to say goodbye to him yet,' she said. 'If you're not rushing off, how would you feel about getting a cup of tea and telling me about him?'

Hattie briefly explained the situation to Nick, who was already gravitating towards the Nell of Old Drury with several of the others, fully intending to bed in for the afternoon, and she and her new acquaintance squeezed themselves into one of the tiny coffee shops tucked into a crevice of Covent Garden.

'I'm Hattie, by the way,' said Hattie.

'Mickey. Nice to meet you. So when did you first meet Steve?'

'Ooh, about ten years ago. We did a North America tour. Some jukebox musical, crap songs, bunch of failed pop stars in the cast, but it was fun enough. Steve ran a tight ship, and I suppose we got on because we shared a low tolerance for silly buggers. It was only near the end of the tour that I realised he hadn't actually been doing it for all that long.'

'That sounds like Steve,' nodded Mickey. 'He'd put his head down and figure it out, not matter what he was doing. Ever since he was a kid. He was a clever boy. Didn't do so well in school, but clever none the less.'

'And he grew up… Portsmouth way, was it?'

'That's right. We're all from there. If I'm honest I was surprised he moved to London. He wasn't really one for all the' – he gestured at the busy street outside – 'hubbub and such.'

'He said he'd moved back out when he… retired.'

'Retired? Hah! People like Steve don't retire. They just move onto the next thing.'

'Did he tell you what that thing was? After theatre, that is.'

'No. But… well, it's been a few years,' said Mickey, looking uncomfortable. 'Like I say, the opportunities were limited what with the grudges and fallings-out and while I bore him no ill will myself… it doesn't come naturally to any of us in our family to extend the olive branch, if you get my drift.'

'I understand,' said Hattie gently. 'It's hard to keep in touch with people. And you don't always know in advance that you're not going to get another opportunity.'

'I'll miss him. He was a bull-headed git but I'll miss him.'

Mickey stared down into his cup for a bit, and Hattie found herself, in the silence, broaching a topic that she hadn't intended to.

'When I spoke to him last' – Hattie tried to ignore the awful thought that she was actually referring to the *second*-last time she'd spoken to him – 'he sounded like some parts of his past weren't sitting well with his conscience. But he never told me much about his past. I just know he worked in some sort of… logistics.'

'He was a thug,' said Mickey simply. 'By the time he was eighteen he had the physique of a heavyweight, he could have *been* a heavyweight if he wanted, but that wasn't his style. Like I say, he was clever, but it wasn't a fast clever. He thought things out. He made plans. It's a dangerous thing, being big and strong and reliable. That makes you useful to the wrong sorts of people. And cos he was only young, he was naive. You could buy his loyalty for a hundred quid and a bit of a fuss made of him. And someone did. Well, a few people actually, over the years. And maybe he'd have got out a lot sooner but his parents tried to *force* him out of it, and if you know anything about Steve you know that's going to have the opposite effect to what you want.

'But he came to his own conclusions eventually. About who he worked for, and what he'd done. So if you say his conscience was troubling him, I say I'm not surprised. It took him long enough, but he got there.'

Mickey paused. Hattie could have filled the silence with more questions, but she got the sense he hadn't said everything he wanted to say, so she waited quietly, and presently he began again.

'I don't know if it balances out. In the end. He had so much promise as a kid. He had ten years of sinking into the muck, then ten years treading water, doing nothing useful but at least not doing what he was doing before. Then ten, fifteen years actually doing something interesting with his life. I mean, theatre, who'd have thought it? Then regrets, and apparently cancer, and a bull-headed exit. He lost his family along the way, made some friends. And on balance… what? Was it a good life? Was it worth it? Did he do more harm than good? I dunno. What do you think?'

Hattie considered.

'You'll have to forgive me if you're religious, cos I'm not,' she said. 'I don't believe that Saint Peter is going to weigh up your rights and wrongs at the pearly gates. It seems to me that a human life isn't something you can do maths on. You can't add up the good things and subtract the bad. You can't weigh up a good deed now versus a bad one twenty years ago, or three days of sadness versus one of joy. It's all apples and oranges. The best you can say it is what it is and it was what it was. It sounds to me like Steve did some bad things, and he did some good things. I think there were times when I knew him when he was happy, and times when he was sad. We don't need to try to give him a final score.'

'Maybe,' replied Mickey. 'I just think back to the kid I knew, the one who broke his arm falling off a trampoline and it took us three days to find out something was wrong because he was too proud to admit he'd hurt himself. If you told him his life would end up the way it did, would he be happy about it? I mean, for one thing… theatre? How'd he have felt about that?'

'Was he into theatre as a kid?'

Mickey shook his head.

'Nah, he thought it was a bit… well, soft, let's say. Thought it was all mincing around in makeup and tights.'

'Well, he wasn't entirely wrong there,' said Hattie, and Mickey laughed.

'He was more outdoorsy. He had a little friend called Ivan, they spent hours in the woods lighting campfires, making bows and arrows and trying to shoot squirrels, carving sticks into spears with penknives. I was a bit sad not to see Ivan here today actually. He wasn't smart but he was loyal. But they went down different paths in life and I suppose they might have fallen out in the end, too. Last I heard Ivan worked in a crematorium, I think. Don't think he'd have ever felt comfortable in a theatre crowd. Although I'd have said the same about Steve, to be honest.'

'So what got him into it, then? Steve, that is.'

'It was his kid,' said Mickey simply, and Hattie nearly choked on her tea.

'I'm sorry. Steve had a *child*?'

Mickey suddenly looked uncomfortable.

'Yeah… well, if he didn't talk about her much it's probably not my place. I dunno. I'd hoped they stayed close at least, but…'

'But she didn't come today either, did she?' said Hattie, suddenly understanding. 'I see. That's a shame.'

'If I'm honest, I think I'd thought maybe he did it for her.'

'Get into theatre, you mean?'

'No, no. I mean, that too in some ways. No, I mean, at the end. I wondered if… God help me, I wondered if he had life insurance. He was dying of natural causes, and he didn't want to wait. That's fair enough. But why go to all the palaver of starting a fire? Best I can think of is that he didn't want it to look intentional, maybe because there'd be an insurance payout for his next of kin, and he definitely wouldn't go to the trouble for *my* sake, but for her…?

'But that doesn't make sense. For one thing, if he cared enough about her to do that you'd expect them to be at least close enough for her to turn up today. And for another, it was a pretty cack-handed job he made of it, wasn't it? No one believes for a second it was an accident. So I don't think it can have been that. I think he wanted to make one last bloody-minded statement. A big "F you" to the world.'

His train of thought was making Hattie feel miserable. She alone knew that Steve's death had been neither an accident nor suicide, and the idea that this man, apparently the only family member who was even remotely close to Steve, would go to his grave misunderstanding what had happened made her tremendously sad.

She needed to say something. She knew it was stupid, but she needed to say it anyway.

'I don't think it was that. Steve was stubborn, and he over-reacted to things, but he wasn't… There was more going on. In his life, at the end. I don't think he went to that yard to kill himself.'

Mickey frowned.

'Why on earth was he there, then?'

'I don't know,' said Hattie, realising she was treading on extremely thin ice. 'I think he was trying something, and I think it went wrong.'

'Like what?'

'I don't know.'

'Sounds like you don't know very much, then,' snapped Mickey.

'I'm sorry,' said Hattie quickly.

But then Mickey sighed.

'No, I'm sorry. That's just… a difficult thing to be told at a man's funeral. You want things to be settled.'

'I shouldn't have said anything.'

'It's all right. But I've probably had enough reminiscing for one day.'

Mickey finished his drink.

'It was a pleasure to meet you, Hattie. I'm glad Steve had a good friend like you.'

'And I'm glad he had at least one uncle he didn't fall out with.'

'It just means I'm lumbered with the paperwork,' Mickey grumbled. 'Actually, that's a point. I've had sight of his will, and there's a couple of names there I don't recognise. Thought maybe they're people he knows from the theatre. Would you mind giving me your number so I can ask for help if needed?'

'Of course,' Hattie replied, and they swapped details. Then they said goodbye, and Mickey made his way towards the tube while Hattie headed for the pub to collect Nick.

'There were some fellas looking for you,' Nick said when he saw her. He was three beers deep, in the middle of a big huddle of techies around pulled-together tables.

'Oh yes?'

'Friends of Steve. I didn't recognise them. Don't think they're theatre people.'

'What did you tell them?'

'I said you were off at a café somewhere but I didn't know which. Gave them your number, hope that's okay. Did they call?'

Hattie realised she had put her phone on silent for the service and forgotten to switch it back again after. She pulled it out of her bag and saw that she did indeed have a missed call from a mobile number. An unfortunate number, really, with a thirteen near the start and a '666' at the end. Hattie supposed that some people would pay extra for a number like that, but probably only moody teenagers who were unlikely to be friends of Steve. Although she was beginning to appreciate just how little she really knew about the man.

'I missed it,' she said. 'I'll call them back at some point. Now, can we head home? I'm a bit worn out.'

But Nick was having far too much fun, and since he'd already got his round in, he considered that staying for a few more was really just getting his money's worth, and in that sense was the only financially prudent course of action. Hattie didn't try to dissuade him, but declined all suggestions by him and the others that she join them. She had no appetite for chit-chat. So she left Nick to it, and limped her way back home.

8

Injuries lead to injuries. A large van was parked just outside the entrance to the flat, and to avoid blocking traffic entirely on the extremely tight road, the owner had pulled up almost all the way onto the pavement. It was by no means impossible for pedestrians to pass, but they had to adopt a narrow gait to do so. Hattie had found that the least painful way of walking was to swing her bad leg out wide. Having to modify her step to get around the van by bringing her bad leg straight forward produced a sudden burst of pain that caused her to flinch and wobble, abruptly rolling the ankle on her good leg. She bit her lip to catch the swear word that tried to escape, and had to endure an agonising hobble to get to her building and then up the steps to her flat.

Once inside, she allowed herself to collapse straight on the floor, and let out the stream of bad language she'd been holding in, albeit under her breath. From her position in the hall, the comforts of the sofa, the kettle, the bed, and the bath all seemed impossibly remote.

'I suppose I'll just stay here then,' she muttered to herself.

She wasn't alone in the hall, though. The other occupant, her suitcase, had been there since Sunday night, and she'd only taken her sponge bag out of it. The dirty clothes remained untouched, in a way that would normally be entirely unacceptable to Hattie. But unpacking them would have meant dealing with what they concealed, and hitherto Hattie had not felt anything like the strength needed to do that.

Now, though, it seemed inescapable. It was right next to her, and for now at least, both legs had betrayed her. And today of all days it was impossible to ignore.

So.

The envelope.

Big Steve had told her to destroy it. He told her to burn it. That was what he wanted her to do. And doing so would respect his wishes.

But he hadn't told her to do that because he didn't want her to know the contents for *his* sake. He told her to do it because he wanted to keep her safe. Because if Conor and his lot caught up with her, the less she knew, and the more she could convince them how little she knew, the better for her. It wasn't a request that she burn the envelope, it was advice.

Hattie sighed. She already knew she was going to open the thing and read it. She could tell, just by listening to her brain put in all the work of trying to justify the decision. And given she was going to open it, she might as well do it as soon as possible, so that whatever she needed to do to the contents, whether that was to take them to the police or to burn them, she could do it as soon as possible.

So she reached out an arm to the suitcase, pulled it over to her spot on the floor, unzipped it, and rooted around until she found the envelope.

No wonder she hadn't picked it up with the other papers. One of the corners was wedged into the gap in one of her spare shoes where the bottom layer of the sole had started to peel away, and she had to tug quite hard to free it. Hattie again felt the wash of shame that, panicked about being late, she hadn't checked she had picked up the right envelope. She was a stage manager for God's sake. If she was good at one thing, it was supposed to be the reliable handling of paperwork in stressful conditions. And she'd messed that up.

Would it have made a difference? If Steve had had the envelope in his hand the last time the men came back, would they have spared him? Could he have talked his way out of it?

It depended, Hattie knew, on the contents of the envelope. So, still sitting on the floor of her flat, legs hooked awkwardly to the sides to push the grief-giving hip and ankle as far away from her as possible, she carefully tore open the flap and pulled out its contents.

She found a wodge of paper, much of it blank.

It was bizarre. There were about ten sheets of A4 graph paper. They had been folded in half to fit them into the envelope, but at some earlier point they had been folded differently, along much more haphazard lines, as a series of diagonal creases remained. Some of the sheets had a couple of scribbles on one side, nothing else, and some were absolutely full of drawings, mostly made in pencil and biro. They seemed to have more intention to them than doodles, but they were highly miscellaneous in both subject and style. One sheet was given over to drawing the muscular parts of animals – a tiger's hind quarters, a gorilla's head, neck and shoulders and so on – one was endless sketches of folds of fabric, another had several sketches of human eyes drawn in black pen, each with a different makeup look coloured in with pencil crayons. Whoever made these drawings clearly had a precise hand and a good eye for detail when they chose to apply it, but they often lapsed into carelessness, particularly at the edges.

Interspersed among the drawings were a few sheets containing scrawls of numbers. They seemed to be costs and quantities, with labels like 'Duffle', 'Broad', 'Doe', and totals added up at the bottom. The numbers seemed to be in the region of a few hundred pounds here and there.

Hattie couldn't make head or tail of it. The drawings themselves were obviously baffling: she couldn't see how they would have anything to do with the actions of a criminal mob. The numbers seemed more promising, although without knowing what the labels referred to it was hard to work out their significance. And the sums involved seemed surprisingly small, ranging from a few hundred to a few thousand pounds per page.

Unless… what if '£10' didn't mean ten pounds, but rather ten *thousand* pounds? That seemed at least possible. In which case these sums took on a greater significance. The handling of sums of money like that could be seen as suspicious if it was something done informally, or in secret. Slipping in the details of million-pound transactions among a series of innocuous drawings could certainly be a sign of someone up to something. And maybe the drawings themselves contained a secret message…? No. If a tiger bottom and some blue eye shadow was code for an illegal purchase or sale then the criminals in question needed psychiatric help.

But nonetheless, maybe there *was* a reason the drawings had been preserved along with the sums. They had obviously been produced on paper from the same pad, probably within a similar time period, probably by the same person. Perhaps it would be easier to identify the author from the drawings than from the numbers. Perhaps, by linking an idiosyncratic drawing style to some shady accounting, these seemingly valueless scraps would indeed be all it took to prove that someone was up to no good.

But equally, perhaps Steve was bluffing. Or wrong. Or had gone mad. Hattie had no idea. And, having inspected the contents of the envelope, she had no clue what to do with it now.

The discomfort of staying on the floor was beginning to overcome the discomfort inherent in the idea of moving, so Hattie decided to pause her ruminations for a moment. She carefully folded up the papers again, and went to put them back in the envelope, only to discover that it wasn't quite empty. Inside it was one small curl of paper, the smallest scrap torn off the edge of something. Hattie fished it out and gave it a closer look. This was different. It was plain, white paper, of higher quality than the graph pad, and it had had text printed on it. It had a landline phone number on it, starting with the area code 01992, and beneath it 'S LIM', with at least one letter missing from the end and possibly some at the beginning too where the paper had been ripped.

It was such a small scrap that it seemed unlikely to have been added to the envelope on purpose. And by itself it had little significance. But the phone number was the most complete, concrete, specific piece of information the envelope contained, and Hattie didn't want to discount it too quickly.

Further examination of the papers yielded no additional insights, so she put all them all carefully back into the envelope and levered herself gingerly upright, letting out two moans and a yelp as she did so. The walk to the kettle was even more painful than she'd expected, and she could feel her ankle starting to swell. So she took herself over to the bathroom only to discover that there was no ibuprofen left in the cabinet. With his neck as it was Nick was going through the stuff at a rate of knots at the moment, and never remembered to tell her when he finished a packet. He'd probably dosed himself up heavily to get through the service.

Hattie sighed. Knowing Nick he'd probably be out all evening now, and she didn't blame him. Being cooped up at home didn't suit him at all. A chance to catch up with old pals and let off steam was undoubtedly going to be good for him, and she didn't want to deny him that. But it did mean that if she asked him to pick up more pills on the way home, then even if he remembered it'd probably be several hours before she got her hands on them.

And she knew her ankle was going to feel a lot worse before it got better.

There was only one thing for it. She needed to go to the shop.

It was right there on the corner of the street, only a hundred yards away, although it would involve both a staircase descent and an ascent, and that was what she found the most daunting. But it was better than the alternative.

So she carefully changed into her comfiest trainers and, regretting having got rid of the crutches she'd been given when she fractured her hip, ever-so-slowly made her way out of her door and down the stairs. The badly parked van was still in her way, and she took extra care as she edged her way around it, but this time she was headed in the other direction, which meant that for the first time she passed the front of the van, and she was surprised to discover that there were two men sitting in it. It seemed a little unfair that, having placed their vehicle in such an inconvenient spot, they weren't actually *doing* anything. Hattie briefly wondered if she should knock on the window and point out just how much of an obstruction they had caused, but a glance at their faces put her off the idea. They were large, angry-looking men. What's more, one of them caught her eye and started forward in a way that made her flinch back and look away, her appetite for confrontation evaporating immediately.

She shuffled to the corner shop, bought a packet of ludicrously expensive but apparently fast-acting painkillers, and shuffled back down the street. As she passed the front of the van she kept her eyes downcast, concentrating only on the placement of her feet. Having one leg that hurt when she moved it and another that hurt when she put weight on it made negotiating the tight space hard enough, and knowing she had an audience meant she was particularly anxious not to stumble.

She was alarmed, therefore, when she heard the van door open behind her.

'Excuse me,' muttered a gruff voice.

She was nearly at the front door. The events of the day and the pain in her legs made her feel drained and overwhelmed, and just this once she decided to let herself off. So she pretended not to have heard, and kept walking.

'Excuse me,' repeated the voice. 'Hattie Cocker, is it?'

Bugger.

She stopped and looked round.

'Yes?'

The man was so big he barely fitted on the small sliver of pavement left by the van. What little hair he had was cropped almost all the way to the scalp, he wore a big black coat, and his neck was covered in faded tattoos that curled up around the edge of his jaw. Hattie knew you shouldn't judge people by their appearances, but the appearance of this man was intimidating. She heard the far door of the van open, presumably as his companion got out on the other side.

'I was hoping to talk to you about Steve Felton,' said the first man.

An image of Steve popped into her head, him lying on the floor, blood everywhere as he urgently croaked at her, *'They're coming back'*.

Hattie stared back at the man, her eyes widening. Adrenaline flooded through her system, and her heart rate doubled, then doubled again. She suddenly found herself turning away again, and bolting, scrambling awkwardly away towards her door on complaining legs.

'Excuse me,' said the man for a third time, his voice firmer now, a note of anger creeping in.

'Now's not a good time…' Hattie muttered as she fumbled with her keys. She was slow to find the right one, but the awkward placement of the van bought her time, as both men had to negotiate their way through the tight spaces around it.

By the time she heard a foot on the step behind her the door yielded, and she pushed herself inside, flinging it closed.

'I just want to talk to you,' said the man, through the door, while Hattie stood, frozen, at the foot of the stairs.

They can't get in. They don't have a key. But they might break down the door. If they try I'll call the police. But the police will take too long. If they start kicking at the door I'll drag myself upstairs into the flat, that will buy me time. But they can break down that door too…

But they didn't start kicking. Ears straining, Hattie heard a muttered 'Now what?' from outside, and a little shuffling, but nothing else.

They'll go away, she told herself, willing it to be true. *They'll give up and go away.*

And then, agonisingly, her phone rang. It wasn't on silent any more, and, standing just inside the front door, the sound must have carried through to the street, making her position clear.

She immediately fumbled her phone out of her bag, and caught a glimpse of an unknown number on her screen, one that contained both a thirteen and a '666'. She rejected the call, but the damage was done.

'I want to speak to you, Hattie,' said the man from outside. 'You're not in trouble.'

Hattie said nothing in reply.

'Fuck this,' said a second voice, and a second later there was a bang on the door.

'Leave it,' muttered the first man. 'He told us to be nice.'

'Yeah? Well she's not being nice to us. I've had it with this shit.'

He banged on the door again. Then again, louder, and Hattie found herself yelling, 'Go away! Go away! I'm not well! Go away! I've hurt my legs!'

She knew her words were barely coherent, but neither were her thoughts at this moment. She turned and hauled herself up the stairs to her flat, double-locking the door once inside. She collapsed back onto the floor, a dizzy, terrified mess, and stayed there for a long time. When her thoughts began slowly to resolve back into focus, she started trying to listen again. There were no noises coming from the stairs, no voices on the street. Occasionally there was the sound of vehicles going past. Some of them sounded like vans, but none of them sounded like an engine being started directly outside the building. Nevertheless, when she eventually worked up the courage to hobble to the window and sneak a look down at the road below, the van was gone.

Act Three

Misophonia is the term given to an irrational and acute dislike of certain sounds. Many people suffer from this in relation to one particular noise, be it cutlery scratching on a ceramic plate, fingernails scraping on a blackboard, or the snoring of a bedroom cohabitant. My own personal bugbear is the sound of whistling. I loathe it, although I couldn't possibly begin to describe why. Thankfully, having chosen a life in the theatre I am largely spared exposure to this horrible noise, at least while at work. This is because of the strong and prevalent superstition that it is very bad luck to whistle backstage.

The reason for this superstition is the very same reason that I would do very badly in the navy: sailors whistle, or at least, they used to. Managing the complex rigging of a sailing ship requires the coordinated work of several people working at different heights and some distance apart. For this group to communicate reliably they need to use sounds that cut through the splosh of waves and creak of timbers. A whistle does exactly that. So sailors of old developed a lexicon of whistling that included instructions to untie certain ropes – to push, to pull, to release, to tie off and so on. And these very same sailors, when their ships were in port, were often hired to run the equally complex rigging systems of theatres, whose purpose was to manoeuvre scenery around during performances. These sailors brought their communication system along with them, meaning that were a hapless actor to wander onto the stage whistling a little ditty, they might unknowingly issue instructions to the riggers above them that would result in a sandbag landing on their head.

The practical use of whistling has faded, but the injunction against its casual use backstage remains, with the result that those such as myself enjoy blessed relief from the sound, until we leave our theatrical sanctums and are exposed to the trillers and tooters without.

– from *A History of Theatrical Superstition*
by Freya Barnsworthy

9

Hattie was having trouble getting hold of Moira. This in itself was not particularly surprising. The prickly costumier was notoriously averse to putting herself out in any way for other people: she would speak to people when it suited her, and not the other way round. This was in many ways a testament to her being extremely good at her job. If she wasn't, then given how hard one had to work just to talk to her there's no way she'd keep being hired.

And hiring her was exactly what Hattie was trying to do. She had now signed the paperwork for Larry Lloyd's production and rehearsals would be starting imminently. She had promised that she would find a costume maker to handle his oddly specific requirements concerning school uniforms, and was fast realising that this was a commitment that she might have some trouble keeping.

The problem was that while, over a career spanning several decades, she had got to know many, many designers and makers, and considered herself on reasonable terms with a fair number of them, the vast majority of the ones she knew who were still working had, like her, been in the game for some time. Unlike her, they had leveraged their extensive experience to move up in the world, were now highly sought after, and could afford to accept only gigs working on proper shows with big budgets and reasonable timescales. A rush order for a heap of school uniforms on the cheap wouldn't appeal to any of them. Hattie knew this, because she had asked, and been rejected or ignored by all of them.

Moira, on the other hand, did small stuff. That famed prickliness had hampered her upwards trajectory, and while she was still highly sought after, it tended to be for work on productions towards the bottom of the theatrical pyramid. And the bottom was very firmly where Larry Lloyd's show sat.

So Hattie had spent the weekend periodically calling Moira, as well as leaving a voicemail and sending an email, all to no avail so far. She had, she reflected on Monday, perhaps been pursuing Moira a little more aggressively than was strictly necessary, but thinking about Moira gave her permission *not* to think about various other things that might otherwise be on her mind. And besides, phone calls and emails were things that she could do, and this was crucial, *without having to leave her flat.*

She had calmed down a lot by the time Nick came home and found her, and her description of the ordeal made it sound, both to her ears and presumably to his, like less than it was: the men hadn't prevented her from entering her building, they hadn't kicked the door in, they hadn't said anything other than that they wanted to talk to her. And she couldn't *prove* that these were actually the men who had killed Steve, or even that they were part of Conor's gang. All she could say for sure was that they had behaved suspiciously, they wanted to talk to her about Steve, and they knew where she lived.

That wasn't enough to justify calling the police, or fleeing the city, or doing anything that was particularly dramatic.

But it was enough to make her quietly arrange her weekend so as to avoid leaving the safety of home. The *excuse* was the chronic pain in her hip and the need to rest her ankle to allow it to heal before throwing herself into the new gig. But that wasn't the reason…

Regardless, by Sunday night she still hadn't heard back from Moira, so she asked Nick to put out feelers for suggestions from anyone else they knew for a decent costume maker who might be prepared to take on these wretched uniforms.

Costumes aside, the pre-production process for *What You Deserve* was beginning to come together. Larry had sent through a cast list, and a script. Well, it was a document that he called a script, but it didn't bear much resemblance to what Hattie considered to be a script. Yes, it described the words that the actors were supposed to say while they were on stage, but the formatting was all over the place, and a lot of the time Larry hadn't made explicit *who* was supposed to be saying each line and it wasn't always clear from context. The dialogue was interspersed with the most bizarre collection of text: a mishmash of what could charitably be called stage directions, some instructions on how the lines should be delivered, and what appeared to be some notes the author had put in for himself about how each scene should be structured and linked, then decided not to take out again. The whole thing swooped erratically between past, present and future tense, and between first, second and third person, and the font size grew and contracted seemingly at random.

This was obviously written by someone who had never previously written, and in all probability never read, a play script before. Hattie did wonder if Larry had ever written *anything* previously. But, buried in all the confusion there was something at least potentially stageable in there. Hattie had diplomatically offered to 'reformat' the script for Larry into 'a template that I find helpful', and, having secured his permission, she patiently worked her way through it over several sessions each lasting several hours, separating out the dialogue and spelling out who had each line, rewriting the stage directions, and banishing everything that didn't belong in the script to a series of endnotes.

By the time she was done, she had uncovered a respectably sized two-act play comprising a series of scenes set in a classroom interspersed with some rather tedious monologues where a schoolchild called George stepped out of the scene and started talking from the perspective of his adult self. Among a gratuitously large list of characters, most of whom were classmates of George whose lines were restricted to things like 'Oh really?' and 'Yes, tell us what you mean,' the action such as it was largely revolved around George, a girl called Fran who sat next to George in class, another boy called Terry who was initially George's friend but eventually deserted him, and a teacher called Mr Unsworth whose sole character trait appeared to be a desire to be anywhere but in school. There wasn't much of a plot: the classroom scenes were essentially just a series of set pieces in which George was bullied by his male peers, with Fran occasionally participating but for the most part ignoring it all. The bullies picked on George's appearance, voice, mannerisms, all the dispiritingly usual things. The monologues talked about George's life after school, and the gist seemed to be that his life was rather disappointing, and that he blamed this on his anxieties and poor social skills, which he in turn blamed on his experiences at school.

It didn't take a great deal of imagination to conclude that this piece might be partially autobiographical, and that George's experience was Larry's experience. Hattie wondered about where the title, *What You Deserve*, came into it. No one in the play seemed do anything particular to deserve anything particular, and even if they did deserve something, they didn't seem to get it. The most depressing interpretation was that at heart Larry was suggesting that grown-up George deserved his unsatisfactory life through his failure to deal with his childhood bullies. Hattie hoped not, though. Children often think they are being bullied due to their own defects, when in fact if there is a defect it invariably lies in the characters of the bullies.

Either way, while it was perhaps an illuminating window into Larry's past, as a piece of theatre it was more than slightly lacking. The whole thing reminded Hattie of a summer gig she had taken once at the South Oak theatre, during which time she had got friendly with the venue's artistic director, a woman called Helen. For the duration of Hattie's show's run, Helen had been holed up in a little office backstage, reading scripts she had received as part of South Oak's 'New Talent' competition. Anyone in the world could submit a script, and Helen had committed to staging the best one they received. However, word had spread rather wider than she had anticipated, and she had been inundated with submissions from budding playwrights, most of which were, she lamented to Hattie, utter tosh.

'It's not their fault,' she explained. 'The problem is they've been horribly misled. The advice every new writer gets given is "write what you know". But most people don't *know* anything. Especially young people. They went to school, they got a boring job, they fell in love a couple of times with mixed results, they now spend their evenings watching telly, and they think *that's* what they should write a play about. I have fifty submissions here about what it's like to have a crush on your flatmate, and fifty more about twenty-somethings experiencing middle-class ennui. Oh, the cleverer ones realise they need more, so they give one of their characters an exciting disease, or they whack in some sort of metaphysical twist where one of the characters turns out to be an angel or something ludicrous halfway through the second act, but they have nothing to *say*. I just wish I could call them up and say, "Forget what you know, write me something about astronauts, or knights in armour, or indigenous tribes of the Kalahari, just please, pick something *interesting*!"'

Helen would have recognised Larry's script, Hattie thought. She might have had some wisdom to share with him. Still, Hattie's job wasn't to improve the script; her job was to help

Larry bring his vision to the stage, regardless of the flaws in that vision. So she finished up re-drafting the script, and sent it back to Larry along with a suggested rehearsal schedule. He accepted both without complaint, so Hattie made a provisional breakdown of which actors would be needed on which day. She sent this too to Larry and, securing his approval, emailed it on to the actors along with a note introducing herself.

Almost as soon as she had pressed 'Send', however, Larry rang her up.

'You've made a mistake,' he said, without preamble.

'Oh?'

'You've left out an actor. Ah. It's okay, but you need to change the schedule. It doesn't make sense.'

'I'm sorry,' said Hattie. 'Who did I leave off?'

'It's Neil,' he said. Neil was the actor playing George.

'Let me just check,' said Hattie. 'I've got my computer in front of me. No, it's okay, I sent it to Neil.'

'No, I mean, you've got his part wrong. He's just playing George, but you've got him down as being both George and the narrator. You've left off Miles. Ah. He's the narrator.'

'I'm so sorry,' said Hattie. 'Perhaps I misunderstood. Are you saying the child George character is played by a different actor to the adult George character? The one with the monologues?'

'Yes.'

'I see,' said Hattie. She was entirely confident that the original script had listed both the child and the narrator of the monologues as 'George', and when she had treated them as a single character in her rewriting of the script and her rehearsal breakdown Larry had made no complaints. But her job wasn't to disagree with the director.

'That's entirely my fault,' she said smoothly, 'and I'm glad we've got this cleared up now before we got too deep into rehearsals. It's easily corrected. So, Neil is playing child George, and the adult George is played by… sorry, did you say it was someone called Miles?'

'That's right. I'll send you his contact details.'

So you're admitting that you've never mentioned this actor to me before, thought Hattie. *In which case, it's a bit much to claim that this is my mistake.*

She updated the script to separate out the two Georges, rewrote the rehearsal breakdown noting which of the two actors was needed when, and re-sent both to the whole cast including Miles, with an apology for her earlier 'mistake'.

The problems didn't stop there, though. It turned out that half the cast were only now learning which parts they were playing, and in some cases, what they had been led to believe through their communications with Larry didn't match up with what Hattie was now telling them.

In particular, a man called Moritz seemed to be under the impression that he had been promised a lead role, and was dismayed to find that his character, Paul, only had three lines in the entire piece, one of which was simply 'Yes'. Hattie double-checked with Larry, then tried to mollify Moritz by promising him (truthfully), that while his character had little to say, he was on stage for almost the entire play, and suggesting (possibly less truthfully) that a significant part of the play was the unspoken action on the stage, details of which would emerge during the rehearsal process.

And, at the other end of the spectrum, an actor called Catherine emailed Hattie and Larry together, very politely but in obvious confusion. When Larry offered her the role he had told her she would be playing a character called Freya. However, having read the script, there didn't appear to *be* a character called Freya. Larry replied saying it had been a typo, and that Catherine would be playing Fran, which evidently pleased Catherine, as Fran was one of the more prominent characters in the piece, arguably one of the leads.

The confusion and grumblings and changes eventually subsided, and by the day before the first rehearsal everyone seemed to know broadly what they were supposed to be doing and when they were needed. Based on what little she knew of Larry's personality and experience, Hattie had initially found herself slightly dreading the rehearsals themselves, but by the time these were due to start she was so wrapped up with worry concerning Conor's people that by comparison, a chaotic rehearsal process didn't seem like too big a problem. And in some ways, it was a blessing. Her impulse was still to hide in her flat and never leave again. But she had a job to do, and her sense of professional responsibility overrode her qualms regarding strange men in vans. So she resolved that, on the day, she *would* leave the flat, she *would* go to the rehearsal room, and she *wouldn't* let herself be held hostage by fear.

In the meantime, the scrap of paper she had found in the envelope was playing on her mind. It was nothing really. She had no reason to ascribe any significance to the phone number, and likewise she had no reason to believe the fragment of text underneath *meant* anything. It was just a bit of detritus that somehow got tangled up with the rest of the papers.

And yet.

And yet it offered a thread to pull on. And Hattie realised just how fervently she wanted a thread to pull on. Because to pull on a thread was to take action. It was to assert one's agency. And when one has been chased into one's home by threatening men who recently killed an old friend, and when one has been told that one should not involve the police or do anything to seek justice, and that these men should be allowed to get away with the awful thing they did, then one's agency can feel suppressed and in need of a good bit of asserting.

At the same time, she knew that if she did pull the thread, it would probably come away in her hand. She would find out that the scrap had been part of a generic piece of junk mail, or an NHS leaflet, or have any one of a million innocuous origins. The thread would be dead, and that would be that.

So she was torn between wanting to pull on the thread, and not wanting the thread to have been pulled on. It was more attractive as an idea, as a piece of potential. So she thought about it all weekend, but didn't do anything.

What tipped the scales was a call she received early on Monday morning. From the number she had saved in her phone three days earlier. *Not* the number with the sixes and the thirteen.

'Hello?' she said, swallowing down a last bite of toast.

'Hello, is this Hattie?'

'Yes.'

'This is Mickey. Mickey Felton. Steve's uncle. It's about his will.'

The call started straightforwardly enough. Steve had made a will, and he had included a small number of bequests to people he had worked with. They made for a rather odd assortment. There was a large and rather powerful projector that for some reason Steve owned, which he left to a video designer called Gareth Kerr, and exactly £347 left to a lighting technician called Laura Harris, noting that 'she will know why'. In both these cases, Hattie knew the intended recipient, and could pass on their contact details to Mickey.

Then Mickey got rather coy for a second, and Hattie wasn't quite sure what it was he was trying to say, or trying not to say. But he eventually seemed to grow tired with his own embarrassment and said rather abruptly, 'He's left you a grand.'

Hattie blinked.

'Really?'

'That's what it says here. After the bequests to theatre people he leaves five grand to his old pal Ivan, then right at the end he's added, "I leave one thousand pounds to Harriet Cocker" – that is you, isn't it? – "a true friend".'

'Well,' said Hattie, flustered. 'That's very nice of him, although I'm sure I don't deserve it.'

It wasn't just false modesty. She really felt like she *didn't* deserve it. Not just because of how badly she had let Steve down the week before, with the envelope. Even before then, while she had been friendly with Steve, she didn't feel she had done anything to merit being called a 'true friend'. When he had retired she hadn't picked up the phone, and before then, while they had been through some adventures together, she couldn't pretend to have felt much closer to him than she did to many of her colleagues.

But apparently it was there in black and white in his will, and it seemed disrespectful to actually decline the money. So after a little more flapping Hattie said that she was very grateful, and Mickey said he would pass her details on to the lawyers, who would handle the administration of the funds once probate was secured.

'How are you holding up?' Hattie asked, as much to change the subject as anything else.

'Oh, you know. I'm getting on with it. Some old faces are being stirred up. Some more welcome than others.'

'Oh yeah?'

He sighed.

'I had a visit from some fellas who should have stayed stuck in the past. I shouldn't say more than that.'

'I see,' said Hattie, her own recently received visit springing to front of mind. She decided to chance it and said, 'Were these by any chance fellows who were connected to a man called Conor?'

'Conor? No, don't think so. Why?'

'No reason,' said Hattie awkwardly.

'I suppose one of them might be called Conor. But these were Tariq's boys. Here, they haven't come and bothered you, have they?'

'No… I was just… I've been trying to piece together a bit more of the stuff I've heard about Steve's past,' said Hattie, improvising. 'I heard about someone called Conor, that's all.'

'Oh. Well. If you want to get into all that stuff, you're best off talking to Nancy. She was in the thick of it, I suppose you'd say. Although… there was a Conor, wasn't there? Used to run his business out of the Queen's Head in Crouch End. Or was that a Colin? It's too long ago for me. Talk to Nancy.'

'I think I will,' said Hattie. 'Can you give me a number for her?'

'Shouldn't think so,' said Mickey. 'She didn't stay close with the family. But she's easy to find. Nancy Duff. She runs a hair salon in Mile End. Called Hair by Nancy, or something like that at least. I'm sure you'll be able to find her.'

'I'll take a look, then,' said Hattie.

They ended the call soon after, with Hattie now the recipient of two new leads into the mystery surrounding Steve's death, in the form of a pub and a hair salon, not to mention a thousand pounds and finally, in consequence, an even more overwhelming sense of guilt. And it was that sense of guilt that prompted her, before she had a chance to put her phone away and let herself off the hook, to go back to the envelope which now sat on the counter in the kitchen, fish out the mysterious scrap of paper, and call the number on it.

'Makerhub Coworking, how can I help?' came a friendly female voice almost immediately.

'Oh, hello,' said Hattie. 'Er. Sorry, what did you say your company was?'

'Makerhub Coworking,' repeated the woman, and then, picking up on Hattie's confusion, explained, 'We're a shared office space. You might be trying to contact one of our tenants?'

'Yes, exactly,' said Hattie, thinking this was as likely an avenue of enquiry as any.

'I can put you through, then. Can you tell me the name of the company?'

'I'm not actually sure,' said Hattie.

'That's no problem. Did they give you an extension number?'

'No, sorry. I think their last name was maybe Lim. Er, S Lim?'

'Hmm. I'm afraid I don't recognise the name, but I don't know the names of everyone who works here.'

'Do you have some sort of directory?'

'I don't have a directory of people, but we do have a list of the names of tenant companies up on the wall here. I could read it out to you over the phone but it's… well, it's quite long.'

'Don't worry about it, then. Where are you, again?'

The woman told her. It was an address up in Enfield, near the reservoir. Hattie thanked her and hung up. Well. An office in Enfield, a pub in Crouch End, and a salon in Mile End. Three places that teased answers, and all of them bloody murder to get to on a bad hip.

But for now they would all have to wait, because the first order of business for the day was a script read-through of *What You Deserve* to kick off the rehearsal process.

10

The first meeting of the cast was, perhaps predictably, a chaotic affair. The rehearsal venue that Larry had hired turned out to be a wine bar whose owner had come up with a creative means of generating some extra revenue before the doors opened to punters in the evening. As a room it wasn't a terrible place to rehearse: it was clean and large, with plenty of lighting. But most of the space was filled with tables, chairs, and stools (as well as, of course, the rather large bar). The manager, who arrived to unlock and let the company in, was fairly inflexible about allowing the furniture to be moved, and even though Hattie promised she could return every item to its proper place at the end of the day, he insisted that the larger tables not be touched. He also warned them that at some point in the day he would need to mop the floor and that they'd all need to stay off it until it dried. Hattie felt that to pay for a venue for a whole day only to be told that for part of the day one was prohibited from using the *floor* was something of a rip-off, but Larry had been the one to negotiate the room and the rate, so she simply smiled and nodded and asked for as much of a heads-up about the timing of this mopping as possible, to which request she received a mere shrug in response.

She didn't have time to dwell on the unsatisfactoriness of all of this, because very soon the cast started to arrive. They were, unanimously, young. And not just young when viewed through the eyes of an about-to-turn-sixty stage manager. They were *young* young, such that some of them could only just barely have graduated drama school, and some of them…

'Hattie?'

Hattie turned and saw a face and had the awkward sensation of recognising it as two different people at once. On the one hand there was Catherine, the actress playing Fran, whose face Hattie knew from the headshot Larry had sent her. The black-and-white photo had failed to communicate, unsurprisingly, the vibrant redness of Catherine's hair, and it was that redness that tipped Hattie off that, on the other hand, she had actually seen this person before, albeit in an entirely different context.

'*Kitty?*'

'Oh my goodness, I *knew* it was you. I mean, I didn't know, and it seemed like maybe too much of a coincidence to be real, but I thought it was unlikely there'd be two stage managers called Hattie, but then when you emailed me and didn't mention anything I lost my nerve and thought I'd best wait until I saw you until I was sure but… Hello!'

'Hello, my love. You've done well for yourself, finding work already.'

'I *know!* I was thinking a lot about it after our conversation, about whether to apply to drama school or not, but then the very next day I got an email offering me the part, and I feel like that's a sign that I'm doing the right thing.'

There were several true things Hattie could have said in response. About how a one-night show at a fringe theatre wasn't likely to get her 'discovered'. About how actors should be looking to learn from every director they work under and that debutant Larry Lloyd was *very* unlikely to have something valuable to teach. About how the casting process for this show seemed to have been rather idiosyncratic, and that success here didn't constitute evidence that Kitty had nailed her audition technique. But none of those things would have been kind, helpful or appropriate, so instead Hattie said, 'Well I'm looking forward to this show even more now that I know you're in it.'

And then more actors swept in and wanted to introduce themselves to Kitty and ask questions of Hattie, and before long the room was filled to bursting with bright young things as the enormous cast assembled in its entirety. There were *just* enough chairs to seat everyone, although the last to arrive had to perch awkwardly on bar stools at the back, and three of the actors had to wedge themselves into a little corner booth with a fixed table, and could hardly see or be seen by the rest of the cast.

Still, it was a more-or-less functional rehearsal room, and the cast were all there and more or less fitted into it, and each of them had a script in hand. The only thing that was missing from this first read-through (apart from all the production roles that Larry had eschewed, like a lighting designer, a production manager and so on) was the director, Larry himself.

Hattie had sort of assumed he would be early (directors often weren't, but producers normally were, and Larry was both), but she had taken it as read that he would at least be on time. So when ten minutes had passed after the allotted hour and there was still no sign of him, Hattie began to wonder, and to worry. She checked her phone several times, but there were no missed calls or explanatory messages, and when she tried ringing him he didn't pick up. At the point when it was beginning to become apparent to the cast that something was amiss, Hattie poked her head outside, just to check that he hadn't somehow been locked out, or something, and there she saw him, hovering on the pavement.

He looked up, wild-eyed, and shrank back momentarily from Hattie before recovering himself.

'Are you all right, my love?' asked Hattie.

'Ah. Yes. Ah,' he said.

'I think we've got a full house now, if you'd like to get started.'

He nodded, but made no move to come in. Beginning to sense what was going on, Hattie stepped onto the pavement, closing the door behind her.

'It's a bit nerve-wracking, isn't it?' she said gently. 'Some of the most experienced directors I know still have a little wobble at the start of rehearsals. There's a lot of people in the room, and it can feel like there's a lot of expectation on you to step in and be their leader, which is a hard thing when you don't know anyone.'

Larry gave a fractional nod, giving Hattie confidence that she had correctly diagnosed the problem.

'Can I let you into a secret?' she said. 'All those actors in there, they are desperate, and I mean *desperate,* to impress you. And each other, but mostly you. They're all young, they're all new at this, none of them have worked with you before, and above all, actors are the most insecure people in the world. And for the first read-through, you're not expected to *direct* them. You're just going to sit back, and let them read your script, and the whole time all they're going to be thinking is, "Am I doing a good enough job?" So you don't need to impress them. You just let them come to you. And I promise you, by the time the first read-through is over, the ice will be broken, and the next step won't feel so scary.'

'Okay. Ah. Okay,' he said. Truth be told he didn't look particularly okay, but at least when Hattie started to move back in the direction of the door he started moving with her. She gently steered him into the building, and thence to the main room where the actors were sitting. The closer ones fell silent as they approached, but the gaggles in the corners were deep in conversation and carried on chattering away heedlessly.

'ALL RIGHT everyone,' Hattie bellowed, getting everyone's attention. 'I think we're ready to get started. My name's Hattie, and I'm your stage manager. This is Larry, our writer, director, and producer.'

A couple of actors started clapping, but not quite enough to reach critical mass, and their applause petered swiftly out. Larry turned an alarming shade of green, and shifted his weight in a way that made Hattie worry that he was about to bolt. So, just to make sure, she put a steadying arm behind his back and used it to shepherd him towards the seat she had saved for him, saying as she did so, 'Perhaps we could go round the room introducing ourselves? Just say your name and the part you'll be playing. Let's start with… you.'

Under the cover of a Mexican wave of introductions, Hattie got Larry seated and put a script into his hand, hoping that no one would notice that she almost had to open and close his fingers for him to get him to hold it. The poor man was *utterly* terrified.

'Right,' said Hattie brightly, just after the last actor had announced themselves, trying to keep all eyes on her while Larry remained in his state of semi-paralysis. 'Shall we jump straight into a read-through? Here we go. "*What You Deserve*. Scene One. A classroom." Neil, when you're ready.'

Neil cleared his throat, delivered his first line, and they were away. Things went largely as Hattie had assured Larry they would: the main cast members devoted ninety per cent of their attention to their own performances, determined to make a good impression, and the other ten per cent to sizing one another up. Those actors with fewer lines spent a rather smaller percentage on the former activity and consequently more on the latter, but crucially no one spent any significant time so much as glancing at Larry, except for when they sometimes looked over just after delivering a line to try to glean from his expression whether or not they had won his approval. Even without much in the way of scrutiny, Larry still looked as though he wished the ground would swallow him, but his face at least had returned to a less medically improbable colour.

After an hour the read-through finished, and everyone

clapped dutifully, and then there was a silence. Hattie had protected Larry for as long as she could; if he was going to direct this piece he really needed to start now. She looked over at him. The wild panic had reappeared in his eyes.

'Thank you very much, everyone. Larry, now that we've all heard the text, perhaps you'd like to share a little bit about your vision for the piece?' she prompted.

'Ah. Well. Ah.' Larry's eyes bulged. 'Well. It's… It's pretty simple. It's about children. In a classroom. And you're all being the children. Except you, you're being the teacher. And you, you're one of the children when he's grown up. Ah. But your bits happen at the same time as the children's bits. Although not exactly at the same time, so you're not talking at once. And it's going to be very realistic, although it won't be in an actual classroom, and some of you look a little bit too old to really be children, but that can't be helped because it's too complicated to hire actual children, and…'

His voice had dropped to a mumble before petering out entirely, and Hattie was alarmed that he really did have nothing more to say about what he was trying to achieve than what he had already said, but, thankfully, Kitty had her hand up, and maybe it was just due to the subject matter of the play but she really did look like a tentative schoolchild. To prevent another awkward silence Hattie said, 'Yes, Kitty?'

'Well, I was just wondering, sorry if this is stupid, but if we're being naturalistic, I wonder if we might use… well, I just happened to read a book on the Meisner technique and I wondered if that would be a good approach to take here?'

'Ah. Meisner. Ah,' said Larry, gawping. 'I'm not… well, look, you can talk about your fancy terminology all you want but… I don't really buy into that.'

His voice became a little stronger, his body slightly more animated as he warmed to his theme.

'Acting is simple, I think it's only overcomplicated by people who want to make it seem harder than it is. You stand in the right place and you say the right words, and if your voice and appearance weren't right then you wouldn't have been given the part in the first place, so that's all there is to it. You won't catch me telling you to use any pretentious techniques.'

'Oh. Sorry. Okay,' said Kitty, looking chastened, and Hattie felt a pang of sympathy for her. Larry's shooting down of her suggestion, and the increasingly aggressive tone in which he had done it, clearly had nothing to do with the merits of the idea (about which Hattie was not well equipped to make judgements, never having paid much attention to different acting philosophies herself), and everything to do with his obvious insecurities and the fact that he had clearly never even *heard* of the Meisner technique but didn't want to admit it to his cast.

This exchange seemed to have sparked something in Larry, though, because he got to his feet and continued, 'In fact, I don't see why it should take us three weeks. I bet we could get most of this done in an afternoon. It's wasteful! You know what? We'll do it right now, and I'll show you. Look, here's the stage, right?'– he gestured to a section of the floor area – 'And here's the audience. So we'll have desks set up here, and chairs. And then the teacher's table will be here. So come on. In the front row we've got Bella and Mike and Lawrence and Kieran and Niamh and Toby. Come on! Come up, bring a chair with you, and sit down where I put you.'

The actors dutifully moved themselves into position, until they were in four rows of six, all on one side of the stage facing Kai, who was playing their teacher, Mr Unsworth, on the other side of the stage.

'Right,' said Larry. 'Now, when grown-up George is talking, he'll be over here, and we'll switch off the lights on the other lot. And that's all there is to it. Honestly, I don't see why we need to rehearse this at all. You know where to be now. You've got your lines. You're not saying them right yet, but I'll just tell you how to say them and then you just need to spend the next couple of weeks memorising them. Easiest money you ever made. Frankly I ought to ask for some of it back.'

Larry seemed to be oscillating between outrage at what he evidently saw as the needless complexity of acting and triumphant glee at being able to eliminate some of it. Meanwhile the actors looked on with expressions of amusement, bewilderment, and, especially among the younger ones, rapt fascination.

'Come on, then. Let's do it from the beginning, and I bet we'll have it sorted by the end of the day.'

Larry stomped over to where Hattie was sitting, in the 'audience' part of the room, and sat down next to her. Then he looked at the actors. Then he stood up again.

'Right. Well we've got to change that. I can only see four of you.'

It was true. With the 'children' arranged in rows running perpendicular to the edge of the stage, the actors on the ends of each row masked all the others sitting behind them. The leads were completely invisible, buried deep inside the pack. Rotating everything by ninety degrees, which was Larry's first proposed solution, turned out not to solve the problem, as now only the front row was visible, and Kai found himself facing away from the audience, expected to deliver his lines directly upstage.

The more enthusiastic cast members were keen to suggest increasingly novel solutions to this problem, and some of them took it upon themselves to direct others to move to particular places, meaning that the whole room dissolved into total chaos for a good few minutes. Hattie could have called them all to order immediately, and arguably as the stage manager that's what she should have done, but instead she took the opportunity to jot down a pencil sketch on a piece of paper, and then gently call Larry aside.

'It's a really tricky one,' she assured him. 'I've worked on shows with classroom scenes before, and you have to balance realism with the practicality of having as many of the actors visible to as many audience members as possible. But you can cheat the angles quite a lot and still have it look okay. One way we've done it in the past is to have the rows of desks staggered, and on the diagonal, like this…'

He took a little bit of convincing, and Hattie readily conceded that, with twenty-four pupils needing to be crammed onto the stage, even with some heavy bending of lines and extreme cheating of angles, even the most carefully crafted staging still meant a lot of obscured faces and a credibility-stretching classroom set-up. But short of cutting some of the characters from the scene, Larry accepted that Hattie's staggered set-up was probably as good as it was going to get.

'Right,' he huffed. 'That's it then. And that's the point, isn't it? That you don't need to get caught up on this stuff. They know it's a classroom. They can see what they need to. Everything else is just self-indulgent. So come on, let's get rehearsing.'

Larry's confidence that, with a sufficiently level-headed attitude, the whole rehearsal process could be reduced to a single day's work, lasted for about another fifteen minutes. The complexities of the placement of chairs were just the start. The next thing to become clear was that Larry had very particular ideas about how each line should be delivered, but did not perhaps entirely possess the language with which to communicate these ideas. Ordinarily a director can fall back to giving a 'line reading' where the director says the line exactly how they want the actor to say it, and the actor just copies their intonation, but Larry, for reasons best known to himself, refused to do this. The cast didn't complain, line readings being generally seen by actors as being creatively limiting, but in the absence of any other medium through which Larry could explain how he wanted his script to be performed, stalemates were regularly reached, and frustrations rose on all sides.

After a couple of hours they had staggered their way through the first scene, at which point Hattie gently recommended a tea break.

'Then shall we run the whole scene again while it's still fresh in everyone's heads?' she suggested. Larry agreed, and after ten minutes in which no one worked out how to get any of the various machines behind the bar to dole out water hot enough to make tea with, they settled into place and, save for a few interjections of 'Not like that!' by Larry, ran the first scene uninterrupted. It was here that Larry learned his next lesson about theatre. Because while, in a secondary school, a ten-minute stretch in which a whole class sits still at their desks and only one person talks at a time would be greeted by the teaching staff as a transcendentally good time, that same occurrence holds considerably less appeal when transposed to a theatre stage.

'Why's it so *boring*?' said Larry to Hattie, looking equal parts affronted and confused.

'Theatre is a visual medium,' said Hattie. 'And visually the first scene is pretty… static.'

'But it's a classroom. They're supposed to be sitting down. It's not realistic otherwise.'

'Realistic isn't always entertaining.'

'So, then,' Larry said, lowering his voice, 'what do I do? I don't want my play to be boring.'

Hattie thought for a second.

'You just need to put a bit of movement in it. What if Fran starts off on the back row and George and Terry are at the front? So when she starts talking to them, maybe she gets up and comes round to them? That would make it a bit more confrontational.'

'But the teacher would see and tell her to sit back down.'

'Not if the teacher was distracted. Maybe the teacher leaves for a bit.'

'But he doesn't leave.'

'It's your script. If you want him to leave, you can just have him leave.'

So they started back at the beginning, this time working out, section by section (and interrupted only by a brief break when someone came and mopped the floor), ways of getting the actors up and about, moving in ways that both made practical sense according to the rules of a classroom and also reflected the dynamics of a script. It was fascinating, Hattie thought, to watch a novice learn in real time and from first principles what directing actually *was*. And to give him credit, Larry at least had the instincts to know when something was wrong even if he didn't have the tools at his disposal to correct them. Aside from his general ignorance the only thing really holding him back was his insecurity. The actors, recognising the problems against which he was struggling, were full of creative suggestions, some of which were pretty good, but only some of the suggesters had begun to learn that if you wanted Larry to accept someone else's idea you had to couch it in the most non-threatening terms possible. Ideas introduced with phrases like 'Surely we should…' and 'Can't we just…' were apt to be dismissed out of hand, normally with a rebuke thrown in to boot. But an idea prefaced by something like 'Do you think it might look good if…' would likely be given a fair hearing and might even be accepted, or at least rejected with grace.

At five o'clock Larry had unambiguously lost his proposed bet that they would 'have it sorted by the end of the day'. However, they had worked their way thoroughly through not just the first scene but also the beginning of the second, putting them slightly ahead of Hattie's proposed schedule. Given how ropey the start of the session had been, Hattie considered it a good day's work all in all.

Larry was clearly exhausted. He had spent the afternoon alternating between sitting next to Hattie and hopping up to the stage with the actors, and as the afternoon wore on Hattie found his returns to her accompanied by an increasing pungent smell: he had evidently been sweating profusely and constantly under his suit. After the actors had been dismissed and once the last of them had trickled out, he collapsed down into a chair and looked like he might never rise again.

'Oh my lord,' he muttered to himself. 'Oh my lord, oh my lord, oh my lord.'

'You've done really well,' Hattie reassured him, and she meant it. Great art this was clearly not, but this was equally not a total car crash; Hattie could appreciate just how hard Larry had worked to get things moving. And yes, in his agitation he had been dismissive and rude at times, and Hattie had made several mental notes to keep an eye, and if possible a lid, on his more unpleasant outbursts, but what director wasn't a bit tetchy under pressure?

'I want to give up and run away. If this wasn't the only thing I have going on in my life right now I probably would. I wouldn't mind curling up and crying for an hour or so now,' he confessed, and Hattie was touched to be shown this little piece of vulnerability. But there wasn't time to either explore this openness *or* curl up and cry, because the owner of the wine bar appeared again and started tutting that the room hadn't been returned to its original state, requiring Hattie's calm reminder that she had the space for another ten minutes, and assurance that the last chairs would be back where they ought to be by then.

Once the room was returned to its required layout Hattie left the bar, and on her way to the bus stop found herself accosted by a timid-looking Kitty, who had evidently been lingering here hoping to catch the stage manager. After the dressing down she had received from Larry about adopting the Meisner technique she had stayed pretty quiet, doing what she was told as best as she could and making no unsolicited suggestions. Out on the street she wasn't looking any more confident.

'Hello, my love,' Hattie greeted her.

'Hi,' she said. 'I was hoping to catch you…'

'Oh yes? What can I do for you?'

'I was just wondering,' said Kitty, her voice a little low, looking around nervously to check that no one else was in earshot, 'was that… normal? For a first rehearsal? Only it all felt a bit uncomfortable, and not like any of the shows I've worked on before, but this is the first time I've ever been paid, and…'

'It was tough, wasn't it? He's an inexperienced director, and he didn't like to admit to all the things he didn't know. I think it'll get easier once we settle in, and I'll make sure he doesn't overstep. Prickly is prickly, but I was always taught that the 'P' in 'professional' stands for 'politeness', and if need be I'll remind him of that.'

'Thank you,' said Kitty. 'I don't really mind that, I just… normally I've worked for directors who made me feel a bit more confident that there's going to be a proper play at the end of it all. I didn't really feel like that today.'

'I understand. Unfortunately, sometimes you get shows that feel like this at the start. And sometimes they turn out great despite everything, and sometimes they don't. I'd say that today wasn't normal, but then again, theatre never is.'

11

Things settled down a bit over the course of the rest of the week's rehearsals. Larry seemed to grow into his role as time went on and, in doing so, overcame some of the insecurity that had been at the root of much of the friction on the first day. He became more confident, both in what it was he was supposed to be doing and that he was capable of doing it, and as a result he didn't exactly relax, but he seemed fractionally less on edge which allowed the actors to be less on edge too. Of all of them, Kitty seemed to wear her heart on her sleeve and her emotions on her face the most, so Hattie watched her keenly as a sort of bellwether for the group, and was reassured that she seemed more enthusiastic, albeit somewhat tentatively so, by the end of the week.

The only thing that stood out to Hattie as a little odd (apart from the fact that she still had no idea why Larry was so keen to stage this piece that didn't seem to have anything in particular to say) was how he treated Miles. Miles was a last-minute addition to the cast, playing the grown-up version of the main character and delivering monologues about his life after school between the classroom scenes. Hattie assumed, from the haphazard nature of his inclusion, that Larry had originally intended the other lead actor, Neil, to play both versions of the character, and didn't want to admit that he had changed his mind. Fair enough. It made sense to split the part, and it was in character for Larry to not want to draw attention to having originally got it wrong.

But what Hattie couldn't quite understand was why, in general, Larry seemed so uninterested in Miles's performance. When it came to the rest of the cast he was a stickler for detail, determined to lock down the intonation of every syllable according to his specific notions of how they should be delivered. But whenever they worked on Miles's scenes, although he still responded to his performance with the same scowls and winces that were his reaction to what he considered 'incorrect' pronunciations by the rest of the cast, he almost never relayed these criticisms to Miles. Instead, all his notes and interventions concerned where the actor should stand on stage, his movements and positioning.

It was a tiny thing, but it stood out to Hattie. Her instincts told her something was going on there, but as yet she had no idea what it was.

Of course, there was another explanation for why she would pick up on this: the appealing thing about this show, from Hattie's perspective, was not what it was but what it wasn't. And what it wasn't was the death of an old friend, or intimidating visits from thugs who may have brought about the aforementioned death. The play was *safe*, and as such Hattie found herself paying it even more attention than was entailed by her professional responsibility. On the bus ride to and from work, while lying in bed at home, in the shower, at all times her mind wanted to stray back to the rehearsal room, because that was preferable to the other places it might wander. With that amount of excess brain power directed to it, it was no perhaps wonder that Hattie was finding unusual patterns of behaviour. She would have found them whether or not they were actually there.

Her intense level of attention towards the production meant that Hattie was taking it particularly hard that she had not yet found someone to do the costumes. Moira had eventually got back to her with a typically Moira-ish three-word email ('Sorry, too busy'). And of the candidates Nick had been able to turn up through his network, only one was available, but he had demanded a fee that made Hattie's eyes water and Larry understandably baulk. Time was slipping away, and Larry was still totally unamenable to the idea of compromise on his school uniforms, and was starting to make nasty noises about Hattie's inability to secure him the costume maker she had 'promised' him. The failure to deliver the goods was weighing on Hattie's mind even more than the peculiarities re Miles.

Despite all these preoccupations, she wasn't *totally* ignoring the Steve and Conor situation. On the Wednesday lunchtime she looked up Nancy Duff's hair salon in Mile End, and tried calling it, but received no answer. And then on the Friday, when rehearsals finished early (as Larry had a dentist appointment in the afternoon), rather than head straight for home, Hattie made her way up to Enfield. It was a tediously long journey to make on public transport, but she wanted to get there during normal office hours, and this seemed like it would be her only chance for a while.

Makerhub Coworking turned out to be a large warehouse building clad in corrugated steel sheeting, and with the organisation's logo printed on a plastic banner mounted slightly lopsidedly in front of some faded lettering spelling out the name of a logistics company, presumably the building's previous owners. The small front door led into a foyer area, whose walls and reception desk had been slapped together out of sheets of chipboard. Most of the signage in this area was handwritten in chalk on blackboards, and Hattie had to tread carefully over various cables running along the floor held down by yellow-and-black striped tape. The overall effect was makeshift but cheerful.

At the reception desk was a woman with thick glasses and green hair slouching behind a laptop screen. She didn't initially acknowledge her new visitor, but after Hattie had hovered in front of her for a few minutes she looked up owlishly.

'Hello,' she said noncommittally.

'Hello,' Hattie replied. 'I wonder if you can help me. I rang earlier in the week. I'm trying to track someone down. The name I have is S Lim, but I don't know if that's the full name or if there's a bit missing.'

'Oh yes! I remember. I was having a think about that actually, and I was wondering if you were looking for Sean. His last name is Lee, not Lim, though. He works for Think Smart, they're an education startup. Could that be it?'

'I suppose so,' said Hattie, doubtfully. 'But the piece of paper I have definitely says Lim. But it might not actually be a person's name. It could be missing some letters at the end. Like "Lime", "Limit", "Limp", that sort of thing?'

'Hmm. I'm not sure. I don't think we've any companies with names like that. You're welcome to take a look yourself.'

She gestured over at one of the blackboards, which displayed a list of office numbers, each with a company name associated with it. Hattie went closer and had a look. There were about fifty companies, none of which had names that started with or contained 'Lim', let alone 'S Lim'. The only one that stood out at all to Hattie was a company called 'Duff Creative Services', and only because she had had Nancy Duff on her mind recently.

'Can you tell me about this company?' she asked, pointing at the name.

'Which? Oh, Roxie?' said the receptionist. 'She's lovely. Costume designer, stuff like that.'

'Oh yes?' said Hattie in surprise. 'I don't think she's who I'm after but as it happens I'm looking for a costume designer. On the off chance… do you think she's in today?'

'I think I saw her… well, if you sign in you're welcome to go take a look.'

Hattie filled in the form at the desk, then, taking note of Duff Creative Services' office number, followed the signs that led down the corridor and into the depths of the building. It seemed as though the majority of the internal walls had been built in the same manner and with the same materials as the reception, a labyrinth constructed from eight by four sheets of particle board and timber battens, with colourful beanbag chairs and somewhat neglected pot plants providing a little bit of visual variety. She soon found the number she was looking for next to a closed door, on which she carefully knocked.

The woman who opened it was very pretty. No, that wasn't quite right. She had chunky, thick-set features and a sturdy frame, and probably wouldn't count as beautiful in any traditional sense of the word. But there was something about her appearance that Hattie found immediately appealing, invoking a feeling of reassurance akin to familiarity. Handsome, Hattie thought. That was a better word for it. She must have been younger than thirty, but there was a confidence to her that felt older. She looked at Hattie with a gaze that suggested neither warmth nor hostility, just slight impatience countered by mild curiosity.

'What's up?' she asked.

'Sorry to trouble you,' said Hattie, 'only I happened to be here on an errand and the woman at the front desk said you might be a costume designer?'

She paused, seeking a word or gesture of confirmation or denial, but received neither, so continued, 'I'm stage managing a show that needs some costume work done, a pretty short notice job, and I wondered if by any chance you had some availability.'

'Oh yeah?'

Again, the delivery was blunt but not aggressive, with nothing given away. It was a little unnerving, and Hattie realised she was in danger of offering a complete stranger with no known qualifications the job simply for the sake of filling the silence. So she collected herself, and tried to reposition.

'So if you have a moment, and if there's a possibility you might be free to take on some costume work, maybe we could have a chat about the show and the sort of thing you do, and see if there's room to work together? My name's Hattie, by the way.'

Curiously, that got a reaction. Not a large one, just a small tilt of the head, but enough to reassure Hattie that her words were actually being heard.

'Roxie,' said Roxie. 'Come on in, then.'

Roxie's workspace was a delight. There were the essentials you'd expect from anyone working with clothing: piles of fabrics, a sewing machine, a tailor's dummy, lots of boxes of beads and buttons and so on. But one wall was also filled by rows of polystyrene heads mounted on spikes, each sporting a different wig, and another was full of pictures of the most gruesome injuries on arms, faces, and torsos, which Hattie eventually realised must be carefully crafted prosthetic special effects. A desk in a corner held pots of putty in an array of flesh tones, and two large clear plastic bottles containing what Hattie had to assume was not *real* blood. And tucked into all the nooks and crannies, and suspended from the ceiling, were all manner of puppets in various stages of completion, marionettes, glove puppets and more.

It was the kind of place that Hattie longed to explore. Every item called out to be examined, and she knew that each must have a story behind it. But unfortunately, she had business to attend to. The contents of the workshop reassured her that Roxie had talents, but the question was whether they were the talents Hattie, or rather Larry, needed.

'Goodness, looks like you do all sorts,' she said.

'Yeah,' said Roxie, 'I used to do puppetry, but there's not much work there. Nowadays it's mostly hair and makeup, and costumes.'

'You're clearly multitalented. And special effects too?' asked Hattie, gesturing at the gory side of the room.

Roxie shrugged.

'When there's demand. Mostly I only get that sort of work around Halloween. But what's it you need?'

Hattie outlined the nature of Larry's production, and his curiously specific requirements about the school uniforms.

'The real problem is time,' she said. 'Ideally we would have had someone lined to work on it up months ago, but this only came to light as a must-have quite recently. I've been struggling to find anyone with availability in the next couple of weeks.'

'I don't think it's too big a job,' said Roxie. 'Get a dozen black blazers, and a dozen blue ones, slice them up and sew them back together as two dozen striped blazers. In terms of how the stripes are laid out, half the blazers would be one way round and the other half the other way, but I doubt anyone would notice. Is there any money?'

Hattie explained about the show's finances, finding professional ways of saying that it was a small-scale vanity project with an unexpectedly high budget, but that the pot available needed to cover both materials and labour, and that Larry sometimes got fussy about spending more on the latter than he had to. When prompted for her hourly rate, Roxie gave a number that Hattie was *fairly* sure Larry wouldn't immediately dismiss.

'It'll be quite a lot of hours, mind,' said Roxie. 'Just sourcing the blazers will be a bit of work on its own. But look, I've got the time at the moment. So if you want me to go for it, I'll go for it.'

'That's excellent,' said Hattie. 'I'll need Larry to sign off, but I think he will, and if he does you may just have saved my neck.'

'Do you think you could let me know by the end of the weekend? If I'm doing this, I'll cancel some other things.'

'Absolutely. I'll speak to Larry about it this evening. Can I have your contact details?'

Roxie handed over her card, and Hattie put it in her bag.

'Perfect. Well, it was very nice to meet you, and I'll be in touch very soon.'

Hattie was pleased as punch, and it was only as Roxie started to shepherd her back out of the room that she remembered that this wasn't the reason she'd come to Enfield in the first place.

'While I remember, do you know many of the other people who work in this building?'

'A few.'

'Does any of them have the last name Lim, or a name that begins with "Lim"?'

Roxie shook her head.

'No matter,' said Hattie. 'There was a production manager I used to know. Fellow called Steve Felton. I think he had some sort of connection to this place, thought it might be to do with someone called Lim. I don't suppose you knew Steve?'

Roxie just shrugged, her face utterly expressionless.

He was like you, Hattie thought. *Didn't waste words.*

'Well, I won't keep you. Thanks for your time, and I'll let you know for sure as soon as I've spoken to Larry.'

'All right.'

Roxie closed the door behind her, and Hattie made her way back to the building's foyer.

'Any luck?' asked the receptionist.

'Yup, she was in. Finding a Roxie makes up for not finding a Lim, I think.'

Hattie signed out and made her way to the bus stop. While she waited, she pulled Roxie's card out of her bag and examined it. Elegant and understated, it had the words 'DUFF CREATIVE SERVICES LIMITED' in clean black lettering against a grey background, along with an email address and two phone numbers: a mobile, and the Makerhub landline. It didn't specify *which* creative services she offered, but that was fairly common among jack-of-all-trade types; you wanted to be remembered as someone who could do whatever needed doing, not pigeon-holed by a single skill or discipline.

Hattie put the card away, but with her last glance she noticed something curious. It was probably a coincidence, but if you ripped off the letters at the edges of 'SERVICES LIMITED', what you'd be left with in the middle was 'S LIM'.

12

Adrenaline affects everyone differently, and the same person can be affected in different ways in different situations. It was a curious feature of Hattie's psychology that, largely unflappable though she aspired to be, when something did manage to flap her, in doing so it occasionally uncovered in her a reckless trait. Which is to say, it was not unknown for her to walk towards trouble, not away.

Take, for example, the situation on the Saturday morning, and the context surrounding it. There was no rehearsal, but Hattie was very much still at work. She was chasing up affordable classroom furniture hire. Desks and chairs are fairly common scenery requirements in the theatre, and as such it is normally fairly straightforward to source some cheaply for a production, but in the case of *What You Deserve* there were two complicating factors. The first was the size of the cast, necessitating an unusual amount of furniture, and furniture that therefore had to be fairly compact in order to fit within the confines of the stage area. The second was Larry's puzzling and unhelpful stubbornness about the exact appearance of said furniture. It wasn't enough to find chairs of the sort that a secondary school in the Midlands in the mid 1990s might believably have used. No, Larry insisted that they needed to be a particular colour, and a specific (and somewhat unusual) style. This despite the chairs in no way featuring in the play other than being where the actors occasionally put their bottoms.

Hattie didn't gripe about it: it wasn't her job to understand a director's creative choices, much less to dissuade them from making them (unless said choices were impossible to achieve). It was her job to facilitate, and if that meant spending her time scouring London for chairs, then scour she would.

Thankfully, Hattie had been sourcing chairs for much of her professional life, and she had good instincts about where to look. She had sniffed out a community hall in north London that had a store of furniture, and the photos of their inventory had met with provisional approval from Larry. Normally the owners rented out the furniture to people who wanted to use it in the hall itself, but they had sounded amenable to an off-premises hire over email. So Hattie had arranged to go see the chairs in person at nine o'clock on Saturday morning.

It didn't make for a particularly early start, but it was still an earlier one than she would have liked for a weekend. The schlep to Enfield the day before had taken its toll on her hip, and worryingly had caused the pain in her ankle from the accident the week before to re-emerge. These two together had made for a bad night's sleep, and Hattie did find herself begrudging the lost lie-in as she made her way north. Her bad mood was compounded by the fact that Larry's response to her triumphant message announcing that she had found a costume maker had been tepid at best. He had grumbled that Hattie had found him a complete stranger without a 'pedigree', and had suggested she spend a few more days looking for other options before he would 'settle for' Roxie. Hattie's attempts to impress upon him via text message that time had run out and that it was likely Roxie or nothing were met with no response at all.

And then the chairs and tables were a bust. The woman who ran the hall kept Hattie waiting for twenty minutes, and when she did arrive she immediately announced that she had thought about it and wasn't prepared to let the furniture be taken away from the hall after all. Bafflingly, she asked if Hattie still wanted to look at them, and when Hattie declined, pointing out that if she wasn't allowed to move them they were of literally no use to her, acted as though Hattie was the one who had wasted both their time.

The sum total of all of this was that by half past nine Hattie was tired, hobbling, frustrated, and in what she would normally call a grump. As she was walking back to the tube, her phone rang, but it had slipped down right to the bottom of her bag and by the time she fished it out it was just cutting across to voicemail. Her surge of disproportionate anger at having missed it was suddenly directed in a different direction when she saw that the number on her screen was the one with the sixes and the thirteen. Conor's lot. The men in the van. Big Steve, lying in a pool of his own blood. Hattie, leaving the envelope behind.

This, then, was the wave of adrenaline in question, the one that spurred her reckless trait into action. It might have caused her to flee homewards, or freeze up on the pavement, or even smash her handset, or any one of a hundred different things. What the wave *did* cause, however, was a search on her phone. Specifically, on her map app. Because Hattie was in North London. And it had occurred to her that Crouch End was just round the corner.

She hadn't consciously decided to go into the Queen's Head, nor had she formulated any sort of notion about what she might do if she *did* go into the Queen's Head. She wasn't really taking conscious decisions at all. She simply allowed her feet to take her to the street in question and, once there, to take a note of where the Queen's Head was and, once noted, to walk up to it and see what sort of establishment it was. Had the door been locked, as by rights it should have been early on a Saturday morning, that might have been the end of it. Met with no obvious next step to take on this course, conscious thought would almost certainly have reclaimed control and Hattie would have made haste away from this place that was apparently the home turf of her antagonists.

But the door was, most improbably, not locked, and was even slightly ajar. And when one is in the grip of a reckless streak, the simple action of pushing gently on a slightly ajar door and walking through it is easily done, even if a moment's reflection would suggest that entering such a door might be extremely ill-advised.

The pub was clearly not open for business. Most of the tables had chairs stacked on top of them and there was no one behind the bar. There was, however, in the centre of the room, a wooden table at which sat two men, one halfway through eating a full English breakfast, the other reading a newspaper. There was nothing particularly sinister about either of these two men, or what they were doing. They were certainly not the two from the van outside her flat. The one with the newspaper was older, with unruly grey hair and thick-framed glasses. His partner on the other hand was young and slight, and his head was bent down, staring at a phone that lay next to his plate.

The newspaper reader, without looking up, said, in a pleasant enough tone, with a gentle Irish accent, 'Now Tad, did you forget to lock the door again?'

'Sorry,' rumbled a voice, and Hattie became aware of a third figure who loomed up out of a corner towards her. This was a bigger man. Was he one of the pair she had seen before? He had a similar build, and a similarly threatening presence. And she'd never really got a good look at their faces.

'We're closed,' he said to her, gesturing towards the door.

'I… yep,' said Hattie, and she would have turned to leave, had the older man not at that moment looked up from his newspaper and fixed her in place with a penetrating, hypnotic gaze. He frowned. Was that a look of surprise? Of recognition? No, it didn't seem to be.

'Unless you're here for a reason, that is.'

Hattie gawped, her mind blank. She was beginning to realise what a dangerous place she had walked into, and for the life of her she couldn't think why she was here.

'You speak English?' asked the other seated man, looking up from his food. 'I don't think she speaks English, Conor.'

'She does,' said Conor thoughtfully. 'She's just frightened. Look how wide her eyes have gone. What are you frightened of, lady? Are you frightened of Tad here? He's a big lad, but he's gentle as a lamb. No? Maybe you're frightened of me, then.'

His voice was so calm, his gaze so continuous, that Hattie found herself almost hypnotised. There was adrenaline racing round her system again, but this time it was pinning her, enforcing a stillness so complete that she could barely breathe.

'Let's keep it simple, shall we? What's your name, my darling?' Conor asked.

'H… Hattie,' she answered.

'It's nice to meet you, Hattie. My name's Conor. But I suspect you knew that, if you've come to my place of business at this hour. Now, I'm guessing that you're here to see me?'

Hattie nodded.

'See, this is what I'm saying,' said Conor, and this was addressed to his seated companion. 'Instincts. It takes a lifetime, but if you can just read people, your life gets a lot easier.'

'Yeah but what's the point? Just tell her to fuck off. Or let me have her. It's ages since I got to cut someone.'

'And what would be the value in that? This creature who calls herself Hattie has come to see me. And yet, finding me, the cat has got her tongue. Don't you want to know why? Doesn't this smack of mystery and intrigue?'

'Nah, it's fucking boring. Slit her throat or chuck her out,' said the younger man, turning back to his food and his phone.

Conor shrugged.

'Forgive him,' he said to Hattie. 'He's a good lad, but he's also an insolent little gobshite. Here I am, trying to resolve the matter of succession for my little empire, literally offering him the keys to the kingdom, and he'd rather indulge in some Saturday morning sadism than take a few pearls of wisdom from the man grooming him for the throne. It's short-sighted, and if he keeps on this way I might lose patience and replace him, but what can you do? You can only lead a horse to water. But now, where were we? Oh yes. We've established that you're Hattie, and I'm Conor. And you're scared of me. But you've come to see me anyway. Which is brave, Hattie. Now, I do have to ask, are you here to kill me? Because I can't lie, that has happened a couple of times. Not the killing itself, you understand, but the motivation. In an earlier time I was a little unruly, and a few people have held a grudge. Are you one of them?'

'No…' breathed Hattie.

'Well then, pull up a chair, and tell me what's on your mind.'

Then the big man, Tad, moved very fast, on the edge of Hattie's vision. There was a blur, and a scraping sound, and something thunked onto the floor, and in that flurry of movement, Conor's hypnotic spell was broken, and Hattie turned and bolted. She was halfway out of the door before she realised that all that had happened was that he had pulled a chair down from the table and set it on the floor for her to sit on, but by that point she was already moving, and saw no reason to stop. She burst out onto the street, chased by Conor's delighted laughter, and didn't stop moving until she had turned two corners and was sure no one had followed her.

She took a few moments to catch her breath and to try to marshal her thoughts, but found she still couldn't think clearly. She just wanted to get away, so she gave in to the impulse and started moving again, vaguely in the direction of Hornsey station. It was only when she had made it onto a train that she began to find it possible to think clearly. First things first: she was stupid, stupid, *stupid*. What on earth had possessed her to walk into that place? It was the home turf of an obviously extremely dangerous man. Sure, he had technically been nothing but courteous, but he was the sort of man who brought a bodyguard with him to breakfast, and by his own admission he had an 'unruly' past such that there were multiple people who wanted to kill him. He had the comportment of a predator, but Hattie had *known* all this even before meeting him, known that that pub was his lair, and she had walked in anyway. It was nothing short of a miracle that she'd escaped. It was only because he'd been seemingly amused by her that he'd let her go. He knew she posed him no threat.

But there was something curious in that. His amusement. His curiosity. It was all based in the fact that he had no idea who she was. He didn't recognise her, which perhaps wasn't surprising. But he didn't seem to have recognised her name either, referring to her as a 'creature who calls herself Hattie', and that *was* surprising. Conor had had Steve killed, possibly even killed Steve personally, and found out that Hattie was associated with Steve, had sent his thugs round to Hattie's flat… yet drew a blank when Hattie gave him her name in person? It didn't make sense.

This line of thought nagged at Hattie the whole way home. She'd missed something. Maybe Conor's organisation was bigger than she thought. Maybe one of his lieutenants was the one who was responsible for tying up loose ends, and didn't want to bother the boss about the details. So was that lieutenant – presumably neither Tad nor the young breakfast-eating protégé – the one who knew about Hattie? Could that be it? Or had Conor been lying just now? Did he know exactly who Hattie was, and was being careful with what he said just in case she was wearing a wire?

Oh listen to yourself, you daft old bint. 'Wearing a wire'? Everything you learned about crime you learned from Brian De Palma films. You're so far out of your depth it's laughable.

She made her way back to the flat, hoping to receive comfort and counsel from Nick.

She received neither, however. He met her in the hall, a worried look on his face. In his hand was an opened envelope. It had Hattie's name on the outside, but no stamp and no address.

'This was in with the post,' he said, handing it to her. 'I got nosy.'

Hattie fished out a piece of paper from the envelope. It had two words on it, handwritten:

BACK OFF

Act Four

It's funny how history repeats itself, isn't it? I have a friend, an actor turned presenter, who recently landed a job presenting a new quiz show. I won't name names, but if you watch much daytime television you may well have seen her at work. Like many quiz shows, the set is a wonderfully high-tech, space-age affair, with glowing columns dotted around, and all manner of panels and beams criss-crossing the background. It's no secret that in recent years producers have, citing cost, eschewed actually building these sets in the studio. Instead they put up a bunch of blue screens in the background, and create a virtual set digitally in post-production. The technology is good enough these days that the audience watching at home never knows the difference. Unless, that is, something goes wrong. In my friend's case, she turned up to work one day wearing a dress that just happened to be the exact same shade of blue as the studio backdrop. No one noticed during filming, and it was only in post-production they discovered that the clever software that replaces the blue background with the fancy space-age set wasn't quite clever enough to avoid also replacing the blue dress with the fancy space-age set, leaving my friend looking like a floating head and hands in a large number of shots. The episodes they filmed that day never aired, costing the production rather a lot of money.

When my friend relayed this to me, I laughed and told her that her colleagues of yester-year would never have faced this problem, for in the past there was a strict injunction against actors ever wearing blue on stage. What started off as sensible accounting (blue being the most expensive dye colour at one time) became a superstition that lingered for centuries. Now, however, the superstition has faded, just in time for it to become sensible accounting again!

– from *A History of Theatrical Superstition*
by Freya Barnsworthy

13

Hattie's one small victory over the weekend was that Larry did eventually, begrudgingly, concede that Roxie might be an acceptable costumier for the show, subject to an in-person meeting and vetting. Hattie therefore rang Roxie and arranged for her to attend rehearsals on the Monday morning. She tried to make it sound like this was a mere formality, afraid that otherwise Roxie might not think it worth the effort, but in doing so was aware that she was encouraging Roxie to cancel any other plans for the week without guaranteed work. She reassured herself that by getting this meeting out of the way first thing on Monday, if it did fall through hopefully Roxie would be in a position to salvage the rest of the week.

Hattie certainly wasn't ignoring the warning she had received over the weekend. Her problem was that she wasn't entirely sure what it was that she was supposed to back off *from*. She had poked her nose into Conor's business, that was true, but the note had appeared at the flat *while she was out doing so*, which made it unlikely to be a prompt for the note itself. She had popped up to Enfield the day before, but all she had found there was Roxie, whose connection to Conor, if any, was entirely unclear, and whose connection to Steve seemed non-existent, and who didn't seem to mind being discovered.

It wasn't hard to infer that whoever had sent the note was in some way connected to whatever Steve had been meddling with, and it would make sense if they wanted her to steer clear of any investigation into who killed him, or what it was that he knew that caused them to kill him in the first place. It was just that Hattie wasn't doing any such investigation, at least not in any significant sense. She'd found herself on the periphery of something that was obviously large and obscure, and had done nothing more than timidly pick at a couple of loose ends. The idea that even this was enough to bring down the ire of… well, someone who may or may not be associated with Conor in some way was terrifying, and Hattie didn't really know what to do about it.

So, in the absence of knowing what to do about that, she did what she *did* know how to do, which was get on with the job at hand. She went to the wine bar on Monday morning, unlocked (after a few days of her being as courteous and professional as possible around him, the owner had been persuaded to trust Hattie with a set of keys), and was gratified to see that the first arrival, a full ten minutes early, was Roxie. Hattie set great store by timeliness (her definition of which entailed never being later than five minutes early for *anything*). She took it as a good sign that Roxie was already living up to her responsibilities in that respect.

'Good morning, my love,' she said. 'Thank you for jumping straight into this.'

'No problem,' replied Roxie. 'It's nice when work falls into your lap.'

'It was a happy accident that I came across you,' said Hattie.

'Yes. Er… why did you end up in my neck of the woods, again?'

'Oh… no reason,' said Hattie uncomfortably. This felt like the sort of thing she was supposed to 'BACK OFF' from, so she didn't really want to start mouthing off about how she had been attempting to understand the contents of an envelope. But equally no one trekked up to Enfield for 'no reason', so by way of explanation she added, 'I was just trying to track something down, but I realised I went to the wrong address.'

'And how did you know I was a costume designer?'

'The receptionist told me.'

'You asked her if she knew any costume designers?'

'No, I…'

Hattie found herself squirming. There was nothing aggressive in Roxie's tone, but she was asking an awful lot of questions, which Hattie hadn't expected: on Friday, she had been notably taciturn.

'It's silly really,' she eventually said. 'I was chatting to her, and I happened to recognise your surname on the board on the wall so I asked about you.'

Roxie frowned.

'My surname?'

'It's silly really,' Hattie repeated awkwardly. 'There's a woman… well, you're not related to a Nancy Duff, are you? Who runs a hair salon?'

'Oh.'

Roxie looked hesitant, and Hattie hurriedly added, 'Not that it's any of my business of course. Sorry, that was a very intrusive question.'

'No, it's okay. She's my m—'

'Are you the tailor, then?'

Larry had arrived and, in his usual bluff way, had marched straight into the conversation just as Roxie was forming a word that Hattie couldn't be sure about but that *might* have been 'mum'.

'That's right,' said Roxie. 'I'm Roxie. Duff.'

That last word was delivered uncomfortably, as though Roxie was in two minds about sharing it, perhaps in case Larry made as much of a fuss over it as Hattie had.

'Larry Lloyd. So. We need two dozen costumes. Ah. Blue and

black blazers. In the next fortnight. Hattie says you can do the job.'

'That's right,' said Roxie. At this point Hattie expected her to outline her idea about cutting up a dozen blue and a dozen black blazers to make the combined sort, perhaps adding caveats about the limited time available, maybe giving an indication of the likely budget. But Roxie did none of those things. She just looked coolly at Larry. Hattie felt herself tensing up. If Larry didn't like this attitude…

But it turned out that Larry *did* like this attitude. He stuck out his hand for Roxie to shake.

'Great. Welcome aboard. What do you need to get started?'

'I'll take some measurements. Are your cast coming in this morning?'

'Half of them,' said Hattie. 'I can get the rest to send me their sizes.'

Roxie shook her head.

'Can't trust actors to be honest about how big they are. If you can tell me what days they'll all be in, I can catch them in person.'

So Hattie and Roxie pored over the rehearsal schedule to work out which days Roxie would need to attend to get every actor's measurements, and then as those actors who had been called for the Monday morning session filed in, Roxie took them each off to one side and measured them up with a tape she produced from her bag.

Hattie found herself liking Roxie, at least on a professional level. She wasn't exactly friendly, but as far as Hattie was concerned, friendliness was an overrated trait in a colleague. What you really needed was calm and efficiency, and Roxie seemed to have both in spades.

But Hattie was also finding herself rather unsettled by what she had just learned. Nancy Duff, who according to Mickey knew all about Big Steve's association with Conor's lot, being connected and possibly related to Roxie, whose company may or may not have been mentioned on a scrap of paper that Big Steve entrusted to Hattie and over which Conor killed him? If all of those possibles were true then Roxie was at the very heart of the mystery around Big Steve's death. Despite that, Hattie felt no closer to any kind of understanding as to what that mystery was actually about. And worse, she had managed to turn Roxie from a stranger to a colleague over the space of a weekend, which seemed to fly in the face of the injunction she had received in her letterbox on Saturday.

There was, however, no time to dwell on this, as the business of the show took over immediately. The great and terrible thing about rehearsals is that they are all-consuming. Maybe it's something to do with actors' personality types, but if you put a bunch of them in a room together, even if you're not working you're still working. Answering questions, asking for quiet, defusing tensions, reaffirming boundaries, asking for quiet again, reassuring insecurities, reminding of schedules, finding new ways of asking for quiet because the actors had seemingly learned to ignore the old ways… Hattie didn't consider herself as particularly good at the pastoral side of things when defining 'pastoral' as 'tending to the general wellbeing of one's colleagues', but if you took the rather more literal meaning of 'herding a bunch of unruly and flighty animals', then she would concede that perhaps this aspect of her job was the one to which she devoted the majority of her attention.

She was still keeping her eye on Miles, the actor playing the grown-up version of George and tasked with delivering all of the soliloquies between scenes. He had more lines than anyone else, and was working hard on them, taking lots of notes and making lots of suggestions, but Larry was now almost completely ignoring the poor man, offering next to no comments on his delivery and giving only the loosest indications as to where he should stand and how he should approach his exits and entrances. It almost amounted to full-on blanking: even when they weren't rehearsing, Larry appeared particularly awkward and almost embarrassed around Miles. He seemed to try to avoid getting into conversation with him full stop, despite making commendable headway ingratiating himself with the rest of the cast.

(The headway was commendable to Hattie's mind to the extent that, Larry being a bit prickly and having got off to something of a bad start to rehearsals, the fact that he was putting in the leg work to try to improve his relationship with his actors was, overall, helping to smooth out the periodic wrinkles in the rehearsal process that his inexperience and insecurity sometimes produced. She did have to concede, however, that his attempts to be charming normally failed: he had no facility for small talk, he struggled to make eye contact, and seemed deeply uncomfortable in engaging in any conversation where the topic was not one he had himself broached. But at least he was trying.)

In one sense this lack of engagement with Miles was helpful. The classroom scenes were inevitably taking longer to get through than they had budgeted, so skimming over the speeches helped to make up lost time and keep them on track overall. But Hattie felt as though trouble was brewing: on the one hand, Miles was beginning to show signs of stress, and Hattie worried about what would happen if he were to start cracking up over his lack of direction. On the other, Hattie simply couldn't believe that Larry, a stickler for almost every other aspect of the play, genuinely didn't care about one of the most central parts of the piece. He might be ignoring it now, but surely he would want to get it right when it came to the performance. Hattie only hoped that by the time he turned his attention to Miles's part it wasn't too late.

One person who absolutely, consistently and obviously was *not* ignoring Miles was Kitty. The young actress was, as one would expect and hope, taking the whole rehearsal process extremely seriously, and her focus was not just limited to her own role. Whenever she wasn't actively rehearsing her part, she was watching the other actors work intently, evidently keen to glean every available scrap of knowledge and insight about the craft from this job. Indeed she would often be found hanging round the rehearsal room during sessions when she wasn't needed at all, simply observing the proceedings. No one seemed to be bothered by this, and Hattie thought it rather admirable: Kitty was at the earliest possible stage in her career, with everything to learn, and while the company of *What You Deserve* wasn't exactly brimming with experience, it was nevertheless an extremely good thing to be exposed to as much of the process as possible, as much to see what didn't work as what did. And equally, it was perhaps unsurprising that Kitty would pay particular attention to the most experienced actors, as they were arguably the most likely to be sources of wisdom. Miles was older and more experienced than most of the actors playing schoolchildren, so it was only natural that Kitty would gravitate to him. But Hattie noticed that the attention Kitty paid to Miles was considerably greater to that paid to Kai, who was even older and playing the part of the form teacher. And it was *perhaps* sheer coincidence that Miles was suave, muscular and handsome, while Kai was stooped and rather plain.

But then again, perhaps it wasn't. The simple truth of it is that actors have a bit of a tendency to fall for one another. And why wouldn't they? Auditions select for charismatic, attractive people, rehearsals entangle them in emotionally intense and vulnerable situations, while performances put them in close proximity in darkened rooms and various states of undress.

There are some pairs of roles, such as those of Hamlet and – awkwardly – his mother Gertrude, where it is so common for the actors portraying them to become romantically (and then anatomically) intertwined that it is almost worthy of note when it *doesn't* happen.

But Kitty was a child, in Hattie's mind even if not in the eyes of the law, and Miles had a good fifteen years on her. While Hattie wasn't at all surprised that the girl found herself vulnerable to his charms, such vulnerability seemed to Hattie to be cause for some concern, and she began to wonder what she could do to inoculate Kitty against them. For the time being, at least, Miles showed no indication of reciprocating the interest, and not much sign of noticing Kitty even existed, but the prolonged, rapt attention of a beautiful woman can play havoc with a normally sensible grown-up's judgement, and there were still a couple of weeks to go.

Hattie found herself inventing entirely spurious errands to send Kitty on, and occasionally resorted to shooing Kitty from the rehearsal room entirely, suggesting, not completely reasonably, that a particular scene might best be rehearsed in private initially, with only those actors who were actually in it needing to be in the room. It was a bit of a stretch, but short of dumping a bucket of cold water on the girl every time she looked a bit moony, Hattie couldn't think of any more effective interventions she could make.

So the week progressed, with rehearsals trundling along as they should, and with Roxie popping in a couple of times to catch the last cast members to get their measurements, before retreating back to her workshop to start on making the blazers. After a couple more false starts, Hattie managed to find a set of classroom desks and chairs that met Larry's requirements, and sweet-talked the owner (a conference management company) into lending her the furniture for free for the week of the show, in exchange for an advert in the show programme. This was the first point at which a discussion regarding whether or not there would even *be* a show programme was in fact broached. Larry initially said he couldn't see the point, but when Hattie suggested that not having to pay for furniture hire was in itself a pretty compelling argument, he acquiesced, and said he would take care of it.

The final piece of the puzzle, Larry having confirmed that he needed no sound effects or incidental music, was lighting. Nick had originally been reluctant to get involved, complaining that it wasn't a 'proper' gig and that besides, it didn't line up with what he was good at. Hattie had to badger him into downloading the Ashwood Artspace's technical specifications document, and could only get him to read the script by forcing it into his hand one evening and blocking the doorway out of the lounge until he read the first scene. But her efforts were rewarded because she noticed him going back to the script over the next couple of days, starting to make notes in the margins at various points. And then at breakfast he surprised her, saying, 'They're quite well stocked, you know. Too many Leko's, not enough Source Fours, but they've got plenty of Fresnels and enough dimmers to be able to do some interesting things. Assuming the document's up to date, which they aren't always in tiddly venues like this. The only thing I'm not sure about is if there's a way of getting decent angles on the downstage area. I think I might do a reccy, see what it looks like in person.'

While Hattie understood more of the words in that speech than the average woman on the street, some of it washed right over her. She grasped enough, however, to be reassured that Nick had now fully engaged with the challenge of doing the lighting for Larry's show, and she rejoiced. She firmly believed that many of Nick's ongoing neck problems were as a result of him not having anything else to worry about beyond the sensations at the top of his spine. A gentle project like this would do wonders for him, she was sure, and hopefully be a big step in his rehabilitation, which would also further the rehabilitation of their household finances, which had been looking more and more ropey as Nick's break from work stretched on.

It was therefore tremendously disappointing to Hattie that when she came back from rehearsals on the Wednesday night, she bumped into him at the bottom of the communal stairs. He was hunched over at an odd angle near the mailbox, and Hattie thought at first he was reading a letter.

'You all right?' she said.

He didn't respond.

'Don't mind me if it's something private,' she tried.

'… Help…' he whimpered, almost inaudibly.

Hattie looked closer, and saw that, while he was hunched up and looking down, there was nothing in his hand that he was looking *at*.

'What's wrong?' she asked.

'Neck… seizedup… onthebus,' he said, the words coming out in pathetic little clusters. 'Ithurtsto… breathe…'

'Oh bloody hell,' said Hattie. 'I thought we'd made it past this stuff.'

'Lookingaround… atthevenue… wasn'tcareful… can'tmove…'

The last utterance came out as a sob. He really was a state.

Hattie sighed, not out of impatience or disappointment, but just as acknowledgement that the next half hour or so was going to be a bit of a challenge.

'Right, are we getting you upstairs or to the hospital?'

'Upstairs. Ifican… liedown… takeapill…'

'All right. I'm going to fetch you a hot flannel and a glass of water, then we'll tackle the stairs, okay?'

'Anychance… medicinal… whisky?'

Hattie grinned.

'I'll see what I can do.'

It took a lot of manoeuvring to get Nick up the stairs using only movements that didn't jolt his neck. The problem wasn't just the pain; as much as anything else it was his fear of the pain that was very obviously (to Hattie; probably not to Nick) causing him to panic and tense up in ways that only made things worse. Hattie's tendency to stumble every time she had to shift her weight off her good leg rather compromised her ability to support her husband, and more than once they came close to tumbling right back down the stairs.

But eventually she got him inside and he tottered over to the bed, creaked his way down to the horizontal, and let out a series of groans so bloodcurdling that Hattie found herself involuntarily vacating the room and seeking shelter in the kitchen. She returned a few minutes later, armed with ibuprofen, some old amitriptyline left over from a previous prescription, a massage ball and, in the interests of being thorough, a small spliff. It took a good hour for the combined effect of these interventions to restore Nick to a state of calm and relative lucidity, but when it did he clicked his tongue sadly and said, 'I don't think I'm getting back to work any time soon, am I? I spent an hour in a theatre, and all I did was *look up*, and rigor mortis set in before I'd even made it home. Am I getting old?'

'Afraid so.'

'Well, it's better than the alternative, I suppose. But what are we going to do?'

'Well, you're going to go see that physio in Belsize Park.'

'What, Zoe's friend? She costs a fortune, she's miles away, and her thing is West End dancers, not crumbly old gits like me...'

Hattie gave him a withering look.

'We're not losing you to an NHS waiting list,' she said. 'And

Zoe says she's the best of the best. So you're going to go see her, and you're going to keep seeing her until you're back on your feet. And I… well, I'm going to start working on the next gig, and try to find something well paid and long term, for a change.'

14

What You Deserve was making significant demands on her time, attention, and energy, but Hattie found herself having to prioritise planning what would come next. She knew that, when it came to publicly advertised vacancies at least, pickings were slim. The last time she'd gone hunting all that she'd found from an intensive search was Larry Lloyd, and nothing new of interest seemed to have been posted since then. On the Thursday morning, not so much in the hope of success as from a desire for some variety, Hattie swallowed her pride and asked around her network of contacts if anyone knew of anyone who happened to be hiring stage managers.

The first response she got back was not so much disappointing as baffling. Kiki Bennett, a deputy stage manager who Hattie had worked with before, replied swiftly:

I heard there's a show coming into the Dionysus that needs an SM... but to be honest I don't think they'd want to speak to you right now. Maybe when things calm down?

The Dionysus was one of the few West End venues that wasn't connected to Geoffrey Dougray, so she had hoped that her falling out with him wouldn't affect her prospects there. And if his reach extended further than she had thought, then it wouldn't be just a temporary trouble: Sir Geoffrey could hold a grudge for years. Things would not calm down.

However, she didn't dwell on this, because to her surprise and delight, she got a lead from the normally elusive Moira:

You've taught before, right? They need a tutor at the Norton.

Hattie could hardly contain her excitement. The Norton Conservatoire was a small but not badly regarded drama school just outside Guildford in Surrey. Hattie hadn't even been aware of them offering a technical training course, and she didn't enjoy tutoring stage management as much as actually doing it, all else being equal, but she did have relevant experience, her various industry blacklists probably didn't extend into drama schools, and teaching was easier on the hips than any of the hands-on jobs she'd been doing recently.

'Could be ideal! Can you introduce me to anyone who works there?' she replied. It was pushing her luck, she knew, but a warm introduction counted for a lot in these circles, in Hattie's experience.

Sure. Head of Wardrobe is a mate of mine.

So, following a swift turnaround of emails from Moira to the Norton's Head of Wardrobe, and from the Head of Wardrobe to the Head of Drama, Hattie found herself scheduled to have a coffee after work that very same day with the Head of Training, a man called David, about their vacancy for a stage management tutor.

As the venue for the coffee was in Guildford, and there was only so late that David was prepared to stick around, it did mean leaving the wine bar early on Thursday, which caused Larry to grumble mightily.

'If I hire you to be in the room during rehearsals, and then you turn around and tell me you can't be there, what am I supposed to think? That you're taking the mickey?'

'I'm sorry to have to do this at short notice, Larry,' said Hattie soothingly, 'and you know I wouldn't do it if it was seriously going to disrupt the work you're doing. But we're well on track, and I'm only disappearing an hour early. And, well, you're scheduled to be working on one of Miles's scenes then, and typically they're less… intensive, aren't they?'

Larry huffed a bit but he didn't disagree. So, not wanting to strain things any more than she had to, Hattie waited until the last possible minute before quietly packing up her things and leaving the rehearsal room, and starting to make her way towards Waterloo station.

David, the Head of Training at the Norton Conservatoire, was a reassuring-looking man: bearded, slightly overweight, glasses-wearing, and possessed of a resting facial expression that suggested a calm and somewhat detached interest in the world around him. He was sitting at a table in the coffee chain at Guildford station when Hattie spotted him, slurping from a paper cup and checking his phone.

'Hello,' she said, making her way over. 'David, is it?'

'And you must be Hattie,' he replied. He blinked at her, and smiled in a brittle way.

She bought herself a tea and sat down to join him.

'So,' he said.

'Well,' said Hattie. She had rather expected him to take the lead in the conversation. This wasn't a formal job interview, not yet at least, but if the context was that he was offering a job and she was interested in it, and she'd come to more or less his home turf, she would have hoped he would take the reins. But if he didn't then it was no problem: Hattie was more than happy to frame their chat on her terms.

'Thanks for taking the time to talk to me. I'd heard you were looking for a stage management tutor, and as I've got some tutoring experience myself, and I'm beginning to step back from touring, I thought it would be interesting to have a conversation to see whether maybe I could be a good fit.'

'Yes. Okay. That makes sense,' said David. There was no denying it: he was curiously unforthcoming. There was nothing hostile about it. If anything, he seemed frozen with shyness, as if he was intimidated by her.

Hattie decided to draw him out.

'If I'm honest I didn't know Norton even had a technical course. Is it new?'

'Yes, brand new. I always wanted to offer one. I started off in production management myself. When ACDA shut down theirs, it made it easier to make the case that we could be the replacement.'

ACDA was the drama school at which Hattie had been tutoring until, for internal political reasons, their technical course was abruptly cancelled. She had to work hard not to wince when she heard the name.

'So you're having to build a teaching team from scratch?'

'Well… not entirely. A lot of the teaching can be done by our in-house technicians, but it's true we're doing quite a big expansion.'

'That sounds exciting!' said Hattie, trying to radiate enthusiasm.

'Yes. Er… so you're looking to move back into teaching, are you?'

'That's right. I—'

'Although you only just left a teaching position.'

'Not out of choice. They shut the course—'

'But you went back into the industry initially.'

'Well, yes, you take whatever work comes up, don't you? There weren't any tutoring positions open at the time,' Hattie explained, hoping she didn't sound too defensive. The truth was that she *felt* a bit defensive, having been rather taken aback by this abrupt avenue of questioning.

'Okay,' said David, frowning slightly. 'That makes sense. Only I'm aware… look, obviously we have a reputation to maintain…'

Hattie's heart sank. She knew she was a pariah in certain circles within the industry – the business with the mask at the Tavistock and her unfortunate clash with Sir Geoffrey Dougray had both caused bad words to be muttered about her in various parts. But she had really hoped that a provincial drama school would have neither awareness of or interest in such things.

'Now hold on,' said Hattie, feeling that she should at least try to defend herself. 'I may have got on the wrong side of a couple of prickly people who happen to be big cheeses, but in an industry like ours, with lots of big personalities, and over the course of a forty-year career it's pretty hard to emerge totally unscathed.'

'Maybe so, but – and forgive me for saying this – there is a line that was crossed, and we at the Norton Conservatoire—'

'I don't think that's fair,' said Hattie, feeling her temper rising. 'I would say that given *significant* mitigating circumstances, about which I would hope you would at least give me the benefit of the doubt if you don't know the details, a couple of slight spats and a raised temper or two—'

'A man *died*.'

'What ma— oh.'

And Hattie got a sudden sinking feeling as she realised that David wasn't talking about the fallings-out with flamboyant theatrical types.

'I don't know,' David continued, 'what exactly happened. I don't want to know, and I don't want to give credence to gossip. I didn't know Steve, and I don't want speak ill of the dead. But it would be extremely difficult for us to justify hiring someone with your… aura.'

'I'm sorry, my what?'

David had the decency to look embarrassed, but it didn't stop him from ploughing on.

'The way you are perceived. Your reputation. Whatever the truth is, and I can only repeat that I do not want to know, we have to think about the wellbeing of our students.'

Hattie felt as though she'd been run over by a truck.

'So why did you even bother meeting me?' she asked weakly.

'Some things are better said in person. I'm sorry.'

David shrugged affably, and Hattie had to resist an urge to throw the remnants of her tea in his face.

By the time she got back to the flat she was raging.

'What the hell did you say?' she asked Nick, as soon as she saw him.

'When?' asked Nick baffled.

'I don't know when.'

'To who?'

'I don't know that either.'

'You're not giving me much to work with, Cockatoo. What did I say about what?'

'About Steve,' Hattie growled, and after a second's consideration Nick's face crumpled into a frown.

'Oh… pants.'

'Tell me.'

'It was after the funeral. We were all down the pub. After you went home. Everyone kept on banging on about how they couldn't believe how Steve had killed himself, and that it seemed so unlike him, and some of them were sort of being a bit mean about it, like they thought less of him. So, you know, I sort of wanted to defend his honour a bit. I definitely didn't say anything specific, I just… well, I may have suggested that there was *possibly* more to it than that. And that you knew some stuff that you weren't telling. I didn't say anything more than that, I swear.'

'Nick, you bloody numpty, you didn't *have* to say anything more than that. You fed them the juiciest bit of gossip the industry's seen in years, and the rumour mill has been spinning ever since. The fellow at the drama school thinks I'm caught up with the mob, he says they wouldn't touch me with a ten-foot barge pole. Kiki too. People think I killed him, or at the very least that I am involved with the people who did, and they're scared that if they hire me I'll show up to the job with a gaggle of murderous gangsters in tow.'

Nick had the decency to look genuinely contrite.

'I'm so sorry. I knew I'd let my tongue slip. I was going to tell you about it. But when I got back, you'd had your run-in with those blokes in the van, and suddenly what I'd said seemed like the least of our problems. Besides everyone had been drinking. I'd sort of been hoping they all forgot about it.'

'Well they didn't,' replied Hattie sourly. 'And now I'm even less employable than I was before.'

'Oh dear,' said Nick. 'I suppose… I suppose you're in a pretty bad mood, then?'

'I'll say,' Hattie snorted.

'So bad it could hardly get worse, eh?'

'That's right…'

'Then now is probably as good a time to talk about it as any: you're going to have to find someone else to do lighting for your Ashwood Artspace show.'

'You what?'

'Well I can't do it, can I? I can't get up a ladder to rig the lights; I can't even tilt my head to look at where the lights are supposed to go. I know you promised your man Larry that you'd sort this for him but you're going to have to sort it another way.'

'Cocker One,' said Hattie firmly, 'you are the love of my life.

My commitment to you is as strong as the day I first married you, and as my life partner I fully intend to stay with you through thick and thin until one of us pops our clogs. Right? So let me say this with all the clarity in the world: if you don't do the show I will bash your head in with the toaster while you're sleeping and laugh all the way to the funeral. I don't care if we have to strap you into one of those Peter Pan flying systems and winch you up to the lighting bars on a pulley. And if you can't do it, then finding someone else who can is your bloody responsibility. You got that? Don't put this on me!'

She had tried for forceful, but somewhere along the way she'd veered in the direction of hysterical. Nick, looking cowed, nodded.

'All right, Cockatoo,' he said gently. 'I'll sort it. Leave it with me.'

The doorbell rang. Hattie and Nick looked at each other. Nick winced, his shoulders rising fractionally, a subtle reminder of his ongoing neck troubles. Hattie gave the slightest incline of her head, an almost imperceptible gesture to draw his attention towards her hip. Nick sighed.

'I'll get it then, shall I? You've been on your feet all day.'

'Thanks, love.'

Nick made heavy weather of making his way to the door, and was slow enough on the stairs that Hattie got bored of waiting and had a look out of the window to see who it might be. What she saw made her heart skip a beat, and she called out, 'Nick! Wait!'

But it was too late. Nick had already opened the door, not having seen for himself the van that was parked up on the pavement, or the two men who had previously been in it and who were now lurking in the doorway. By the time Hattie made it out into the hall at the top of the stairs, they were still there, in the doorway, and one of them had Nick by the throat.

'… and you tell her… ah,' he was saying, catching sight of Hattie as she appeared. 'Hattie, yeah? I need to speak to you.'

The man who spoke was the same one who'd accosted her before: same short hair, same tattoos, different coat. When they'd come before, his tone had been restrained but it was clear now that he was done with social niceties.

'Let him go,' said Hattie, aware of just how badly her voice was quavering.

'Ngh…' gurgled Nick.

'If it's me you want to talk to, you can let my husband go,' said Hattie, more firmly this time.

The man shrugged, and released his hold of Nick, his eyes fixed on Hattie the whole time.

Nick slumped against the wall for a second, then turned and scuttled back up the stairs. Halfway up he froze, and the entire top half of his body tensed up.

'Bugger,' he muttered. 'My neck…'

'Just get inside,' said Hattie.

He stumbled up clumsily the rest of the way, and once he was inside Hattie was tempted to follow suit and bolt the door behind her. But, perhaps sensing her intention, the man shook his head.

'When we came to see you before, about Steve Felton, we were very polite, and you weren't very polite back, were you? You slammed a door in my face. But we didn't make a fuss. It was the day of his funeral, after all. We were being respectful. This time though it's quid pro quo, isn't it? If you're polite to us, we'll be polite back. But if you slam a door in my face…'

'… then maybe this time we'll slam your face in a door, make it even,' finished his colleague, thoughtfully.

The first man took a step towards the foot of the stairs.

'I don't know anything, and I haven't done anything!' Hattie called down to him, panic rising in her chest. 'You tell Conor, or whoever, that I don't know anything about anything and I don't want to. You told me to back off; well I would, but there's nothing I can back off from. I'm just putting on a show, and I needed a costume designer, and Roxie's a costume designer. That's all…'

Something was wrong. Or if not wrong, exactly, then something was *off*. As she'd spoken, the man had been looking at her with quizzical amusement. *He doesn't know what I'm talking about*, Hattie thought. *Not about Conor, or about backing off.*

But then, when she mentioned Roxie, there was a change. Just a slight shift in his body language, a fractional adjustment of his facial expression.

'Huh,' he grunted thoughtfully. 'Well we'll tell… *Conor*… that you don't know anything about Steve. You're just putting on a show. With… *Roxie*. Thank you for your time. You have a good night, now.'

And with that, he stepped back, and closed the front door.

Hattie was rooted to the spot by terror and confusion for a second, then, snapping to, raced back through the flat towards the living room window. From here she could just catch the sounds of the conversation between the two men below as they walked back to their van.

'… Roxie, then?' said the second man.

'I'll tell you on the way. Tariq'll do his nut,' replied the first.

Then came the sound of van doors opening and closing, an engine starting, and the van driving away.

15

Roxie worked fast. By Friday morning, despite having only started the job on Monday, she already had the first prototype blazer stitched together to show to Larry. Hattie was relieved; with the performance only a week away, now would be a very bad time to discover that Roxie wasn't able to move at the necessary speed. And the necessary speed was fast.

Hattie's pleasure at seeing Roxie appear, in the rehearsal room, with Neil's blazer, was almost enough to offset the uncomfortable reminder of her encounter the night before. She didn't have a clear sense of what had actually happened, but she couldn't help but worry that somehow she'd dropped Roxie in it.

Roxie seemed in good form, however. She had, very sensibly, got the prototype blazer to a good state of completion, so that Larry was given a very clear idea of what the end result would look like and couldn't quibble. And the blazer did look very good. In fact, the only surprising feature was that she'd added a thin pink ribbon to the edge of the lapel.

Larry spotted it at once, and was horrified.

'I didn't say it should have pink! Why did you put pink on it?'

Roxie shrugged. Her phone was buzzing in her bag, and she picked it out distractedly and silenced it.

'I thought it looked nice. I can take it off if you like.'

'Yes, get rid of it. There can't be any pink!'

'Okay, no problem. Apart from that, does it look all right?'

'Well, ah, yes. Get rid of the pink and everything else will be fine.'

'Cool. Leave it with me,' said Roxie, and as she did so her eyes drifted across the room, making passing contact with Hattie's, and Hattie was sure she spotted a tiny ghost of a smile flit across her face.

Roxie double-checked a couple of measurements with the actors, then packed up swiftly to head back to her workshop. Hattie caught up with her as she was leaving.

'What were you hiding, then?' she asked conspiratorially.

'What do you mean?' asked Roxie innocently.

'The ribbon… that was a blue duck, wasn't it?'

It had been Big Steve who first told Hattie the story: a scenic painter, whose job involved painting the big backdrops for productions every season at a prestigious Italian opera house, had realised that no matter how good her work, the set designers always found something to complain about and force her to correct. So she started deliberately introducing a blue duck into her paintings somewhere, small but completely out-of-place-looking. The designers invariably saw it and asked to have it removed, but in doing so satisfied their urge to meddle, meaning that the only correction the painter ever had to do was the relatively easy job of painting out the blue duck, and the rest of her work was allowed to go unchanged.

Roxie smiled. Her phone was buzzing again, but she ignored it.

'The stripes are a bit wider than he asked for, but I can't really fix that without trashing the whole jacket and starting again. I wanted to give him something else to focus on.'

'Clever girl,' said Hattie. 'Listen, I… I wanted to check in with you about… Oh Lord, this is a bit… Sorry, do you want to get that?'

Roxie's phone had briefly stopped buzzing, but then started again.

'All right, gimme a sec,' said Roxie. She turned away, and picked up her phone. Hattie tried not to listen. Well, she tried not to listen too obviously, at least. She heard Roxie mutter, 'Look, it's fine. It's *fine*. D— I'll call you later.'

Then she put the phone down, and turned back to Hattie, her expression unreadable.

'Sorry,' said Hattie, not entirely sure what she was apologising for. 'Er, look, I… do you know someone called Tariq?'

Roxie gave her a long look.

'No,' she said slowly.

'It's just that I know that you know Nancy, and someone I met called Mickey knows her, and he said he had a visit from some people connected to someone called Tariq, and then… well, last night *I* had a visit from some people connected to someone called Tariq, and… I may have accidentally mentioned your name, and one of them seemed to recognise it, and I don't know what any of it means, but they… they didn't seem like nice people,' Hattie finished lamely.

Roxie gave a thoughtful grimace, and then nodded.

'Thanks for letting me know,' she said.

'I… well,' said Hattie, unsure if she'd said enough or indeed if she'd said too much.

'Hattie! I need you!' called out Larry behind her.

'Just a se…' started Hattie, but Roxie was already walking away. Feeling uncomfortable, Hattie turned her attention to Larry.

'I need you to go to the Artspace,' he said. 'There's a bunch of paperwork that needs signing today. Health and safety stuff.'

'I think you'll need to do that,' said Hattie. 'As the producer, you—'

'Congratulations. You're a producer now.'

Hattie frowned. 'The venue's just round the corner. You could come along in the lunch br—'

'No. You do it,' said Larry, and there was a note of something unexpected in his voice. He was being gruff and brusque as ever, but Hattie had learned how to read him better over the past couple of weeks, and she thought she detected what might in fact be a little whine of panic.

So, not wanting to make any more trouble, she acquiesced, and made her way over to the Ashwood Artspace. It looked closed this time – the café that ran semi-independently inside the building's foyer didn't open until later, and the main door was shut – but Larry had assured her that there were people inside. So she rang the discreet doorbell placed to the left of the entrance, and waited.

After a few moments she was rewarded for her patience by the sound of a deadbolt being drawn back, and the door opened to reveal a woman dressed in comfy black clothes with a laptop balanced on her forearm. She had a mass of beautiful red hair, much like Kitty's, but she had at least twenty years on the young actress.

'Can I help?' she said.

'Hullo,' said Hattie. 'I'm Hattie, I'm the stage manager for a show that—'

'I think I met your husband, didn't I? Couple of days ago? Bad neck?'

'That's the one,' Hattie said, smiling.

'Come in, come in,' said the woman. 'I'm Freya. You here for the paperwork?'

They settled down in Freya's office, where a mass of forms awaited them. It was all standard stuff: health and safety disclaimers and waivers. Hattie was the rare sort of person who actually believed in reading this type of thing before signing, so that rather drew out the process, as did Freya's realisation, halfway through, that the documents she'd produced were of the *old* format that they'd replaced with a *new* sort a year ago, as she'd absentmindedly got out the paperwork from the old "to shred" pile, instead of the new "to use" pile.

While Freya assembled the correct documents, Hattie took a look around the office, and her eye was immediately drawn to a collection of several copies of the same book on the shelf behind her. The title of the book was *A History of Theatrical Superstition*, the author one Freya Barnsworthy.

'That you?' Hattie asked, nodding towards the shelf.

'Hmm? Oh, yes, yes that's me. I wrote it a few years ago. By my reckoning since then I've sold enough copies that if I flogged those spares behind you I'd only double my total sales. I'm a huge disappointment to my publisher, but there we are.'

Hattie smiled sympathetically.

'It's pretty good going to have published a book at all, regardless of sales.'

Freya gave her a condescending look.

'That just the sort of thing someone who's never written a book would say.'

Then she waved her hand.

'Oh I know, I know, I'd just hoped it would be a platform to other things. I thought it was my ticket out of this place, for one thing. But never mind, I'm leaving soon anyway.'

'Really?'

'Well, it's the revamp, isn't it?'

'I hadn't heard about a revamp.'

'Oh yes. They've secured a big dollop of funding, and they want to start producing their own work. So they're splitting up my role – which is mostly just paperwork – into an artistic director and a venue manager, who's basically a glorified caretaker. And I mean obviously I applied for the AD role, but they gave it to… well, it doesn't matter. Some man.'

Freya pulled a face, then continued. 'They offered me the venue manager position, but it's basically just the worst parts of my current role, plus a bunch of technical stuff that's no fun at all. No offence.'

'I'm not technical myself,' said Hattie. 'I'm just a stage manager.'

'Well that's more or less the same… Either way, time for a change. I'm out of here. Just got to get through a showcase night for local dance schools, a couple of lower-tier touring comedians, and of course whatever on earth your lot is putting on. Something about a school, is it?'

'That's right,' said Hattie, surprised at Freya's apparent lack of knowledge about or interest in Larry's show. 'New writing, a first-time playwright—'

'Vanity project, eh? I've never met him in person, he just paid to hire the venue for a night, did everything by email, didn't even come to inspect it beforehand. Let me guess: written by, produced by, directed by and starring a middle-aged career-changer who's halfway through a mid-life crisis?'

'Well he's not starring in it,' said Hattie uncomfortably. It was true that Freya was otherwise entirely on the money, but this wasn't the right way to talk about shows in one's own theatre. It wasn't professional, not in Hattie's book. Perhaps Freya's unconcealed disdain was because she was leaving soon and allowed herself to let her standards slip.

'It's an interesting piece,' Hattie said, trying not to sound too defensive. 'It's looking at the relationships—'

'Oh don't tell me, he made me promise to watch the performance. Wouldn't even send me the script beforehand, said he doesn't want to "spoil the surprise" for me. Mind you, looking at the ticket sales it might just be me in an empty auditorium. I'm hoping he's a better playwright than he is a publicist. All right, here we are. I need you to read *these* ones, and sign *these* ones.'

Hattie swiftly became absorbed in this second round of paperwork, and was secretly grateful for an excuse to avoid further chit-chat. Freya was a little bit abrasive, and Hattie found herself uncomfortable in her presence.

When the last document was signed and counter-signed, Hattie took her leave and, armed with a little packet of papers for Larry's records, headed back to the rehearsal room. They'd finished lunch early, and were looking at the final scene. Larry was berating Neil for putting the emphasis on the wrong syllable in the word 'controversy'.

'You lot spend all your time watching Netflix and swooning over American influencers. The British pronunciation is contr—
– they for me? Put them in my briefcase – it's controversy, right? You'll be a laughing stock if you get that wrong.'

Hattie, whose raised hands holding the paperwork from Freya had prompted the remark about the briefcase, did as she was told, and retreated to the back of the room where Larry left his things. She opened up the briefcase… and abruptly closed it with a barely stifled gasp.

'Larry,' she said.

'Hold on, Hattie. I don't care how they say it on the news, I—'

'Larry!' Hattie barked again.

'What? I… oh. Ah.'

Larry looked over at Hattie and she immediately knew that he had realised what she had seen. His face flushed red.

'Can I talk to you for a second? Straight away?'

Hattie led Larry to the far corner of the room, where a door led to the toilets. She hovered in the doorway, so that she could have a private conversation with Larry while still keeping her eyes on the briefcase.

'Larry, why is there a handgun in your briefcase?' she muttered urgently.

'Ah. Well. It's only… it's not real. It's a prop.'

'A prop.'

'Yes.'

'Why? There's no prop gun in the script.'

'No. But I thought it might work. In the final scene. Ah. As a metaphor.'

'A metaphor.'

'Ah. Yes.'

Hattie frowned. Larry had never before mentioned anything about a gun, and every other prop in the play was a piece of classroom paraphernalia. The sudden introduction of a metaphorical gun was surprising to say the least.

'And when you say it's just a prop, what do you mean?'

'I mean it's a prop. It doesn't actually fire.'

'Now I want to be very clear on this Larry: can that gun fire anything at all? A blank, a pellet, that sort of thing?'

'Well…'

'Because if there is any sort of firing mechanism then we are going to have a problem. There are very strict rules about—'

'No, it can't fire. It's a model. It's a harmless model. Do you think I'm an idiot?' Larry's face darkened. 'The only idiot here is you if you think I'd have brought a dangerous weapon into a rehearsal room. Where would I even have got it from? Use your head, Hattie, this isn't America. You're as bad as this lot not knowing how to pronounce words the English way. Honestly, I don't know why I waste my time with you all.'

Larry was, as he so often did, covering embarrassment with aggression, and Hattie found that she wasn't entirely reassured.

'All right, Larry,' she said. 'I'm sure you can understand that that was a very unpleasant surprise, so forgive me if I'm a bit rattled. If you want to use a prop gun—'

'No, forget about it. If you're going to overreact like that, I can't imagine what the cast will do. We won't use it. Forget you saw it. I'll take it away tonight and you won't see it again. Now, can I get on? I have a play to rehearse, you know.'

Hattie hesitated, then nodded. 'Righto.'

They got back to rehearsing. Hattie felt shaken, and Larry obviously was too. He was grouchier and more critical of the actors than usual, and he kept shooting resentful glances over at Hattie. Hattie couldn't make head nor tail of it. Try as she might, she couldn't believe that the point of that gun was to be a prop for the play. Especially given how quickly Larry had abandoned the idea. So why did he have a gun in his briefcase? And was it really, definitely, actually not real?

The day wound to a close, and by five o'clock they were more or less where they needed to be, which was having rehearsed more or less everything. The following week was the run-up to the performance, which meant they would no longer be able to spend much time on the nitty-gritty of individual scenes, needing instead to focus on the flow of the show as a whole, and the practicalities of how to move from one scene to the next. With the continuing exception of Miles's monologues, they had spent the previous fortnight doing enough nitty-grittying that it seemed to Hattie they were in a good place. Larry evidently thought so too, because while he wasn't exactly outwardly happy, he at least wasn't haranguing the actors about not working hard enough as they put their scripts away and packed up their belongings for the weekend. That was an improvement on the previous day.

The wine bar owner arrived and made his usual fuss about getting everyone out and the room reset so that he could open up for business at six. Hattie made her usual polite noises, and stayed behind after everyone else to make sure that the chair positioning was inch-perfect. She noted that Kitty engineered it so that she happened to be ready to leave just at the same time as Miles was, and the two of them walked out together. The last glimpse of them Hattie caught was of Kitty laughing and flicking her gorgeous hair in response to something Miles had said. It all seemed very ill-advised, but once they were out of the rehearsal room they were beyond Hattie's jurisdiction.

Once the room was as it needed to be, Hattie packed up her things and was the last one out of the door. She had a little bit of work to do over the next couple of days, but nothing too strenuous, and she was looking forward with some intensity to the prospect of a quiet weekend.

But as she made her way to the bus stop, she found herself prickling with unease. Something was amiss. Had she forgotten something in the rehearsal room? She stopped, patted her pockets, checked her handbag and holdall. No, everything was where it should be. Had she seen something out of the corner of her eye? She couldn't think what, but it wouldn't be the first time that her subconscious had warned her about something without giving any additional information. She looked round, but nothing seemed off: the street was fairly quiet, a car and a couple of buses pootling down the road and a few pedestrians skittering about, none of them appearing out of place. It was getting dusky, though, and there were several patches of darkness she couldn't see into.

Her bus stop was just up ahead, and deserted. Still feeling out of sorts, she walked up to it, and was just about step under the shelter to lean up against one of the little not-quite-a-seat rests when she heard a noise close behind her. Looking round, she had just a moment to realise that someone was walking up fast behind her before the man in question had caught up to her, pulled her round to face him with a rough hand on her shoulder, and pushed something into her hands. But the push was more a shove, and Hattie found herself toppling backwards over her weak ankle, a cry of dismay escaping her lips, and then landing awkwardly on the ground, twisting her knee as she tried to protect her bad hip, and the cry of dismay morphed into a yelp of pain.

It took her a second to get her bearings, discombobulated by her hurt leg and her sudden shift from standing to sprawled on the ground. When she had her wits about her enough to look round, the man was gone. It had all been so sudden she could hardly believe it had really happened, and she immediately started mistrusting her memories. Had she seen a man? Yes. Yes, she had. His features were obscured by a hoodie, sunglasses and a disposable face mask, so she had no idea what he looked like. He had been tall, and heavily built… or was he? Was that just her mind remembering how easily he had shoved her to the ground and trying to fill in some blanks?

A bus pulled up beside her, and the doors opened.

'You all right?' called out the driver.

'I was knocked over,' said Hattie distractedly.

She gingerly started to pick herself up. Seeing her struggling, a passenger on the bus, a woman in her twenties, hopped off and helped her.

'Thanks, love. I don't know what happened. A man just came up behind me and knocked me over. Then he just walked off.'

'Are you hurt? Do we need to call you an ambulance?'

'No, I'm all right,' Hattie replied, suddenly feeling flustered. *She's treating me like a frail little old lady. I suppose I look like one.*

'This bus going to Lewisham station?' she asked, to cover her embarrassment.

The woman nodded, and offered Hattie an arm to help her get on.

'Thank you. I don't need—'

'Is that yours?'

The woman was gesturing towards something on the ground. Looking where she was pointing, Hattie saw that it was an envelope. She stooped to pick it up, but halfway down her knee started to wobble and she let out an involuntary gasp. The woman picked it up for her and handed it to her. Hattie took it, but ignored it until she had got herself onto the bus and into a seat. She was very aware that every other passenger was looking at her, and her face was flushed, not just from the exertion of the last few minutes.

The bus moved off, and the other riders went back to their phones, and Hattie got her breath back and turned her attention to the envelope. It was unlike either of the other envelopes that had come her way recently. This was smaller, and brown. It wasn't sealed, and it wasn't empty. It certainly wasn't Hattie's. It must have been the thing her anonymous assailant had shoved at her. With a glance around her, Hattie opened it. Inside it contained a single piece of paper, on which was scrawled:

STAY AWAY FROM ROXIE. DON'T CALL HER. DON'T VISIT HER. FINAL WARNING.

The handwriting was the same as the note she had received the previous weekend.

'How am I supposed to stay away from her?' she said, and only belatedly realised she had done so out loud. She could feel the eyes of the man opposite flick across to her, but she was now too distressed by the note to be embarrassed. It didn't make any sense. She couldn't avoid Roxie, they were doing a show together. This was the problem with corresponding via threatening anonymous notes delivered in passing by threatening anonymous thugs: it was only possible for information to flow in one direction. There was no easy way to request clarifications.

To say nothing of the fact that the *first* note had said nothing about Roxie at all, and if she was the thing that Hattie was supposed to have backed off from then it would have saved everyone a lot of time and stress (and now a very sore knee) if that had been made clear in the first place.

Hattie found herself looking around irritably to see if by any chance she could spot her masked assailant out of the bus window. She wanted to give him a piece of her mind about some very questionable communication choices. Then she realised how silly she was being, and sighed. It was all the after-effects of sudden spike of shock and fear and pain. Big emotions surging round her body, with nowhere to put them. She needed to start thinking rationally. She was in a dangerous situation, with dangerous people, and if she wanted to stay out of trouble she needed to make sure she didn't cross them. But to avoid crossing them, she needed to know what it was they wanted, and so far she was being thwarted in that by the fact that she had no idea who these people actually *were*.

Steve had told her to worry about Conor's men, and when two men had come to see her, she had thought that was who they were. But the last time she had seen them, they hadn't reacted to the name of Conor, but instead had said something about Tariq. Tariq, who had apparently sent his boys round to see Mickey as well. They had said they wanted to talk to her about Steve, but as soon as she mentioned Roxie they changed their minds. Meanwhile, Conor hadn't seemed to have a clue who Hattie was when she confronted him.

Then on top of that, someone (else?) had started sending her notes as soon as she made contact with Roxie, and was trying to get Hattie to stay away from her. Whether this someone had anything to do with Tariq, or Conor, or Steve, was unclear. And Roxie's connection to Conor was equally unclear, and evidenced only by a scrap of paper in an envelope of things that were apparently related to Conor's business dealings, but mostly just looked like sketches. And Roxie had a *very* indirect connection to Steve, in that Steve's uncle Mickey said that a woman called Nancy knew about Steve's past, and Nancy may or may not be Roxie's mother.

All of which meant… nothing. Hattie was completely stumped. She was caught in the middle of a lot of people whose motives were obscure, and she had no idea how to extricate herself.

All in all, it was high time for a spliff.

16

The weekend did very little to bring Hattie relief, illicit Friday night self-medication excepted. She wasn't sure how to leave Roxie alone, and all of her thoughts around how to negotiate a way of leaving Roxie alone involved speaking to her, which meant, in the short term at least, *not* leaving Roxie alone. She knew that her best option was to do nothing, but the idea of doing nothing while in an already unsatisfactory situation held scant appeal.

And speaking of unsatisfactory situations, Hattie was uncomfortably aware that after *What You Deserve*'s one and only performance the coming Thursday night, she would be out of paid employment, and Nick's neck, while no longer causing him the constant agony it had inflicted on him when he first hurt it, was still a long way from where it needed to be for him to go back to work. Over her morning coffee on the Saturday, her mind still oozing back into shape after the night before, Hattie allowed herself finally to think the discomfiting thought she had been attempting to ignore for the past week: it might be time to consider trying for a non-theatre job.

There was no shame in it. Of course. Everyone always said so whenever a colleague fell on hard times and ended up doing temp work, or shop work, or hospitality work. The industry was small and there wasn't always room for everyone, and an honest day's work was an honest day's work no matter what the work was. And so on.

But deep down, Hattie knew that taking a job that wasn't a theatre job would feel like an enormous failure, and she could imagine turning up to work in a café or a shop with no more pleasure than she could imagine crawling over broken glass. She was a theatre person, and had been all her life, and, in a role that is always about being the scapegoat, bearing the brunt of other people's big feelings, the only validation that she was any good at it was that she had, for forty years, managed to keep getting work. If she stopped being Hattie-the-stage-manager, she would just be Hattie. And she wasn't sure, if you took away the stage manager bit, that very much would be left behind.

She couldn't accept that it was time to give up. Not quite yet. So she spent a few more hours trawling the same job websites, looking at the same listings, and even having a go at applying for some of the jobs she'd previously written off, just in case the blacklists weren't as total as she feared.

Nick, trying to be helpful, offered to scour the print edition of *The Stage* for her, but, being Nick, he kept getting distracted by the articles.

'Hey, there's a piece about the Ashwood in here.'

'Oh yeah?'

'Well, a paragraph. They've announced their new, and first ever, artistic director.'

'Oh yes, Freya told me about that. She's gutted that she didn't get it.'

'Did she tell you who did?'

'She just said it was "some man".'

'Well, that might be true, but it's a man you know, you know. At least, I think so. Hashi Hassan?'

'Small world.'

Hashi was a director Hattie had worked for a couple of years earlier, coincidentally on the last show that she had worked with Big Steve on. It had been a chaotic and scandal-hit production, made more difficult at every turn by Hashi's diva-esque traits and frequent temper tantrums. Admittedly, over the course of the show Hattie had developed a certain fondness for the man: behind the bluster, he really did try to do a good job, and against the odds he had rather made a success of the show. But his career was continually thwarted by his knack for falling out with people, and Hattie knew that artistic director of a backwater Lewisham theatre was a far cry from the sort of positions he had been aspiring towards when she knew him. Still, he had secured a job, which was more than she could say for herself.

'Good on him,' said Hattie. 'I think he'll do good work there. Don't suppose they've announced a season of shows there yet? With vacancies for a stage manager?'

'Afraid not. Would he hire you?'

'I don't know. I don't think by the end he disliked me any more than he seemed to dislike *everyone*.'

'One to keep tabs on, then.'

The focus on new jobs and her worries about Roxie didn't mean that Hattie's responsibilities around her current job could take a back seat. The following week was performance week, with the show happening on the Thursday night, a dress rehearsal on Thursday in the daytime, and all the necessary technical preparations by Hattie and Nick at the venue having to be squeezed in on Wednesday. Of these preparations, the one looming largest over Hattie's consciousness was the lighting. She had told Nick to handle it, and he had said that he would handle it, and therefore it wasn't Hattie's problem so she ought to be able to forget about it.

But.

Since that conversation with Nick she had seen no evidence that he *was* handling it, and he'd certainly declined to give her any indication of *how* he was planning to handle it, and she couldn't help but worry that, despite his assurances to the contrary, he *wasn't* actually handling it.

Every time she raised the subject, he simply told her he had it under control and offered no further information. When she pressed him, he reminded her that she had given him clear, verging on strict, instructions not to burden her with the details of the lighting, and forcefully changed the subject, leaving Hattie to stew in her own worried juice. It wasn't that she didn't trust Nick. It was just that occasionally his response to a difficult situation was to wish for a positive outcome and leave it at that. Which did work for him surprisingly frequently, but which didn't jibe well with Hattie's pragmatic, pessimistic stage managerial sensibilities.

Eventually she could bear it no longer, and over their Saturday night curry she confronted him.

'I was wrong. I want to know what's going on with the lighting. If you've found someone to handle it, that's fine, and if you haven't found someone yet that's also fine, but not knowing what's going on is making me worry more than knowing would.'

'Well, at least you have the self-awareness to spot it, I suppose,' replied Nick. 'All right. I needed to rope you in at some point to help me anyway, it might as well be now. I'm going to indulge in the time-honoured practice of delegation. I shall be on the floor, and some of your actors, who I'm assuming you can spare on Wednesday, will be running up ladders for me. My superior intellect, combined with their superior physiques, will result in great success all round. So I just need you to send two or three of your finest actors my way. Does that put your mind at ease?'

'Not entirely, my love. Assuming I've got a bunch of actors free on Wednesday is… a pretty big assumption.'

'Oh. Are there any free then?'

'I'll have to check with Larry. I told him I'd be in the theatre all day, so he'll be doing run-throughs and so on without me.'

'Well, I'm sure just a couple of actors won't be missed. He's got hundreds of them, hasn't he?'

Hattie shook her head in frustration. Nick could be annoyingly blasé, and the worst part was that he was probably right. Larry *did* have hundreds of actors, and he probably *could* spare several of them. It was just that if this was what Nick was dependent on, he really should have been checking this stuff a week ago. Whereas now it was on her to make a last-minute request to Larry, that would make him grumpy and her look unprofessional.

But it was better to know than not to know, she supposed. She fired off a quick email to Larry outlining the situation. He replied an hour later, grumpy as expected, but acquiescing, also as expected. The only unusual thing was that for some reason the email didn't come from Larry's normal email address, but rather one under the name of George Grose. It was the full name of the main character in the play, and Hattie idly wondered whether Larry had set up a new address as some sort of marketing ploy. Freya had said that ticket sales had been poor so far, so maybe he was preparing some sort of publicity campaign. Hattie in general took a very dim view of theatrical marketing. The correct reasons to go see a play, in her opinion, were either that you knew someone involved, or you'd seen a positive review, or that the company had a good reputation. Everything else was just advertising, and advertising, in Hattie's mind, was pretty close to being synonymous with 'lying'.

She spent the weekend ticking off tasks on her show to-do list, and by the end of it felt that she was on top of everything she could be on top of, which unfortunately allowed her mind to return to the list of things she was *not* on top of, and the name at the top of that list was Roxie. Why was she supposed to stay away from her, what would constitute a breach of that, and how would that affect the show? She really wanted to call Roxie to try to work through the last and possibly the first of those questions, but she had a pretty strong notion that the answer to the middle one forbade it.

Who else could she call? There was one other person who might be able to offer at least some insight. Hattie hadn't managed to get through before, but there was no harm in trying one last time, was there?

She rang the number, and was gratified to have her call answered on the third ring.

'Hello?' said a suspicious voice.

'Hello, is that Nancy Duff?'

'Speaking.'

'Hello. My name's Hattie Cocker. I wonder if you can help me. Er…' Hattie dithered, unsure where to begin. 'A man called Mickey told me to look you up. He says you used to know Steve Felton. Is that so?'

'Yes.'

Nancy sounded suspicious, and Hattie could understand why. Her own experiences of strangers accosting her and asking to talk to her about Big Steve had not been entirely positive ones.

'I'm so sorry to intrude, but I've got into a bit of a tangle regarding Steve. Since he died. I was a friend of his. We worked together. Only somehow I seem to have got involved with… another part of his life. And I don't quite know what's going on. I met Mickey at the funeral, and he said you might know a bit more about… it…'

'I see,' said Nancy. 'I should have come to the funeral, I suppose. But Roxie told me to stay away.'

'I'm working with Roxie at the moment, as it happens. She's… your daughter?' hazarded Hattie.

'That's right,' confirmed Nancy, and Hattie nodded to herself, tucking that away. She would need to come back to that later.

'I suppose she had her reasons,' continued Nancy. 'I doubt I'd have been welcome among his family.'

'There weren't many family members there, beside Mickey,' said Hattie, grateful to have broached a topic that elicited more than single-word responses from Nancy. 'It was mostly his friends. Well, friends from the industry. I don't know that he had many friends outside the industry. Apart from someone called Ivan. But he wasn't there.'

Hattie realised she was babbling, so she stopped.

'I remember Ivan. I'd have thought he'd have turned up out of, I dunno, professional interest or something. Anyway, what is it you want to know about? It must be ancient history if you're coming to me for it.'

'It's about some people Steve used to work for. When he was a young man. A… well, it sounds like they weren't an entirely legal operation, but it was back when Steve was young and maybe didn't know any better.'

On the other end of the line Nancy took a deep breath.

'Ancient history,' she repeated. 'You're best off not dragging any of that stuff up.'

'I didn't exactly intend to. But I think Steve did some dragging of his own not so long ago, and somehow I've managed to get involved.'

'Then you want to be careful. They were dangerous people, and some of them still are.'

'You're not the first to tell me that. But I don't really know who or what they were. I know they were involved with transporting something from the coast to London, and I know there was someone called Conor involved, but—'

'Conor? You really are in a tangle,' Nancy snorted. 'Conor's a jumped-up Paddy thief who learned how to run his racket from *Oliver Twist*. His lot never got much beyond stealing cars in London and smuggling them out of the country to sell on in Poland. Steve helped them out for a couple of months while he was trying to work out how to go straight. Last I heard they'd given up on cars, they just snatch phones instead. Conor's a nobody.'

'Oh,' said Hattie, confused. 'I thought—'

'No, Steve didn't have much business with Conor. If you're talking about the people he got his start with, you're talking about Tariq.'

'Tariq?'

'That's right. Steve started working for Tariq as a teenager, stayed with him for years, running his vans up from Portsmouth to London, handling distribution from there.'

'Okay,' said Hattie, trying to get her bearings. 'And this was drugs, was it?'

'At first. If only it stayed that way,' Nancy replied. 'Look, you got a car?'

'Yes…'

'Well, do you ever take your car to a car wash? One of those hand wash outfits that sets up in a clapped-out former petrol station forecourt? And the people who wash your car never smile, and they don't speak much English, and they work furiously hard like their life depends on it? And it's always a group of skinny men, isn't it? And there's always one guy, better fed, who never does any work, just sits there watching the others. Get my drift?'

'Not really, I'm afraid.'

'Well to spell it out… Hang on, you're not police, are you? Because this is just hearsay, right? And I'm not part of any dealings of material convenience, or whatever you call it, so you can't—'

'I'm not the police,' said Hattie. 'I'm just a stage manager.'

'A what? Oh, that's a theatre thing, isn't it? Look, why are you asking about this stuff anyway?'

Hattie didn't really have a good answer. She didn't know enough about Nancy to trust her with the whole sorry story. So she decided to fudge a partial truth.

'I had a visit from some people after Steve died. I thought

they were connected to Conor, but now it sounds like they were connected to Tariq. They scared the wits out of me, if I'm honest.'

'They'll do that, Tariq's boys.'

There was a pause. Hattie decided to just come right out with it.

'Is there any connection between Tariq and Roxie?'

'Why?' asked Nancy, sharply.

'It's just something one of them said.'

'Bloody hell, you're raking up all sorts now. Yes, Tariq knew Roxie. When she was a baby. I've got photos of her sitting on his knee. But me and her were out of there before she was out of nappies. To my knowledge they've never come across one another since. I can't see how they would. But then again she never tells me anything about her life, so what do I know? You know Roxie. Just like her father, isn't she?'

'I, well… sorry, I don't actually know. If it's not too personal a question, who is Roxie's father?'

'What's that supposed to mean?' said Nancy, her tone surprised and a little hurt.

Hattie felt her grip on the conversation failing entirely.

'I'm sorry, I didn't mean to cause offence. I genuinely don't know.'

'Oh for God's… You really are lost, aren't you? Steve. Steve was Roxie's father.'

Act Five

A good actor gives their all to every performance, and takes the job of enthralling and delighting the audience just as seriously whether that audience is two pensioners at a Wednesday matinee or a full house on Christmas Eve. To that extent, all performances matter equally. But it is nevertheless inevitably the case that the first performance matters ever so slightly more. Everyone wants a good show on opening night, to provide a boost to morale that will carry them through the rest of the run.

In the run-up to opening the stakes are high, and everyone is jittery, and the whole company desperately wants reassurance that things will go well. Conversely, the start of a run of performances is when things are in practical terms most likely to go badly, as the actors haven't yet had a chance to get fully into the flow of performances.

Therefore it's perhaps unsurprising that, as a salve to the worried minds of actors everywhere, a superstition has arisen that a bad dress rehearsal portends a good first performance. Whenever there's a car-crash dress, you'll hear actors insisting on the truth of this, and deriving great comfort from it.

Curiously, though, whenever a show has a notably good dress rehearsal, the implicit converse of the bad dress/

good first night superstition is conveniently forgotten, and never mentioned...

– from *A History of Theatrical Superstition*
by Freya Barnsworthy

<h1 style="text-align:center">17</h1>

The atmosphere in the rehearsal room on Monday was strained. Larry looked like he hadn't slept all weekend. He was scowling and terse, verging on monosyllabic, and the cast quickly picked up on his unease. Actors always feel insecure in the run-up to a show opening, and the director acting like something terrible was happening quickly convinced some of them that something terrible actually was happening, and that the terrible thing was, in fact, *the show*. Perhaps it wasn't a conscious thought process, but Hattie noted a sudden rise in suggestions coming from the performers about how they could do things differently, and proposals for line tweaks and changes in delivery. Larry, to no surprise of Hattie's, responded very badly to these pitches. He didn't like the implication that anything about his show needed fixing, and he snarled dismissals of every idea that was put to him. Unfortunately, his rejections, not being accompanied by any reassurances that the show was in a good state, only served to agitate the actors more, causing some of them evidently to arrive at the belief that their proposed fixes were only failures in that they weren't radical enough. More fundamental alterations were consequently raised, which only served to antagonise Larry further, eliciting more stinging rebuffs, and the cycle continued.

Hattie was slower in interceding than she should have been. She had slept badly, and all of her pains and sprains seemed to be flaring up simultaneously. She was also continually distracting herself with thoughts of Steve and Roxie, his daughter. His daughter who had refused to come to her father's funeral and even denied knowing him when Hattie first met her.

When Hattie thought about it, it was *obvious* that Roxie was his daughter. She had her father's reserved confidence, and was reassuringly capable, just like her old man. And the physical resemblance was… well, it wasn't pronounced. Steve had a face like a bag of walnuts, after all, and it would be a very unfortunate woman who bore a close facial similarity there. But there was *something* similar about them.

And yet Steve had never mentioned a daughter. He was a private person, and it sounded from what Nancy had said as though he had her very young, and Nancy and he had gone their separate ways when Roxie was just a baby, so it would make sense that he wasn't at all close to her… but if so, why was a piece of paper with her company name and phone number on it in the envelope of evidence he put together on Conor's lot?

And that was the other thing, wasn't it? She had believed, from the night of his death, that Steve had been killed by Conor, or by people who worked for him. But at every step that belief had been challenged, as Conor didn't seem to know who she was, as the men who came to visit her following Steve's death didn't seem to know who Conor was, and now, as the final nail in the coffin, Nancy told her that Steve had barely worked for Conor at all. It now sounded as though Tariq was the man who had had Steve killed. So why had Steve kept mentioning the name Conor? Had he just been confused?

By now Larry was in an outright shouting match with Kai and Moritz, and Hattie knew she needed to get out of her head and sort things out.

'Can I make a suggestion?' she called out, politely but loudly enough to secure the attention of the others. 'Would it be a good idea to have a quick tea break and then try a full run-through so we can see where we stand? It seems like there are some concerns about what various scenes *might* be like, but if we run it we'll be able to see what they're *actually* like, and that might make for a more productive starting point for some of these discussions.'

The suggestion was grudgingly approved. It helped that a full run-through was part of the plan for the day's rehearsal anyway. So Hattie set up the room as it needed to be for the top of the show, and after a brief break they got down to it.

It wasn't a hugely encouraging exercise. That is to say, while the run-through was a car crash from a practical perspective, that was only to be expected, and Hattie knew far better than to judge a pudding before it had finished baking. But, looking past all the things that weren't working simply because they weren't working *yet*, there was no getting away from the fact that the piece didn't really hang together as a play. There was no *development*. Child George was picked on at school; adult George felt that these childhood experiences predisposed his adult self towards failure. But there was no progression, no conclusion. The play didn't really have an ending, it just stopped at a certain point.

This didn't impact Hattie from a professional perspective: her job was the same whether the play was good or bad. But as someone who cared about theatre, it saddened her that they hadn't found a good show here. And as someone who, despite herself, had grown rather fond of Larry, she was sad that his show, which he so obviously cared so deeply about, was not likely to be the success he wanted it to be.

Such concerns had to give way to more practical considerations, though, when Larry said, at the end of the run-through, 'It's not very believable, is it? None of you look like schoolchildren. We really ought to be doing this in costumes. Hattie, ring Roxie and find out when she's going to have those jackets done. She said she'd have them over to us this morning.'

'Oh. Er… Okay,' said Hattie.

Larry looked at her expectantly.

'Now, please.'

'Right,' said Hattie. She picked up her phone and walked out of the room, to get away from his inquisitive eyes. Once outside she looked at her phone uneasily. She wasn't supposed to contact Roxie. Would doing so really incur the wrath of the bus stop shover? And if so, what might he do about it? Would his next move be more than just a shove?

She wanted to be brave and determined, but she had done a lot of being brave recently and it had cost her more than she cared to admit. So she found herself dawdling on the street for a minute, before putting her phone back into her pocket and stepping back inside, telling Larry that she couldn't get hold of Roxie. In one very specific sense of the word "couldn't" that was technically true.

'Oh. Did you leave her a message at least?'

'Er… yes.'

(There were no senses of the word "yes" that made that one anything but a bare-faced lie.)

The matter of the costumes remained unresolved for the rest of the day, and the day after as well. Over the course of Tuesday's rehearsal Larry became increasingly agitated as Hattie kept reporting back that Roxie 'wasn't picking up'. Sensing a possible loophole in her injunction, Hattie tried suggesting to Larry that *he* might try contacting Roxie, but he insisted that he was far too busy.

'You found her; you manage her,' he retorted, and Hattie nodded uneasily, wondering how on earth she was going to get around this one.

'He's not paid her yet, has he?' asked Nick that evening.

'He's given her the money for materials, but I don't think he's paid her fee yet. He certainly hasn't paid mine.'

'And she'd promised she'd have the costumes done yesterday, right? And then went radio silent.'

'Well, she didn't promise, but yes, she'd said she'd have them done, and she hasn't got in touch to explain the delay.'

'So tell him she's upped and fled, and get him to use the money he would have paid her to buy some supermarket school blazers.'

'But they won't have stripes.'

'Better not to have stripes than not to have jackets at all.'

'True… but what if she *is* working on the jackets? What if she's going to drop them off tomorrow? I can't diddle her out of her fee.'

'Well if you can't get hold of her—'

'I *can* get hold of her! Well, maybe I could. I don't know, I haven't tried because finding out is the very thing I'm supposed not to try to do.'

'Oh yeah,' sniffed Nick. 'Sorry. Would they *really* know though?'

'I've no idea. Maybe they're monitoring her phone. Maybe they're monitoring mine.'

'Is that a thing that people can really do?'

'I don't know.'

Nick scratched his nose.

'Hold on,' he said. 'You said the lady at the reception of the warehouse she works in knew her, right?'

'Yes.'

'Well then, give me her number then. I hope they're open late.'

Nick pulled out his phone and Hattie, a little hesitant, read out the number, which he dialled.

'Oh hello, excuse me,' he said, when his call was answered. 'I'm just trying to get hold of…'

'Roxie Duff,' mouthed Hattie.

'Yes, Roxie Duff. Do you happen to know if she's in at the moment? Oh really, not at all? Well, not to worry… Certainly, tell her a Mr Min-Su was trying to contact her about her home insurance renewal. All right thank you, goodbye.'

He put his phone down.

'She hasn't been into the workshop at all this week, apparently. Was last seen over the weekend collecting some bits. I think it's safe to say your costume maker has made a break for it.'

'Oh,' said Hattie, not knowing whether to be relieved or disappointed. 'Do you think she's all right?'

'My love, I have no idea.'

'No, fair enough. Me neither. I suppose that's it then. I'll have to tell Larry that she's flaked out, and get him to let me buy some cheap blazers as a fallback. Oh he won't like that. I might need a cup of tea before I make this call.'

'Good idea. And?'

'And what?'

'And thank you Nick for using your quick thinking and initiative to get me out of a tricky situation?' he suggested with an expectant shrug.

Hattie smiled, leaned over and planted a kiss on his cheek.

'You're a better husband than I give you credit for, my love. Thank you.'

Hattie didn't end up calling Larry, however, because almost as soon as she got up to put the kettle on the doorbell rang. She grimaced, cursing her luck. A quick look out of the window revealed that there was no van on the street, but she couldn't see who was standing on the pavement thanks to the angle of the porch awning. That was reassuring, in that two big burly men wouldn't have been able to both fit in the little blind spot. But it did mean this warranted further investigation. And since she was actually on her feet, and she'd just acknowledged a favour from Nick, there really was no way she could get out of answering the door herself. For the millionth time she thought about how nice it would be if the landlord could be persuaded to install a proper buzzer system with a video camera. Then she grudgingly made her way down the communal stairs, taking each step one by one as she tried to shield herself from twinges in various parts of her legs.

By the time she made it to the front door, whoever had rung the bell had long since left. There were no pedestrians on the street. Several large, heavy-duty carrier bags had been deposited on her doorstep, but Hattie didn't at first pay them much heed because her attention was caught by a car that was driving away, nearing the junction at the end of the road. It was quite an eye-catching car, a little three-door runaround, bright pink in colour. But more than that, it struck Hattie as familiar. She had seen that car before, or at least one very like it. She didn't immediately remember where. It was only as it turned the corner and disappeared that the brief glimpse of it from the side jogged her memory: there had been a little pink runaround parked outside Desi's yard the night Steve died. It was an unusual enough car that it couldn't be a coincidence that it happened to just be passing the flat soon after someone else rang the doorbell.

The thought that someone who had been present at Steve's death might have just knocked on her door brought her attention back sharply to the bags they had left behind. She already had her suspicions; a quick poke around in the nearest bag confirmed them.

'Nick!' she called back up the stairs.

'What?'

'Will your neck let you do a bit of carrying?'

'Depends how heavy. What needs carrying?'

'Funny thing, that. It's a couple of dozen school jackets.'

*

While the circumstances surrounding their arrival was somewhat alarming to Hattie, the jackets' presence itself was a source of comfort. The next day she had Nick drive her and the bags over to the rehearsal room, so that the cast could try them on. It did occur to her that if any of them were seriously ill-fitting there was very little she could do about it, but thankfully Roxie had done a very professional job (Hattie couldn't help but marvel at how quickly she'd managed to pull it all together), and nearly everyone fitted into their allotted blazer. Larry was delighted.

'Finally, you're starting to look the part! Maybe the play will start to make sense. Right, let's do another run-through, and I hope this one works better than Monday morning's.'

'I do need to borrow a couple of your actors to do the get-in at the venue,' Hattie reminded him.

'Oh right. Take Moritz, and Darren, and Miles.'

'Won't you need Miles for the run?'

'It's fine. Ah. I'll read in his lines.'

'If you're sure…'

Moritz and Darren had the fewest lines of anyone, so they were obviously expendable. (And Moritz was possibly being punished for his increasingly tendency to argue back and criticise Larry's direction.) However, it didn't make any sense to Hattie that Miles, the narrator, who had more lines than anyone else, should be absent from the run-through. And certainly Miles looked crestfallen to hear it. But it was what Larry wanted, so it was what would happen. Hattie supposed that Miles's scenes happened in isolation, so in one sense it was less disruptive to remove him than some of the 'schoolchildren'.

The three actors piled into the back of Nick's car, and together they all drove to Artspace, where Freya was waiting to let them in.

'Right, you lot, you're with me,' said Nick, walking through to the auditorium with a large A2-size lighting plan rolled up under one arm and the old yoga mat Hattie's physio had made her buy when she first hurt her hip rolled up under the other. He marched to the front of the stage, unrolled the mat, and lay down flat on his back on top of it, unrolling the plan and spreading it across his chest. Substitute the mat for a towel, and the plan for a broadsheet and he'd have looked ready for a day on Margate Main Sands.

'Gentlemen, today is a good day, for today you graduate from lowly actors to lofty techies,' he called out, as his new assistants hovered uncertainly behind him. 'It will start off bewildering, but it'll quickly get easier because I'm going to spoon-feed you instructions. Then it'll get harder as I start asking you to use your initiative. Then it'll get easier again when you begin to understand how everything works. Then harder again, because once I'm done with you, you'll need to go back to acting and you'll discover that the place in your brains where you normally remember things like what your lines are has been replaced by a bunch of much more practical information about stage electronics and the Stanley McCandless method of lighting design. But that's a problem for your future selves, and I'm sure they're smart enough to figure it out.

'Now, first things first; Moritz, I want you to head to the lantern store behind the lighting booth over there, and start bringing out everything that looks like a light and lining them all up at the back of the stage,' he continued. 'Miles, there should be a ladder somewhere backstage, tall enough to reach the lighting bars. Go sniff it out and bring it out here. And Darren, I need you to go into the lighting booth itself and find the patch panel. It's a little bank of plugs that connects the switches on the desk to the sockets in the ceiling, get me? Stay by it, because I'll be telling you to start plugging stuff into it in short order. All right, hop to it everyone.'

It couldn't possibly work. You couldn't delegate an entire

fit-up to a trio of young men who had no idea what they were doing, and you certainly couldn't do it while lying down the whole time, functionally paralysed, on the stage floor. It was a daft idea. And yet the three actors scurried away to complete the first of their assigned tasks, and Hattie found herself relaxing fractionally, because deep down she had total confidence that Nick would, somehow, make it work. He wasn't exactly a natural leader, but when he asked things of other people those things tended to happen, if only because no one could ever bear to let Nick down if they could possibly help it.

So she decided to trust her husband and turn her attention to her own responsibilities, and before anything else that meant getting acquainted with the auditorium. Hattie liked what she saw: it was a proper theatre. Tiny, mind you, and badly maintained, not to mention an impractical shape, but a proper venue nonetheless. It felt right. It *smelled* right.

The building had once been a church – not the beautiful gothic-arches-and-clustered-columns sort, but still a church – and a certain unmistakeable churchiness had survived the fairly thorough conversion job. The transept (where the two strokes of a lower-case 't' intersect) now housed a stage, and the chancel (the top of the t') now formed the backstage area, but here a problem with the original layout of the venue presented itself: the stage extended more or less the full width of the body of the building, which meant that the wing spaces on either side of the stage, housed inside the extremities of the transept (the sticky-out bits of the 't'), were cut off from the main backstage area: the only natural way out of them was to come back onto the stage. This made entrances and exits harder, so the architects of the conversion had installed staircases in either wing, which led up to a small catwalk that ran above and around the edges of the stage, linking the wings to each other and to another stair that allowed for safe descent behind the upstage curtain into the chancel. In some ways this was a hugely convenient innovation, as it allowed access to much of the lighting rig via staircase rather than ladder, which certainly would make Nick's lackeys' jobs easier. But it also meant that actors (and stage managers) needing to get about backstage quickly during performances would have to descend and ascend staircases to do it. Hattie found herself rubbing her hip in anticipation just looking at the things. Worse, the wing staircases had only partial handrails, due to the awkward positioning of some lighting bars. There were places on either side of the stage where, if one was particularly clumsy and in a rush, it would evidently be possible to step off a step and onto empty air, and then tumble a good couple of metres before hitting the ground. This had been painstakingly drawn to Hattie's attention in the documents Freya had had her sign. The theatre's position was that (a) it was the performing company's duty to mitigate the risk of accident, even though (b) there was nothing the theatre could do to add barriers and that (c) the performing company wasn't allowed to add any form of barrier either (such unsanctioned backstage fixtures ironically constituting a potential fire and/or trip hazard). What it came down to was that Hattie and Larry needed to brief their entire company extensively and exhaustively about the dangers, but even if they did, if an actor did fall and hurt themselves it would be Hattie/Larry's problem, not the actor's, and certainly not the theatre's.

So Hattie sighed and hauled herself up and down the stairs on both sides to inspect the bits of missing barrier, all the better to point it out to the actors when they eventually arrived. She was in the middle of this when Freya appeared, a sheaf of printed papers in her hand.

'I've had the programmes he emailed through printed. I thought you said he wasn't acting in it?'

'Who? Larry? He's not.'

'That's not what this says,' said Freya, handing Hattie the printouts.

Hattie looked at what she'd been given. Sure enough, in the section for the cast it just said:

Starring
Larry Lloyd
Other parts by
The Ensemble of the Larry Lloyd company

Hattie frowned.

'That's not right.'

Freya shrugged.

'That's what he wanted printing. If he wants something different, he'll have to print it himself. But I'd recommend you get on with it if it needs changing. You don't want to be having to sort out programmes at the last minute.'

So Hattie took her phone out and called Larry.

'What?' he answered, grumpily. 'I'm in the middle of a rehearsal.'

'Er… I just wanted to check in with you about the programmes,' said Hattie.

'Ah. Printed, are they?'

'That's right. And they say "Starring Larry Lloyd". Er.'

'Ah. Yes. Ah, well, that's because I've had to step in. To the role of George.'

'Grown-up George?' asked Hattie, bewildered. 'Or child George?'

'Grown-up George.'

'But… what about Miles?'

'He, ah, is unwell.'

This was so obviously not true Hattie had to stop herself from audibly scoffing.

'Larry, he's here with me now. He's fine.'

'Well. Ah. That's just how it is,' said Larry, his voice tight and uncomfortable.

'Have you told him?'

'Ah. You say he's with you?'

'Oh. No. Larry I'm not going to—'

'Just explain it to him for me.'

'Explain what? I don't know what's happened!'

'It's a recasting, Hattie,' Larry huffed. 'It happens all the time. I'd have thought even you would understand that. This is just how the industry is. Ah. So get on with it.'

Once again, Larry was hiding embarrassment behind anger, and Hattie knew that there was no way she'd get him to back down from here. She couldn't work out what on earth he was playing at, though.

'You know that you're still going to need to pay him, right?'

'Of course I'll pay him! I'll pay all of you first thing in the morning. Stop making this about the money.'

Curiouser and curiouser. It flashed through Hattie's mind that perhaps Larry had *always* planned on playing grown-up George, and he'd simply been hiding it for some reason. He'd hired Miles at the last minute, then ignored him for the entire rehearsal period. He had clearly been planning on dropping him for some time, at least since before he sent the wording for the programmes through to Freya. But *why*, though? Why did he want to play the part himself? And why was he embarrassed to admit it? Could the man even *act*?

Larry's motives had to take a back seat, however, as Hattie was faced with the unenviable task of breaking it to Miles that his acting services were no longer required. To his credit, he took the news with equanimity.

'I knew something was up,' he said. 'He would barely even look at me. Never answered any of my questions. He was always going to do this, wasn't he?'

'I'm so sorry,' said Hattie. 'You've been treated truly horribly.'

'Do you think I did something to upset him on the very first day? Because even at the end of the first read-through he was already treating me differently to the others.'

'I don't think so. I think… well, I think Larry is a complicated and troubled person. I don't know what was going through his mind.'

'Well, that's that then. I'll tell my girlfriend not to bother coming to see it.'

In other circumstances Hattie, still feeling protective of young Kitty, would have been delighted to hear that Miles was spoken for. Right now that was the least of her worries.

'If it makes you feel better, he has promised you'll be paid as agreed.'

'That's something.'

'I'm sure, given the circumstances, you can take the rest of the day off. It's not fair to make you do the get-in for a show you're not even involved with.'

'Don't worry about me,' said Miles with a shrug. 'I'm quite enjoying this. I'm having a laugh, and Nick's teaching me all sorts that I never knew about lighting.'

Hattie couldn't help but smile. Nick's never-failing ability to get on with people undeniably came in handy.

'All right, we're certainly glad of the help, but any time you want to head off, you go right ahead.'

The five of them spent the rest of the day carefully working towards getting the venue ready for a performance. Nick's assistants took to their new roles with enthusiasm while Nick, his neck protected from further injury or aggravation by his supine position at the centre of things, had them rigging, focusing and plotting at a rate of knots. Hattie took delivery of her painstakingly sourced tables and chairs and set them up on stage. By knocking off time they had done everything they could to set themselves up for success in the following afternoon's dress rehearsal.

And yet, despite all of that, the dress rehearsal managed to be a complete and utter car crash.

18

There are many things that can torpedo a dress rehearsal. An inexperienced director, for example, who doesn't know the standard processes and so does unintentionally harmful things like denying the cast the necessary preparation time to get into the right headspace. Venue scheduling restrictions that preclude a meaningful technical rehearsal to get the lighting cues properly established. Having bespoke costumes but not having the person who made them on hand to deal with emergency repairs and alterations (with the stage manager explaining their absence with a vague excuse about a family crisis). All of these can cause problems, but all of them pale into insignificance when compared with a last-minute recasting of arguably the lead role and replacing an experienced actor with someone who, despite intimate familiarity with the text, has no noticeable acting abilities, no stage presence, poor vocal control and diction, and a difficulty, when flustered, in remembering lines, stage directions and apparently, in extreme cases, how to breathe.

It made for a miserable hour and a half. Any momentum that was built up in the classroom scenes evaporated the moment focus switched to Larry, shuffling around awkwardly on his side of the stage, trying to deliver his lines as adult George. He needed prompting for almost every alternate sentence, and as he forgot more and more his face went redder and redder and his delivery got quieter and quieter until Hattie could no longer feed him his lines effectively because she couldn't hear where he had got up to. And when he limped to the end of his scenes the lights would shift back to other actors who then spent the first half of their next scene trying to rouse themselves from the horrified stupor that he had induced in them.

They made it to the end, and when the final line was delivered, and Nick cued the final blackout, Hattie asked the cast to remain on stage so that Larry could rehearse the curtain call before giving notes on the performance. But when the house lights came up, Larry was nowhere to be seen.

'I think he went backstage?' said Kitty.

'Would you mind nipping back and fetching him?' asked Hattie, and Kitty scampered off, only to return soon after looking sheepish.

'I can't find him,' she said. 'I think he went out the fire exit.'

'I don't blame him,' muttered Moritz.

'Did you see his face? I thought he was going to have a stroke,' said someone else.

'From the way he was talking I thought maybe he'd already had one.'

'Do you think he'll come back?'

'First Roxie disappears, then Miles goes, now Larry… it's all getting a bit *Mary Celeste*.'

'If he doesn't come back do we still do the show tonight?'

'ALL RIGHT EVERYONE,' called out Hattie loudly and firmly. 'I'm sure Larry will be back in a little bit. In the meantime we have a job to do. We're professionals, and we do the work we're paid for.'

And paid they had been. Most unusually, Larry had seen to it that everyone was paid, in full, first thing in the morning, before they'd even done the performance, let alone received the proceeds from ticket sales from the venue. Hattie's bank balance was looking healthier than it had in months, and she had to admit that up until her phone made the 'ping' noise to tell her about the deposit in her current account, part of her had quietly feared that Larry would back out at the last minute. Being paid renewed her determination to do a proper job, regardless of the quality of the show.

So Hattie took over the orchestration of the curtain call, they ran through it a couple of times, and then, in the absence of any directorial notes, she delivered a brief (and entirely disingenuous) reassurance that everything would certainly come together for the performance itself, reminding them that a bad dress famously presaged a good show. Then she sent them away to get out of costume and get some food, giving them strict instructions to return in good time for any last-minute rehearsals Larry might want to do before the evening's performance.

'Thanks for your hard work, today and throughout, and I'll see you in a little bit,' she finished.

Right, she thought to herself as the actors drifted off the stage. *Time to find out where the bloody hell my director has run off to.*

She tried calling him, but received no response. She made her way backstage and poked about, but it was pretty obvious pretty fast that he wasn't around: the Artspace was small enough that, short of crawling into an equipment cupboard, Larry could have had nowhere to hide where Kitty, and then Hattie, would not have immediately spotted him. There was a fire exit, so Hattie slipped out through that and found herself in the loading yard at the back of the theatre. This too was empty, so she made her way to the street beyond and looked both ways, just in case he happened to be loitering. He wasn't. There was, however, on the street, a man who Hattie thought perhaps she did recognise. He looked rather like the companion of the man who had had Nick by the throat on her doorstep the previous week. But in the daytime, in a different place, by himself, she suddenly found herself unsure if it was him or not. He spotted Hattie staring at him, and gave her a cool glance in return, giving no sign of recognition and making no attempt to approach.

He's just some punter, and I'm just jumpy, thought Hattie. It was unsurprising that her nerves would be playing up.

She sighed and walked back to the fire exit, where, just as she was about to go in, she bumped into Kitty on her way out.

'No sign of him?' asked Kitty anxiously.

'Not yet, but I'm sure he'll turn up soon.'

'It's all falling apart, isn't it?' said Kitty abruptly. 'I should never have taken this job. I knew it was too good to be true, paid work landing in my lap as soon as I started looking. And the wheels have been falling off since day one. I feel so stupid. I invited everyone I know: my parents, my friends, oh God and Uncle Julie. It was supposed to be my big professional debut, and now I don't know what's worse: it not happening at all, or it happening and being... well, being like that dress rehearsal.'

She looked as though she might be about to cry. Hattie took a deep breath, then stepped forward and folded the young woman into a big hug.

'Don't you fret, my love. It'll all be all right. And even if it's not all right, it'll still be all right, if you get my meaning.'

'Not really,' said Kitty, her voice muffled by Hattie's lapel.

'I mean... look: worst case scenario, for some reason we have to cancel the performance tonight. And if that happens, and your friends and family have made the trip for nothing, find a pub, buy them a drink, sit them down and tell them all about it. It'll make a funny story.

'On the other hand, if the show goes ahead, then yes, maybe it'll be terrible. Maybe it'll be unwatchable. But *you* won't be terrible. *You* won't be unwatchable. You'll have given a decent go to the part you've been given, and at the end of the day that's all the job is. I don't know any actors who haven't been involved in a total turkey somewhere along the line. There's no shame in it.

'But I also want you to think about the other shows you've done, the drama club productions and the school plays. Are you really going to tell me that you've always had total confidence in a piece on the day of its first performance?'

'Well, no…'

'Well then. This is the point where it's *supposed* to feel like a car crash. That's how you know it's theatre. Does that make sense?'

'I suppose so,' said Kitty, with a sniff.

She didn't seem very convinced, so to take her mind of things, Hattie suggested, 'If you don't have anything urgent on at the moment, why don't you come with me to see if we can track down Larry? I wouldn't mind the company.'

Kitty agreed, so the two of them pottered back through the theatre building to the front of house area. That too was Larry-free, so Hattie suggested, for the sake of something to do more than from any conviction, 'I wonder if he's popped in to see Freya.'

She led Kitty through to the office, where Larry wasn't, but Freya as it turned out was.

'Hullo,' said Hattie. 'I don't suppose Larry has been in here in the last few minutes?'

'No,' said Freya. 'But if you see him, tell him he needs to check in with me about pre-sales. Goodness, I love your hair.'

She was, Hattie realised before opening her mouth to thank her for the unexpected compliment, talking to Kitty, who replied, 'Thanks! I love yours.'

Hattie thought it was a slightly self-congratulatory exchange: the two women had very similar hair. In actual fact, they had similar heights, builds and freckles. They could believably have been mother and daughter.

'This is Kitty, she's playing Fran in the show tonight. This is Freya, she runs the theatre.'

'It's nice to meet you,' said Freya.

'You too. Oh, I think that explains it,' said Kitty.

'Explains what?' asked Hattie.

'When Larry first cast me, he told me the part I'd be playing was called "Freya". I got horribly confused, because there's no mention of Freya in the script. But maybe he got muddled between a redheaded character in his play called Fran and a redheaded colleague called Freya. They're similar names, after all.'

'Cute theory,' said Freya with a mirthless smile. 'But I'm not his colleague, and we've never actually met. So unless he's a stalker he probably doesn't know my hair colour.'

'Oh,' said Kitty crestfallen, and Hattie felt a pang of sympathy. It had been a slightly improbable theory, and she suspected that this was Kitty's best attempt at making a memorable and positive first impression on someone she considered to be a potentially influential contact in the industry. It had been a little uncharitable of Freya to shoot her down immediately like that.

'Well, we won't keep you,' said Hattie.

'Righto,' said Freya.

They'd failed to rustle up Larry, but Kitty seemed at least a little bit more chipper, so Hattie considered the time not to be entirely wasted. She sent the young actress off to get some food, then decided to do the same herself, remembering at the last minute that Nick, who had been operating the lighting desk for the dress rehearsal and was probably there still, would doubtless be hungry too, and it was not unreasonable that he might expect his colleague *and spouse* to pick him up a sandwich if she was buying one for herself. That was the problem with working with your husband, she decided: she was so used to his presence she found it easy to forget he was even there, which was fine when at home, but led to some strangeness when on a job together.

So she picked him up an egg and cress from the shop down the street and then brought it to the booth, where she found him topping up on medication for his neck. Thanks to his drastic preventative measures the day before it was in reasonable nick, and his duties today wouldn't place too many demands on it. But were it to seize up during the show it would be a disaster, so Hattie and he had agreed that a controlled overdose of painkillers was in order.

'Any sign of him?' Nick asked.

'Not yet.'

'Bother. He's so short, somehow everywhere he walks on stage he manages to find the dead spots and his face is completely in shadow. But as I don't know where he's planning on actually standing for the performance it's hard for me to fix. I can't believe he's going to shuffle around quite as aimlessly as he did in the dress, is he?'

'I wouldn't put it past him,' Hattie muttered. 'The man has the stage presence of a hamster.'

'Ha! You always this mean when you're working?'

Hattie sighed.

'No, and I need to stop it now. It's unprofessional.'

'You're too hard on yourself.'

'Isn't that the job?'

'Nah, the job's mostly keeping everyone else happy. Speaking of which, is this a sandwich I see before me?'

They munched their sandwiches in silence for a little while, listening to the ambient noises of the theatre: the dripping pipe, the hum of the lighting equipment, the coffee machine in the foyer's miniature café, the occasional bleating of Freya's phone.

'How are you doing, anyway?' asked Nick, suddenly.

'How do you mean?'

'Well… broadly. In general. This gig. The next gig. The hip. All the mess around Big Steve. Holistically speaking, in the middle of the maelstrom, how is Cockatoo?'

'That's not the sort of question you normally ask.'

'Well, you're used to home Nick, not work Nick. Work Nick makes time for his colleagues, and tries to be an empathetic presence in the workplace.'

'Oh yeah? So where's all that empathy go in the evenings, then? Why's home Nick so preoccupied and selfish?'

'Well, home Nick is pretty worn out from being work Nick all day. He needs some Nick time.'

'Seems a bit unfair… although I suppose I know what you mean. Something to work on, I would suggest. For both of us.'

'Agreed. But you've not answered my question.'

Hattie considered.

'Mostly I just miss him. Big Steve. It's bad enough that he's dead, but all this chaos around it, all this mystery, it makes it hard to let go, you know? The fact I don't even know who killed him, and all I know is that someone did… I feel guilty. I feel like I ought to be doing something about it. The younger me would have. She'd have kept on at it, kept asking questions until it made sense.'

'The younger you never had to deal with hardened criminals. She might have ended up dead,' said Nick.

'Maybe. But I'm a bit sick of feeling old and scared.'

'I do get it. It's over now, though, isn't it? With each passing day it'll start to fade.'

'I hope so. I should probably burn that envelope, eh? I just hope Roxie's all right. I can't believe he never told me he had a daughter.'

'You never know, you might see her again one day. Then she can tell you all about it.'

The door swung open behind them. Nick looked round.

'Alternatively,' he added, 'maybe she could tell you now.'

'Hey?'

Hattie spun round. Sure enough, standing at the back of the auditorium, there was Roxie.

'Crikey, are you okay?' asked Hattie.

'Fine,' said Roxie flatly. 'How're the costumes?'

'Oh. Er. Seam's come undone on Neil's jacket, Darren's is a bit long in the arm, Kai forgot to bring a shirt so he's nipped out to Primark. Other than that, costumes are the least of our worries.'

'All right, I'll fix Neil's seam. I should have time to shorten the sleeves too. Curtain up in a couple of hours, right?'

'Listen, is everything okay? I'm not entirely sure you're supposed to be h—'

'I've got a job to do. I'm going to do my job,' said Roxie, and in that moment she looked and sounded *exactly* like her father. Stubborn as a mule, willing to take a stand against the world on principle alone. She strode off towards the dressing room, leaving Hattie and Nick gawping at each other in her wake.

'Does this mean I'm supposed to leave?' muttered Hattie.

'You can't leave. We've got a show to do.'

'Do we? Our writer, director, producer, and, as of yesterday, *star* is AWOL.'

'The first three of those roles are redundant this late into the game. As for the last, well, we could get Miles back, couldn't we?'

'God, can you imagine? *"Sorry we fired you yesterday, will you come back and be the star today?"*'

'Wouldn't be the first time in showbiz,' Nick pointed out.

'Let me try ringing Larry again, see if I can find out where on earth he ran off to.'

She dialled his number and, to her surprise, this time he answered.

'Ah. Hello.'

'Hello, Larry. Er… are you all right?'

'Yes. Ah.'

His voice sounded very small indeed.

'And are you… coming back?'

'Ah. Yes.'

'Good,' said Hattie quickly. 'We've rehearsed a simple curtain call, and the cast are all out getting some food. Roxie's here, doing some costume work and—'

'Ah. I suppose you're wondering…. Ah. I mean… I know it wasn't… Well…'

After a couple more false starts Larry stuttered into silence. Whatever it was he wanted to say, it wasn't coming out on its own.

'I know the dress rehearsal must have been very difficult for you,' said Hattie gently. 'I think it was a very brave choice to act in the piece yourself, and I'm guessing it was a shock running through it for the very first time under lights, in costume and on stage. But the good news is, you've been through it now. You know what's coming. Tonight will be easier.'

'Ah… yes. Yes, tonight will be easier. My… My life is very empty,' he confessed abruptly. 'This show is the only thing of any value that I have. I've been working towards this for a long time.'

'I bet you have,' said Hattie, struggling to think of appropriate things to say.

'I know I've been quite demanding. I just wanted it to be right.'

'Of course.'

'Thank you. In fact, I'd like you to say thank you to everyone for me. For their work. After the show.'

'I'd be very happy to, but I'm sure they'd rather hear it from you directly,' Hattie suggested.

'Ah. Yes. Of course.'

'Oh, while I remember, Freya said she wanted you to drop by her office to talk about ticket sales. Will you be able to do that before the show?'

'No, I'm afraid not. I shan't be back until nearly curtain up. You need to do it.'

'Oh. Can you not—'

'And, ah, remind her that she needs to sit and watch the show. It's very important to me.'

'All right, Larry.'

'Goodbye.'

He hung up. Hattie turned to Nick.

'Well I don't know what to make of that. He says he's coming back to do the show, but he won't be here till the last minute.'

'Probably avoiding the cast. He knows they know how crap he is, and he can't bear to face them, so he's going to walk in right before his first entrance, then slip away again at the end. I'm not sure whether it's cowardice for hiding, or bravery for actually doing the show despite knowing how badly it'll go. It's certainly unusual. But he's an unusual man.'

'That he is. Well, I suppose I'm in charge of things then.'

'You're a stage manager. You're *always* in charge. It's just that mostly people don't realise it.'

Hattie went to talk to Freya about ticket sales (there were no real decisions to be made or actions to be taken, she just seemed to want to voice her disapproval about how ineffective Larry's marketing efforts had been), and secured her assurance that she would watch the show ('I suppose I have to; if I duck out that's ten per cent of your audience gone'), and by the time she was done the actors were returning to the theatre and it was time to start preparing for the performance itself. She did the rounds, explaining that Larry was indeed returning, but that he had been unavoidably held up, and that therefore he wouldn't be available to give notes or answer questions prior to the show.

The actors were understandably taken aback and perturbed by this news, but Hattie did her best to put a brave face on it and assure everyone that they were as ready as they would ever be, and that further directorial intervention at this point was not strictly necessary. She felt a little bit slimy trying to convince her team that something weird and alarming was actually normal and unsurprising, but squared it with her conscience on the grounds that on balance, this way was likely better for morale, and therefore would result in a better show and happier actors.

For the most part, with a bit of grumbling, they bought it. In an odd way, the reappearance of Roxie, who was stoically plugging on with her repairs and tweaks, seemed to help calm everyone. She had a very grounding presence, Hattie thought with approval. Although she couldn't *say* anything approving to Roxie because she was still trying to obey her instructions to avoid her. Which seemed mad and daft, but somehow she didn't dare do otherwise.

The pace picked up as the actors warmed up and got into costume. Hattie was running round making sure all the desks and chairs were set in the right places and the classroom stationery was all available in the places needed, and that the actors all remembered where their entrances and exits were. Nick was barking out requests every few minutes for one actor or another to nip up a ladder and nudge a light left or right a bit, or to stand at a particular point on stage so he could check that both sides of their faces were equally lit.

And then, in the blink of an eye, Freya was poking her head backstage to let everyone know that the stage needed to be cleared as the house was about to open. Hattie hurried to the back of the auditorium for a last confab with Nick.

'When Freya closes the doors she'll give me a nod, right?' he said. 'And then she'll go sit down, and I'll give it a few seconds then pull the house lights.'

'Did you manage to get the cue light working? It'd be helpful to get a warning backstage.'

'Sorry, didn't get to it. Keep your phone on you, I'll ping you a message.'

'Righto. Clean show, Cocker One.'

'Clean show, Cockatoo.'

She made her way back to the front, managing to get across the stage just in time before the first audience members drifted in. She hauled herself, wincing, up the staircase and round to one wing and then the other, and finally backstage, in each place calling out softly, 'Ladies and gentlemen of the cast, the house is now open.'

The cast were milling round all over the place backstage. They seemed nervous, although on opening night there's nothing particularly unusual about that. Some were fussing over their costumes, and Roxie was doing the rounds, snipping dangling threads and flattening unruly collars. There was, understandably, a lot of quiet chatter about Larry, and whether he would return. Hattie didn't see him anywhere. She also caught a couple of other snippets of conversation that made her ears prick up.

'… a mask, did you see him?'

'Maybe he had COVID…'

'… creeped me out…'

She wanted to stop and ask further questions, but there was no time. She was the stage manager. She had a job to do. She completed her rounds. A few minutes later she had to do another one, this time announcing, 'Ladies and gentlemen, this is your five-minute call.' There was still no sign of Larry, and she started to get nervous. He had said he would be there at the last minute. It was now the last minute. He should be there. But it had taken her so long to get round the last time that it was already time for her next and final announcement. So she set off once again, this time calling out, 'Ladies and gentlemen, the show is about to start. Beginners to stage, please. Break a leg everyone.'

This time, to her intense relief, she saw Larry, in costume, pacing in anxious circles just outside the dressing room, his briefcase in his hand. She wanted to go up to him and say hello at the very least, but she didn't have the chance, because at that moment her phone juddered in her own hand and she looked down to see a message from Nick: Showtime.

19

It was clear to Hattie that something was wrong from the moment Larry opened his mouth to deliver his first line.

That was a little unfair. From the moment Larry opened his mouth it was clear that something was *different*, and the difference manifested itself in Larry actually giving quite a creditable performance. He was finally projecting his voice, his shuffling was reduced to a minimum, and he was more or less remembering his lines. The only mistake he kept making, which betrayed his anxiety, was that every time he was talking about the Fran character, he called her Freya. Which, given that the other actors were still referring to her as Fran, would surely confuse the audience, and none more so than the real Freya, who was watching from somewhere in the stalls.

Oh, and then there was the briefcase. He had had it in his hand when the house lights went down and had absentmindedly brought it on stage with him. He was pretty much stuck on stage for the entirety of the show, confined to a small corner that wasn't taken over by the classroom furniture, so he wouldn't have an opportunity to get rid of the case. But there was nothing particularly odd-looking about him holding a briefcase – his character seemed to be a businessman of some sort, after all.

All in all, from the audience's perspective, the show they were watching was more like an actual proper show than it had ever been in the rehearsal room. In some ways, everything was under control.

But to Hattie, watching from the wings, knowing what she did about Larry, and what this play was, remembering every little oddity that had played out over the course of the rehearsal period, there was definitely something amiss. Larry's new attitude was alarming: something had shifted, and it made everything else around him feel wrong.

It was, Hattie realised as the performance progressed, something about the play itself. She had always felt that as a script it lacked a point and a purpose. The show had been so beset with other problems that it had been easy to overlook this one thing. Now, however, with the piece finally firing on all cylinders, it actually felt like a play. With four scenes to go the intensity of the interactions in the classroom scenes was building minute by minute, and the rhetoric of adult George's monologues ratcheted up likewise. Which was good and all, except that Hattie knew that it wasn't going to go anywhere. The end of the play was a fizzle-out, and as such it seemed increasingly incongruous.

Three scenes to go now. She caught a movement in the opposite wing from the corner of her eye. Presumably it was Roxie, although the figure had seemed taller than Roxie. But that wasn't a pressing concern just this second.

So what should the ending be? How was a piece like this supposed to end? It needed some sort of resolution. But that was pretty much impossible: the stuff that needed to be resolved was what had happened in the classroom, and the conceit of adult George reflecting on it all, years later, by its mere presence ensured that the classroom stuff *couldn't* be resolved. Not unless George developed a time machine. No, the formative events occurred, and George was formed by them. He was bullied. Maybe not viciously, maybe not as badly as some, but now the piece was playing out in front of her, she could see that in some ways the worst of it wasn't the taunts by the other boys but rather the studied disdain of Fran, who, especially when portrayed so ably by Kitty, was more cruel through the *absence* of a reaction than with any words she might have said. And while that cruelty might not have even been noticed by someone a bit more resilient, it clearly affected George.

Two scenes left. The final classroom scene, then the final monologue.

So what sort of resolution was left? Perhaps George could make peace with the past. Perhaps he could find something else to rebuild his confidence. Perhaps, with a little schadenfreude, he could learn that Fran and her cronies hadn't done so well for themselves in their adulthood, and the knowledge that they could no longer set themselves above him would give him peace. Maybe there could even be some form of comeuppance for Fran. Maybe the audience would feel happier for George if we knew that Fran got what she…

… deserved.

Ah.

The cogs in Hattie's brain started to spin. That was the title of the play, after all. *That* was the intended ending, it had to be: Fran's character had to get what she deserved eventually, in order for adult George to get some semblance of closure. Except that she couldn't, because adult Fran didn't appear in the play.

But Larry wasn't calling her Fran. He was calling her Freya.

The ensemble was wrapping up now. They'd had the bit where one of the children started playing with the nickname 'Gross George' (a play on his surname, Grose), and Terry began using it too, and child George started crying. Soon they'd be onto the final speech, where adult George revealed that it wasn't the nickname nor Terry's adoption of it that made him cry, but rather the fact that even with the nickname, Fran/Freya ignored him: the idea that he was so dull to her that she couldn't even be bothered to mock him. The speech started: 'That was the moment when she did it. That was the moment when Fran broke me.'

As per the script, the classroom scene ended. As they'd rehearsed, the lights went down on the kids and came up again on Larry. But the line he actually said was, 'That was the moment when you did it. That was the moment when you broke me.'

For the first time since the start of the performance, Larry stumbled over his delivery, and his voice again faded to the mumble he'd used throughout in the dress. Hattie, almost within touching distance as she hovered in the wings, could see that he had tears in his eyes, but also that those eyes were locked onto a very precise spot in the audience.

He was also fumbling with his briefcase.

In that moment Hattie understood what was about to happen. She understood what Larry's plan had been all along, and why someone quite so untheatrical as him had engaged in such an unlikely theatrical endeavour. Worse, she understood what was in the briefcase, and why, almost touchingly, Larry had taken the unusual step of making sure that the cast and crew had all been fully paid in advance of the only performance of this show there would ever be. And she understood that she had to act.

She could have called Nick and had him kill the lights. She could have set off the fire alarm. She could probably have just run onto the stage screaming. But she was a stage manager, and some rules were sacrosanct. You don't stop a show. You *can't*.

But you can improvise.

Not giving herself time to think about why it was a bad idea, she took a step forward, and then another, and then two more put her onto the stage, in full view of the small audience. With the spotlights in her eyes she couldn't make out Freya, or anyone else for that matter.

Larry hadn't seen her. He was still fumbling with the briefcase, mumbling through his lines, only Hattie could hear that they weren't really his lines, but an agonised stream-of-consciousness rant that was almost inaudible to anyone besides himself.

'… waited this long and now I can't even do this right but I'm going to do it anyway, and if I can't do it this way I'll do it another and you're probably laughing at me right now but you can laugh all you like because you won't be…'

'You don't have to do this,' Hattie called out.

Larry's head snapped up and around.

'Ah,' he gawped at her.

'Er. It's me. Fran. I mean, Freya,' she said, in the vain hope that she could pass off her intervention as a part of the show. 'Er. I know we didn't get on very well at school—'

'Stop it! She ruined my life!' he hissed.

'I don't think she – I – did. I think maybe I ruined your adolescence. Children can be mean, and sometimes the things they do that hurt the most are the ones they don't even notice doing. But you're not a teenager any more. You're a grown-up with a lot of bad memories, but if you let those memories control you… well, that's on you.'

'Look at me,' Larry moaned. 'I'm a hollow shell. I'm a broken toy. I'm a little grey smear. I can never be anything. I've never done anything. I'm so tired. I don't want to do this any more.'

In his surprise at Hattie's appearance, he had temporarily stopped fussing with the briefcase. But now his fingers returned to it once more.

'Then do something different, George,' said Hattie urgently, desperate to keep his attention on her and away from Freya and the case. 'You've got nothing tying you down. You can walk out of here tonight and take yourself off to anywhere on earth. This time tomorrow you could be anywhere, doing anything.'

'I don't want that! I just want it to be over.'

It wasn't working. Hattie knew she had nothing she could say to change his mind. She had hoped that the mere act of disrupting his speech, of letting him know that she knew what he was planning, would be enough to knock him off course and cause him to reconsider. But it hadn't, and now she realised she was potentially only seconds away from a murder.

'Nick!' she yelled. 'Blackout! Now!'

Bless him, Nick, confused though he must have been, didn't hesitate. Almost immediately the lights went out; Hattie used the second of afterglow from the fading bulb to line herself up, and in the darkness she charged at Larry.

He must have taken a step to the side, because she didn't make full contact, but by sheerest luck her hip – her bad hip inevitably – clattered into the hand that held the briefcase and she heard it slide away on the floor as she and Larry tumbled down to the ground together. Then she was overwhelmed by a surge of pain from her leg, and it was a few seconds before she could think clearly again.

When she could, the first thing she became aware of was sounds of confusion that were beginning to crescendo into panic. It was a small audience, but it was a large cast, and between them there were enough people that, if they collectively lost their nerve in the darkness, they could do quite a lot of damage to one another.

'Can we have some house lights please?' she called out over the din, and once again Nick obliged from the booth, swiping the faders to illuminate an awkward tableau. The cast were in disarray. Some had remained frozen in place, some had started making their exits, and some had lurched uncertainly towards Hattie and Larry. Larry, for his part, was crawling round on his hands and knees, evidently searching for his briefcase. Several members of the audience were on their feet, some heading for the exits, some clambering towards the stage. Hattie searched the stage floor for the briefcase and couldn't see it. Then she looked up a little, and saw the case, clutched in the awkward arms of Kitty.

'Kitty, my love,' said Hattie, in the moment of silence that fell after the lights went up and everyone took stock. 'Please, whatever you do, *do not* give that briefcase to George.'

Kitty frowned.

'Er...'

'Sorry, I mean Larry. George is his real name.'

'Oh. Yes, I suppose that's not very surprising, is it?' said Kitty.

George was now standing up.

'Ah. Can I have my case please?'

'Don't give it to him,' Hattie warned.

'Er, why not?'

Not keen to say a word that would incite immediate panic, Hattie tried for discretion.

'It's got something dangerous in it, and George isn't in the frame of mind to make good decisions right now.'

George turned to look at Hattie.

'I just want to go home,' he said.

'I think that sounds like a very sensible idea.'

'Just give me my case and I'll leave.'

'You know I can't do that.'

'It's not... Ah. I don't, ah, think... Look. I just want my case. It's mine. You can't keep it from me. That's theft.'

He had set his jaw, and was beginning to get that petulant note in his voice. Hattie knew that he would only get harder to deal with from here.

'Tell you what. Let's go somewhere quiet, have a quick look-see in the case and get rid of anything dangerous, and then you can take it home and be done. Does that seem fair?'

'I don't see—'

'All right, ladies and gentlemen!' called out Hattie to everyone else, cutting off George before he had a chance to protest. 'The evening's performance is now over. If you would kindly make your way to the exits, thank you for coming, and I hope we'll see you back at the Artspace soon. Now, Kitty, would you come with me backstage? Neil too, and maybe Moritz?'

Hattie, George and the three actors made their way backstage. Neil and Moritz had picked up enough of what was going on that they didn't need to be instructed to insert themselves between George and Kitty. As they left, Hattie heard Freya, over the murmurings of the cast and audience, saying confusedly to someone, 'I'm *sure* he was in a different year to me...'

The old church had had two vestries in the chancel, one stage left, which was now the main dressing room, and one stage right, which was now used as a store cupboard. Hattie led the way to this latter one, knowing that the rest of the cast would probably be wanting to get changed in the former. Once they were all inside, she closed the door, turned to face them all and said, as gently as she could, 'Now, I know that everyone is probably a little bit confused about what's going on, but now isn't the time to get into it all. So that we're all clear, my understanding is that there's a loaded gun in that briefcase, and I believe George was planning on using it tonight, in a way that none of us want. So I propose that we open the case, take out the gun, hand George the case, let him leave, and then pass the gun on to the authorities. Does that sound fair?'

She expected shock and alarm on the faces of the actors, and she got it. Kitty in particular nearly dropped the briefcase, and as soon as she had reclaimed her grasp on it she thrust it firmly at Moritz, who accepted it with the enthusiasm of an uncle who has been passed a baby long overdue a nappy change. Hattie also expected something from George: a protest, a plea, anything. But instead he simply shook his head.

'Moritz, my love, would you mind very carefully opening the case?' she asked.

Moritz put the case on top of a tub of cables and very gingerly did as he was asked. He lifted the lid, looked down… and frowned.

'Er… there's a knife,' he said, then turned the case round to show Hattie. Sure enough, the briefcase contained a few scraps of paper, and a kitchen knife.

'I wasn't going to kill *her*,' said George, in a quiet voice. 'I just wanted her to have to watch… me… with the knife…'

'Oh,' said Hattie confused. 'But the pistol in the rehearsal room…'

'It was just a replica. I liked the idea of it, wanted to imagine what it would be like, but it wasn't possible. I told you. This isn't America. Where on earth would I find a real g—'

He was interrupted by two loud bangs coming from somewhere outside the building. The influence of the current topic of conversation on her imagination notwithstanding, Hattie had no doubt that they were the sounds of a gun being discharged.

'Stay here,' she warned the others, and stepped out of the vestry, nearly bumping into Roxie as she came out the door. The younger woman looked very upset, the fear on her face conveying a level of emotion that Hattie had never seen from her before, and she was backing away from the fire exit, which was slightly ajar.

'What happened?' asked Hattie.

'He's coming for me,' Roxie hissed. 'Shit! Dad was right.'

Then she sprinted away towards the stage and the safety of the auditorium.

'What's going on?' asked Kai, poking his head out from the changing room.

'Stay in there!' Hattie replied sharply. 'Close the door. Don't let anyone in.'

Kai's eyes widened in alarm, but he nodded, and did as he was told, leaving Hattie temporarily alone backstage. She hesitated, then started making her way towards the fire exit, unsure if she intended to go through it or close it. As she got close, though, she heard slow, methodical footsteps approaching on the other side. Hattie stopped again, then turned and fled to the staircase, the one that led to the gantry that allowed access to the wings. She dragged herself up the steps, stifling a groan as she did. Just as she reached the top she heard the fire door swing open behind her, and she bolted to the left, knowing she was making a horrible racket on the metal platform, but desperate to get away from whoever had just entered the building. She rounded the corner and hurled herself onto the upper steps of the staircase that led down to the wing space, then had to scramble frantically to find a handhold to stop herself plummeting straight through the gap in the railing that had been the source of so much paperwork.

Bloody deathtrap, she thought to herself. *If I get through this, I'm never coming back to this theatre again.*

She stood for a moment, hanging onto the railing, catching her breath, ears straining to listen to what was going on. She could hear muffled noises from beyond the stage. The last of the audience must still be leaving the auditorium, or else milling in the foyer just beyond. Hopefully Roxie had headed that way too, and could seek safety in the crowd. There was no sound of the cast coming from either of the vestries. Good. If they kept the doors closed and stayed quiet that was their best chance of keeping safe. That just left Hattie up here in the wing, the unknown man backstage and…

Oh God. And Nick. What would he be doing right now?

As if reading her mind, at just that moment she heard her husband call out, 'You all right, Cockatoo? What's going on?'

She didn't dare say anything to warn him. She didn't dare move. But she knew that if she did nothing he would come closer to investigate, putting himself in harm's way.

And then, she saw movement. A man in a hoodie, his face obscured, padded across the stage and stepped into the wing space below Hattie. She could hardly breathe. He didn't seem to have noticed her.

'Excuse me!' called Nick. 'Are you supposed to be back there?'

Nick must have seen the man crossing the stage. How did he not realise the danger he was in? He needed to be getting away, not provoking a confrontation.

The man froze, then turned back.

'Come out of there please!'

What on earth was Nick doing? Oh. He was trying to protect Hattie, that was what. Stupid bloody idiot.

The man turned, and took a step back towards the stage. Then another one. He was now almost directly beneath Hattie. He was the man who had shoved her at the bus stop, she was sure of it. Was he one of Tariq's men? Or Conor's? Whoever he was, as he turned to step out onto the stage Hattie saw that he had a gun in his hand.

She didn't let herself think. She stepped out through the gap in the railing, and simply fell, straight down, on top of him.

They both cried out in unison as Hattie landed on him. He went down, and Hattie felt her full weight land on his leg, which made a deeply unpleasant cracking noise. Then they were both sprawled on the floor a couple of feet apart, and it took Hattie a few seconds to realise that she *wasn't* in a lot of pain. His body had largely broken her fall.

The man, by contrast, was rolling about in apparent agony.

'Ow, bloody hell!' he moaned.

Hattie sat up blearily. She recognised that voice. She squinted at him. He was still wearing sunglasses and a face mask, but now that she knew who she was looking at he was unmistakeable. Impossible, but unmistakeable.

'Steve?'

20

'All right. Well. Thank you very much,' said Hattie to a still-shell-shocked-looking Freya, hovering in the doorway of the fire exit. 'The van should come at about ten o'clock tomorrow for the furniture. They'll load it all up themselves, so all you need to do is open the door for them and point them towards what they need to collect. If there are any problems, get them to ring me.'

'Right… And La— I mean, George?'

'He went home a little while ago. There's nothing else you need from him, is there?'

'I have… questions… I mean, I sort of remember him, but I really don't think we had much to do with one another. He can't… he can't really blame me for… well, for his whole life, can he?'

'I shouldn't worry about it if I were you. He needed to get something off his chest with this show, and he did it. I doubt you'll hear from him again.'

Hattie found she believed what she was saying. The last she had seen of George he was shuffling off into the night, briefcase in hand (the knife having been removed and given to Nick for safekeeping out of an abundance of caution). Whatever vision he had had for what the night would be, whether that was elaborately slashing his wrists in front of Freya and a deeply confused audience or something else entirely, it had not come to pass. What he would do now was anyone's guess. But realistically, it was out of her hands. She had more pressing matters to attend to.

'And what about the shooting?' said Freya, frowning.

'Gave us all a scare, didn't it? I don't think that's much to do with us. Maybe it was a gang thing. Obviously if the police come round asking questions you can tell them what you heard. Anyway, I know Nick wants to get home so I'd best be off. Thanks for everything, and I hope your last few weeks here go well!'

Hattie backed away awkwardly, then hobbled towards where Nick had pulled up the Astra on the kerb. Their combined ailments had made it an easy decision to drive to the theatre instead of taking a bus on the day of the show, having anticipated that they'd be tired and uncomfortable by the time they were finished, and Hattie was deeply grateful that they'd afforded themselves that luxury, for both its foreseen benefits and its unforeseen ones.

She opened the passenger side door and got in, sitting down with a sigh.

'Right,' said Nick. 'Where to?'

He was answered by a groan from under the blanket on the back seat.

'I don't suppose I can take that to mean "a hospital", can I?' asked Hattie dubiously.

'Christ no,' said Big Steve, through gritted teeth. 'I know someone. Can you get me up to Mile End?'

'We can go via Greenwich, and the Blackwall tunnel,' said Nick.

'Rotherhithe will be faster this time of night,' said Steve.

Nick opened his mouth to disagree, but Hattie cut him off with a firm 'You're the boss.'

Nick pulled out onto the road, and as the rear wheel came

down off the kerb the back of the car gave a big bounce that caused Steve to let out a cry of pain.

'Hurts, does it?' asked Hattie.

'You broke my leg.'

'Yes.'

'We're sorry about that,' said Nick awkwardly.

Hattie snorted. 'No we're not.'

'Doesn't he deserve a bit of sympathy?'

'I dunno,' said Hattie. 'Do you?'

'No,' said Big Steve.

'There we are then.'

'Oh,' said Nick.

They drove for a little while in a silence broken only by Steve's periodic sharp intakes of breath each time the car slowed down too abruptly or turned too sharply.

'I know I'm being thick,' said Nick after a while, 'but would someone mind telling me *why* we're not being sympathetic? I'd sort of thought we'd mostly be glad he turned out not to be dead, but the atmosphere in here is a little bit less than celebratory.'

'I'm very glad Big Steve isn't dead,' said Hattie solemnly, 'but I am also extremely angry with him.'

'I see. Er…'

'Do you want to tell him why, Steve?'

'It's because I lied,' muttered Steve.

'Lied, yes. And?'

'And I put you in harm's way.'

'Harm's way, yes. And?'

'And…'

'And you gave me a very upsetting experience, Steve. I thought you died in the most horrible way imaginable. I thought I *watched* most of it. I've been having nightmares about it, Steve. In the small hours of the morning I have had *flashbacks*. I don't think I will ever forget that night as long as I live.'

'It had to be convincing,' mumbled Steve.

'No it didn't. It didn't have to be convincing at all. You wouldn't have had to convince me of anything if you'd simply told me what it was you were trying to do.'

'But if I told you you'd have—'

'I wouldn't have gone along with it, that's right, because it was a bloody stupid idea and anyone with half a brain in their head could have told you it wouldn't work. And I *would* have told you so if, again, you had told me the plan instead of throwing me under the bus.'

'… sorry…'

They drove in silence for a little while longer. A couple of times Nick opened his mouth to speak, then evidently thought better of it and shut it again. Eventually Hattie relented.

'Look, he faked it. The whole thing. He didn't go stirring up trouble with Conor, he didn't arrange a meeting with him at Desi's yard, and he didn't get beaten up and set fire to. He just wanted everyone to believe he was dead, and he wanted me to believe the specific details of how he'd died. And it had to be me, didn't it? Or at the very least, someone very like me. Because I'm sensible. And I'm reliable. Which means I'm predictable. That's why you charged back into my life after a year of silence and got me involved with this horrible mess. You knew if you set things up in the right way I'd behave the way you wanted me to.'

'Didn't pan out like that, though, did it?' muttered Steve.

'Okay,' said Nick, frowning. 'And this was all in aid of what exactly? An insurance scam? A tax wheeze?'

'Nah. If it was something like that, he could have thought things through at his leisure, and he might have come up with a less *stupid, reckless plan*,' said Hattie, tilting her head to deliver those last words with venom towards the back seat behind her. 'He was in hot water, and he needed to improvise. Because he didn't go stirring up trouble with Conor, who was just some petty crook he did a bit of business with back in the day, but he *did* go stirring up trouble with someone much, much worse. Tariq. Ain't that right, Steve?'

Steve grunted.

'Tariq, who's a drug dealer?' said Nick.

'Tariq, who's a people smuggler,' said Hattie.

'Tariq, who's a modern-day slaver,' said Steve. 'I've felt guilty about what I did for him for twenty years. I wanted to make amends.'

'But you underestimated him, didn't you? As soon as you started buzzing round him, he decided you were trouble, and he's got no qualms about troubleshooting, does he?'

'I messed up. I thought I had some leverage. I didn't,' said Steve.

'I get it. So he wanted Tariq to believe he was dead, so Tariq wouldn't come after him,' Nick said, and then faltered. 'So… he staged it to look like he'd… killed himself?'

'To make it look like he'd been kicking up trouble both with Conor's lot *and* Tariq's gang, and that Conor had got to him first. But he had to balance it carefully. If the official story was that Conor had had him killed, the police would have investigated and the lie would have probably fallen apart straight away. Whereas if the official story was an accident, or suicide – which was it you were going for, by the way?'

'Suicide,' said Steve miserably.

'Well, if that was the official story, the police probably wouldn't dig too deep. They knew about the canc… oh God. Steve, do you actually have cancer?'

'What answer would upset you more?'

'Being lied to again,' said Hattie immediately.

'Then yes, I do actually have cancer. It was the kick up the arse that got me started on this whole thing.'

'Well I'm very sorry to hear it,' said Hattie.

'I know.'

'But as you expected, I told the police about the cancer, and didn't tell them about Conor. My statement made the public version of your story very easy to swallow. That and the fragments of charred bone they found, of course.'

'Jesus, I forgot about that,' said Nick. 'Where'd you get bones from?'

'I've got a friend, works in a morgue,' muttered Steve.

'That's right, Ivan, isn't it? Lives not far from West Rimesdale. You'd just been to see him when you dropped in on me. What, did you have a femur or two in your boot that night? Did you go home and toast them to a crisp in a bonfire to make sure they wouldn't be good for a DNA test?'

'Jesus,' Nick repeated horrified.

'I had to be thorough,' Steve croaked, wincing in pain.

'You wanted everyone to believe it was suicide, and you got your wish. Well, you wanted everyone except Tariq to believe it was suicide, because he's far too cynical to buy that. You wanted him to believe that it was murder, and so you made *me* believe it was murder, and then you sent Tariq after me. Once again, you were counting on me being predictable: if thugs turned up at my door I'd crumble and tell them everything I knew, in particular that you'd got on the wrong side of Conor and he'd offed you. Tariq would believe that, especially if it came from a scared little old lady who truly thought she'd witnessed it.'

'You mean that whole thing at Desi's yard was staged just to traumatise my wife?' said Nick sharply. 'And those men turning up on our doorstep and nearly throttling me were part of your plan? I'm beginning to see why you're so angry, Cockatoo.'

'I *thought* there was something unreal about the wounds. She's good, I'll give you that, but fake is fake. If it wasn't for all the scene setting you'd done I might have smelled a rat.'

'Wait, who?' asked Nick, bemused.

'Roxie. She sidelines in special effects makeup alongside all her other talents. Very handy for this sort of thing.'

'So she was in on it?'

'From the start. I even saw her car outside Desi's yard, although of course I had no way of knowing it was hers at the time.'

'I told her to move that thing,' said Steve. 'She never listens.'

'She's headstrong. Like her dad.'

At that moment, Steve's phone pinged.

'Speak of the devil… Right. Detour. I need you pop into Bermondsey. Corner of Southwark Park.'

'Really?' asked Nick.

'It's important,' Steve grunted.

'More important than a broken…? All right, all right.'

They worked their way up to Hawkstone Road. Steve had Nick pull in to a roadside parking bay, then sent a message on his phone. A few minutes later a familiar figure approached the car. Hattie wound down her window.

'I'm glad to see you're all right,' she said.

'Likewise,' replied Roxie coolly.

'We need to talk,' called Steve from the back seat. 'Privately.'

'Let's go for a walk,' Roxie suggested.

'That's not happening,' said Steve.

Roxie shrugged.

There was an awkward pause, then the penny dropped.

'Come on,' said Hattie to Nick. 'You and me are heading to the Tesco at the end of the street.'

The two of them got out of the car, and Roxie got in.

'Are you sure we should be leaving them alone together?' asked Nick quietly, massaging the sides of his neck with both hands.

'Of course. I trust… well. Maybe. You didn't leave the key in the ignition, did you?' Hattie muttered back.

'Not likely.'

'Then I'm sure it's fine. Come on.'

They walked in silence down the road. Hattie found her mind running back over the events of the last month. Steve's reappearance had recontextualised all of those events, and she had very rapidly come to a new understanding of what had been going on, but that understanding was raw and incomplete and had lots of sharp edges and frayed ends. She tried to imagine what it must have been like for Steve: trying to make amends for mistakes made a lifetime in the past, realising with a shock that he was completely out of his depth, fearing for his life and, despite facing an illness that was going to get him soon no matter what, being grimly determined to go out on his own terms. He'd scrambled to come up with a plan, involving the few people he could trust – Roxie, Ivan, Hattie – and even then, keeping them in the dark where possible. It had been a desperate, stupid plan. But it had nearly worked.

In Tesco they bought a bottle of orange juice for Hattie, a scotch egg for Nick, and a packet of ibuprofen for Steve.

'It was very brave of you,' Hattie said to Nick as they walked back. 'When Steve appeared earlier on stage, and you tried to accost him. Foolish, given the gunshots. But brave.'

'Well, I thought my lady wife was in danger,' said Nick gallantly. 'But you were the one who launched herself off the fly floor onto him. That was braver than me. And more foolish. Speaking of foolish… I'm still getting my head around all this, but what I do understand is that Steve lied to you, tricked you, and put you in harm's way in several different ways. He's committed all sorts of crimes, and he's involved with some terrible things. And he's in the back of our car. Should we really be helping him?'

'I did break his leg. I owe him at least—'

'You don't owe him anything,' said Nick firmly.

'You're right,' acknowledged Hattie, then she sighed. 'But

after all this he's still my friend and I'm going to help him anyway.'

'I hope you're not inviting more trouble down onto our heads. This Tariq fellow sounds a nasty piece of work.'

'I don't think we have to worry about Tariq any more,' said Hattie slowly. 'I think—'

They had reached the car, and at that moment the door opened and Roxie got out. The dim street lighting only partially illuminated her face, but it was enough for Hattie to see that she had been crying.

'Are you all right, my love?' asked Hattie softly.

Roxie nodded vigorously, as if trying to shake away the tears.

'He's a stupid old man who never thinks about other people,' she said gruffly.

'You're not entirely wrong,' said Hattie. 'We need to get him patched up. Do you want to come along? I'm still trying to work out what happened, thought you might be able to help fill in the blanks.'

'No, I'm done with him. I won't fix any more of his messes, it always just gets me in trouble.'

'All right,' said Hattie. She was disappointed. Steve didn't have many allies, and Hattie had hoped that Roxie would be one of the few. 'Well, take care of yourself. Hopefully we'll cross paths again someday.'

'Yeah,' Roxie nodded, then added, in an unexpectedly small voice, 'Just… take care of him for me, will you?'

'I'll see what I can do,' said Hattie, with a small smile.

She and Nick got back into the car.

'That didn't go so well,' said Steve, as Nick pulled back out onto the road. 'I don't think I'll see her again.'

'I'm sure you will. She does love you,' Hattie tried to reassure him. He said nothing in reply.

They reached the Rotherhithe tunnel and while the car briefly dipped into the subaquatic tube of artificial light, its occupants briefly dipped into the silence of reflection, each no doubt ascribing different weight to the different parts of the evening's revelations.

'And that's another thing,' Hattie continued when they were above ground once again 'Why did you never tell me about her? We worked together for *years*, Steve. And you didn't even say you had a daughter!'

'She wouldn't let me,' said Steve. 'I wasn't around much when she was a kid, but I got to know her more once she was grown up. It was her being into theatre that got me interested in it as an alternative career. But I went into the management side of it, and pretty soon I was working in the sorts of jobs that involved hiring and firing people like her. She didn't want any favours, I could understand that, but she didn't want even a possibility that someone might *think* I'd done her a favour. So as long as I had any influence I wasn't allowed to acknowledge that we were related, in case someone else felt like they should hire her as a favour to me, or assumed she'd only got a gig because I put in a word. I went through fifteen years of her not speaking to me. I didn't want to risk another fifteen. So I kept my mouth shut.'

'That proved handy in the end, didn't it?' Hattie pointed out. 'No one knowing you and she were associated. Your colleagues in the industry didn't know about her, and your family didn't know you two were in touch because you mostly weren't in touch with them. I'm guessing you thought there was no way she'd get sucked into this, even if you got her to help you.'

Steve laughed ruefully.

'Yup. That's what I thought. And then you came along.'

'I'd apologise, but I'll remind you for the third time that *if you had told me what was going on* none of this would have happened. Even if things had gone smoothly on the night, even if I hadn't made a mistake, there's no way things would have panned out exactly as you'd planned in the long run. There were too many variables.'

Nick frowned.

'I'm confused again. What mistake? What was actually supposed to happen?'

'What was supposed to happen,' Hattie explained, 'was that after the funeral, Tariq would come a-calling – presumably you left him some sort of clue that would lead him to me? – and when he did, I would wobble around and tell him everything I knew, or rather everything I thought I knew, about Steve and Conor, and Tariq would buy the story and you'd quietly sail off into the sunset and live out your remaining years on a Caribbean beach or something.'

'Months, not years,' said Steve quietly, and Hattie suddenly found herself thinking back to Roxie's tears and Steve's assertion that he wouldn't see her again. 'Cancer, remember? And more likely Brittany than Barbados. But yes, something like that. Only next thing I knew, you were offering Roxie a job. How the hell did you find out she was involved so fast?'

'Well, that was the mistake, wasn't it? I did what I always tell my actors off for doing: I left a prop behind when I went onstage. In my case it was that envelope. Because that's all it was, wasn't it? A prop, whose sole purpose was to give me a reason to come to the yard so I could be in the right place at the right time. You got Roxie to stuff some scraps from her recycling bin into an envelope. I was supposed to hand it back to you and then it would never be seen again. Only I left it behind.'

'I was terrified you'd hand it over to the police, or to Tariq when he came to see you, and that would make my whole story unravel.'

'But I didn't do that. Instead I opened it, and I took a look, and among all sketches and her notes about fabrics and quantities was a scrap of an old invoice of Roxie's. The irony is that even after I found her, I had no idea she was involved. I couldn't puzzle out the connection. And if you hadn't started trying to warn me off her I might never have mentioned her to Tariq's men when they came back to see me again. But that was when it really started to go wrong, wasn't it? Up until that point, I was doing exactly what you expected of me: panicking, and mentioning Conor. If they'd asked me any more questions I'd have squawked out everything I thought I knew and they'd have gone away believing that you'd done the same thing to Conor that you'd done to Tariq, only he'd got to you first meaning they no longer needed to worry about you. But then I mentioned the name Roxie. And that got their attention, because they knew that name, and if she was involved with any of this mess it was presumably as your accomplice. Which meant she might know everything about their operation that you did. And that suddenly gave them an incentive to find her and get rid of her in just the same way they'd wanted to get rid of you.'

'I was hiding out in her flat on Friday morning, and they turned up outside and started banging on the door. Scared the shit out of me when I thought they knew I was there. Scared me even more when I realised they didn't.'

'I can imagine,' Hattie sympathised. 'I was there when you called her to tell her about it. So they started sniffing round her, and at that point all bets were off, and you made her go into hiding?'

'Tried to,' Steve corrected her. 'She didn't believe the danger. Insisted on finishing the job she'd started with your show. And Tariq, who'd been keeping an eye on your movements by the way, as part of keeping an eye out for her, got word she'd turned up at the theatre tonight, and came down to see her. He wouldn't have… he wouldn't have been gentle with her. I had… I had to—'

Steve let out a ragged gasp, and Hattie wasn't entirely sure it was down to the pain in his leg.

'It's all right, Steve,' she said gently. 'He was a very bad man, I believe that. You don't have to justify anything to me.'

'Justify what?' said Nick.

'Well I'm not sure,' admitted Hattie. 'But I heard a couple of gunshots earlier, and I notice that Steve wasn't on the receiving end of them.'

'They won't find him immediately,' said Steve. 'Last I saw him he was crawling away behind a bin like a wounded rat. But he won't have gone much further than that. I got him in the gut. Twice. He's done. He's done.'

'Have you got a gun on you right now?' asked Nick in alarm. 'Has he still got a gun?'

'Ditched it,' said Steve. 'Wiped it down and ditched it. Had that bloody thing for thirty years. Tariq gave it to me himself. Never fired it until today. Glad to see the back of it.'

Hattie looked back at Steve. He was sitting more or less upright in the back seat, but his head was lolling back, and his eyes were closed. Hattie knew that he must be in a tremendous amount of pain and, her initial anger having worn off at least in part, she could now find a little more room in her heart for sympathy with him. She imagined him, cold with fear, patrolling outside the theatre all evening, waiting for the devil to come and try to take away his daughter. The daughter who he had put into harm's way through his own pigheadedness, and then who he'd been unable to keep safe through *her* pigheadedness. Hattie had never met Tariq, never even seen what he looked like, only learned of him through hearsay, but she could readily believe that he would not, as Steve had said, have been gentle with Roxie.

No, Hattie wasn't angry with Steve any more. He had taken a life to protect his daughter's and had been landed with a broken leg for his trouble. For now, at least, she could no longer remonstrate with him. Except…

'Steve?'

'Yes?'

'When you shoved me over at the bus stop the other day. That really, really hurt.'

'I'm sorry. I was terrified you'd recognise me and I overdid it. I wanted to get away as quickly as possible. I should have been gentler.'

'Yes. You should have.'

They approached Mile End, and Steve directed them to a street with a tower block on it, and gave them a flat number.

'Who's here?' Hattie asked. 'Ivan?'

'God no,' said Steve. 'He'd never come to London. And besides, the price of the kind of favour he did for me is that I never get to see him again, let alone ask him for more favours.'

He didn't offer anything further. Nick pulled up opposite the building, and Hattie got out and rang the buzzer.

'Hello?' came a crackly response.

'I've, er… I've got someone here who needs your help,' said Hattie.

'Yes?'

It was a woman's voice, but beyond that Hattie could make out very little about who she was talking to.

'Er, he's been injured, and he said you'd be able to help him,' she explained, realising as she did how unconvincing she sounded.

'I'm sorry, I think you've got the wrong—'

'It's Steve. Steve Felton,' she said, lowering her voice lest anyone else should hear.

There was a pause, and then the voice said, 'I'm coming down.'

A couple of minutes later the door opened and a woman walked out, casting furtive glances to either side as she did so. She was probably in her late forties, her hair and makeup immaculate, the overall look let down only slightly by the very weathered fleece dressing gown she had wrapped around her. She caught sight of Hattie and frowned.

'Who are you, then?'

'My name's Hattie. I'm a friend of Steve's.'

'Oh yes. I remember,' said the woman.

Hattie was initially taken aback by the response. But then she thought about where they were, and suddenly she recognised the voice.

'You're Nancy, right?'

Nancy nodded.

'Steve's in the car over there,' Hattie continued. 'He's broken his leg. He said you could help.'

'So he's alive, then.'

'Yes.'

'But he's not supposed to be.'

'Er…'

'Meaning he can't go to a hospital.'

'Oh. Yes. Exactly.'

Nancy rolled her eyes.

'Best bring him in, then.'

The two women walked over to the car. Nick got out, and opened the back door. Between them they managed to haul Big Steve off the back seat and, with his arms across Nick and Nancy's shoulders, they shuffled him across the street, through the tower block door, and into the lift in the lobby.

'I've got it from here,' said Nancy. 'You two piss off before anyone sees you.'

Steve was leaning up against the corner of the lift, all his weight on his good leg. Upright, it was obvious that something was deeply wrong with the other one, and not just from the growing blood stain around the knee of his trousers. The angle of his calf compared to his thigh was all sorts of wrong.

'Hold on,' he called out hoarsely. 'Hattie, the police. They'll find Tariq. They'll ask at the theatre. Some of the actors… they'll trace things back to you eventually.'

'I won't do any more lying for you, Steve. I'm pretty sure they can do me for harbouring a fugitive or something.'

'Don't lie for me. Say whatever you like. Feel free to say I made you drive me here at gunpoint. They're welcome to try to catch me if they can. I reckon I can stay out of their way for as long as I've got left anyway. But… is there a version of the story you can tell that doesn't mention Roxie?'

Nancy shot Steve a suspicious look.

'What have you got my girl wrapped up in?'

'Oh don't start, I—'

'Don't start? Don't start?! First I see of you in ten years you turn up, supposed to be dead, on the run, and the first thing I learn is that you've put my daughter in danger?'

'*Our* daughter, and she's not in any danger any more,' croaked Steve.

'What the hell's that supposed to mean?'

'I'm sure,' Hattie interjected, 'that I can leave her out of it.'

Steve looked relieved.

'Thank you. But Nance is right. You'd better get going.'

Nancy pressed the lift button, and as the doors began to close, Hattie saw her turn to Steve and say, 'How oh how did you manage to piss so many people off that you had to turn to *me* when you needed patching up…?'

And then they were gone, and in that moment Hattie remembered that she had never thanked Steve for the £1000 he'd left her in his will. It was too late now. Hattie realised that she would almost certainly never see him again, and she found herself mourning the loss of her friend. But she'd already grieved for him once; she didn't want to do it again. In some ways, she thought, best to think of him as still dead. He'd died that night in Desi's yard, ducking out early to avoid letting cancer do it the slow way. Everything else was just tying up some loose ends.

She'd still miss him, though.

Hattie and Nick wordlessly returned to their car, and started the drive home.

Epilogue

The morning brought with it two messages on Hattie's phone. The first was a short note from Kitty, thanking Hattie for all her help. Hattie approved. Not, it had to be said, that Hattie had done very much to help Kitty, apart from steering her away from Miles at every opportunity, which she suspected the young actress wouldn't necessarily appreciate fully. But theatre was very much an industry where getting on with people mattered, and the instinct to part on good terms with everyone in the company was a wise one. Kitty hinted, without saying anything specific, that she was perhaps more open to the idea of going to drama school than she had previously been, and of this too Hattie approved. It would do her good to learn about the proper way of doing theatre, which was very different to the way things were done on *What You Deserve*. The truth was that theatre in venues like the Ashwood Artspace was a very mixed bag: there would certainly be some companies that knew what they were doing and took things seriously, but there would also be a bunch of chancers and no-hopers who, at best, would be making things up as they went along. Formal training would be better for her than bouncing around in companies on the theatrical fringe.

Hattie sent back a friendly reply, wishing Kitty well and expressing the hope that they would work together again one day. A slim hope, she thought, given that she was having a hard time imagining ever working again at the moment.

But before she could get too maudlin about her employment prospects her attention was caught by the other message: an email, received at four in the morning, from George. From his actual, personal email address, the one that she'd only ever received one message from, not the one he'd used for his alter ego.

Well, at least he was still alive at 4am, Hattie thought to herself, and then felt horrible about it.

She opened the email.

It began: I'm not dead.

Hattie couldn't help but laugh. George's bluntness was, in its own way, reassuring. She read on:

I know I made a fool of myself. I know it was a disaster. I know everyone thinks I'm a weird, sad idiot.

But people have always thought that about me. If I have one superpower, it's tolerating the ridicule of others.

I can't carry on the way things were before. It turns out I can't just quit either.

So I'm going to take your advice and do something different.

And I've decided what that is: I'm going to put on another play. A better one.

Why? Because the last few weeks may have been awful, but they were also the closest to happiness I've come in years.

You probably won't see me again. You can think what you like about me. But you should know this isn't the ending.

Hattie found herself laughing again. Laughing with relief, laughing because it was easier than crying. She wondered whether it would be arrogant of her to interpret George's message as some sort of thank you. Maybe. Either way she wished him well. She was sure that his next foray into theatre would go better than his debut. It could hardly go worse.

Nick got up, and the two of them had breakfast. Neither of them had anything particular they needed to do for the next couple of days, so they shared a rare morning spliff and allowed themselves to bask in the early spring sunshine streaming through the sash window as they settled back comfortably into a warm, muggy haze. They didn't say much. There wasn't much to say.

After a while Hattie was pulled out of her reverie by the buzzing of her phone. What she saw there gave her a jolt that immediately chased the fug from her brain: the number on the screen had a treble-six in it, as well as a thirteen.

'Oh bloody hell,' she mumbled. 'I thought it was over.'

'Who is it?' asked Nick.

'It's… well, I thought it was Conor's lot. Then I thought it was Tariq's lot. Then I thought it was Steve. I'm honestly not sure at this point.'

'You going to answer it then?'

Hattie looked over at Nick, annoyed. She couldn't just *answer* it… or then again, could she? What more trouble could she possibly get into?

Just before the call was redirected to voicemail, she tapped the little green icon and held the phone up to her ear.

'Hullo?' she said cautiously.

'Hattie?' asked a high-pitched man's voice.

'Yes?'

'Thank God! Darling, I've been trying to get hold of you for *weeks*. What on earth have you been doing with yourself?'

She knew the voice. She knew she knew it. She could half-visualise the face that attached to it. But she couldn't place the person behind the face, and her memory wasn't yielding a name either.

'I've been busy,' she said. 'I just did a show at the Ashwood Artspace.'

'No!'

'Er… yes.'

'If I was a superstitious man I would take it as a sign. Sod it, I am a superstitious man and I *do* take it as a sign. Darling, I've just been appointed the new Artistic Director at the Artspace!'

Hattie's brain finally began to click into action. She knew who the new AD at the Artspace was. Nick had told her. Which meant that this person on the phone was…

'Hashi?'

'I know! Little old Hashi Hassan finally got his own theatre! I mean, it's an utter hellhole, isn't it, but when you've spent this long in the wilderness you take what you can get, and it'll make for a good chapter in the memoir.'

Hattie remembered what Hashi had been like when she had worked for him a couple of years earlier. He was a diva of the first order, and while undoubtedly talented as a director, his aptitude for rubbing all and sundry the wrong way meant that his career to date had been rather stilted. Hattie had a soft spot for him, in the way that she had a soft spot for almost every flawed theatrical type she had got to know well.

'Congratulations,' she said genuinely, and then, less genuinely, 'It's a lovely venue.'

'It will be by the time I'm done with it. Now, this brings me on neatly to why I'm calling. I need a venue manager, and you were the first person I thought of. I need someone I can trust, someone who knows how I work, and someone who's going to be a grown-up about things like pay and working conditions. I was hoping to get this all thrashed out weeks ago but then I couldn't get hold of you so I nearly hired someone else, but he just pulled out because he couldn't make the finances work. So what do you say?'

Hattie had to stifle a laugh. He couldn't have made the job sound less appealing if he tried. Working in close confines with abrasive, obnoxious Hashi, on what was evidently an unliveably poor salary, in a theatre that he himself described as an 'utter hellhole'. Who would possibly say yes to that?

Hattie thought about her own experience of the theatre. It was miles away from home, it was impractically shaped, with more stairs in the backstage area than her hip would stand, plus it had those deathtrap railings gaps that would absolutely one day be the death of her. Or at least the death of someone.

Then there was the job itself. Venue manager. That was far too far removed from the actual theatre. It would involve sitting in an office all day. At best she might be, as Freya had put, it a 'glorified caretaker'. It was utterly, utterly unappealing.

Then Hattie realised that she was having to work quite hard to convince herself that she didn't want the job. And it wasn't just a kneejerk desire for employment at all costs. She thought back to how she had felt when she first walked in to the Artspace. It was, she had recognised immediately, a proper venue. If she worked there, it would be *her* venue. It smelled right. Somehow, that counted for more than anything else.

Hattie Cocker, Venue Manager, the Ashwood Artspace.

She didn't hate that as an epithet.

'Well? I *do* have other calls to make today, you know.'

'Of course, Hashi. Yes, I want the job. Count me in.'

Acknowledgements

Huge thanks as ever to my agent James Wills, and to my editor Carolyn Mays and the wonderful team at BSP. Being allowed to write these books is a true privilege, and I am deeply grateful for the hard work that goes into making it possible.

About the Author

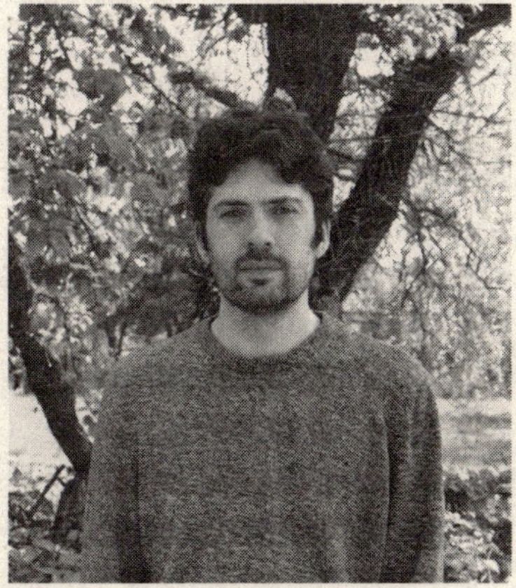

Photo courtesy of Patrick Gleeson

Patrick has a degree in philosophy and classics, another one in technical theatre and stage management, and one more in business administration. He has worked as a theatre sound designer, an 'interpretive naturalist' at an aquarium, a software developer, a business mentor to fledgling entrepreneurs, and a voice actor.

He composed the music for a musical about taxidermy that *The Stage* said 'put to shame the hackneyed standards of the contemporary musical scene', and has been performed in London, Edinburgh, Suffolk and, weirdly, Alaska. In 2012 he built a giant mechanical octopus that played the xylophone rather badly.

He now lives in Norfolk with his wife, two children, and two extremely clumsy cats who have accumulated more severe leg injuries than even Hattie.